GET TO KNOW THE INTERNATIONAL BESTSELLING SERIES
FEATURING DETECTIVE HELEN GRACE.

"Grabs the reader by the throat."
—Crime Time

"Thrilling and enjoyable...a shocking twist at the end."
—The Crime Scene

"A fast-paced roller-coaster ride."
—Life Through Books

"One of the greatest heroes to come along in years."
—*New York Times* Bestselling Author Jeffery Deaver

THAT'S THE WAY THE MURDER GOES....

PRAISE FOR
EENY MEENY

"[A] gripping debut. . . . Helen Grace [is] a flawed but winning heroine. . . . The pages fly by." —*USA Today*

"Dark, twisted, thought-provoking, and I couldn't turn the pages fast enough. Take a ride on this roller coaster from hell—white knuckles guaranteed."
—Tami Hoag, #1 *New York Times* bestselling author of *Cold Cold Heart*

"No doubt about it! *Eeny Meeny* debuts one of the best new series detectives, Helen Grace. Determined, tough, and damaged, she must unravel a terrifying riddle of a killer kidnapping victims in pairs to send a particularly personal message. Mesmerizing!"
—Lisa Gardner, #1 *New York Times* bestselling author of *Crash & Burn*

"M. J. Arlidge has created a genuinely fresh heroine in DI Helen Grace. . . . He spares us none of the dark details, weaving them together into a tapestry that chills to the bone." —*Daily Mail* (UK)

"With an orchestration of tension that is always sharp and cinematic, M. J. Arlidge's debut novel grabs the reader by the throat." —Crime Time

"A fast-paced roller-coaster ride. Every chapter holds new developments, new murders, new clues. . . . I would highly recommend it for any crime fiction fans and I am giving it four stars out of five. A truly wonderful debut novel." —Life Through Books

"A thrilling and enjoyable read . . . a shocking twist at the end."
—The Crime Scene

"This taut, fast-paced debut is truly excellent." —*The Sun* (UK)

continued . . .

Also by M. J. Arlidge

Detective Helen Grace Thrillers

Eeny Meeny

POP
GOES THE
WEASEL

A DETECTIVE HELEN GRACE THRILLER

M. J. ARLIDGE

 NEW AMERICAN LIBRARY

NEW AMERICAN LIBRARY
Published by New American Library,
an imprint of Penguin Random House LLC
375 Hudson Street, New York, New York 10014

This book is a publication of New American Library. Previously
published in a Penguin Group (UK) edition.

First New American Library Printing, October 2015

For more information about Penguin Random House, visit penguin.com.

LIBRARY OF CONGRESS CATALOGING-IN-PUBLICATION DATA:

Arlidge, M. J.
Pop goes the weasel / M. J. Arlidge.
pages cm.—(A Detective Helen Grace thriller; 2)
ISBN 978-0-451-47550-3 (softcover)
1. Policewomen—Fiction.   2. Women detectives—Fiction.   3. Serial murder
investigation—Fiction.   I. Title.
PR6051.R55P67 2015
823'.914—dc23   2015015604

Printed in the United States of America
10 9 8 7 6 5 4 3 2

POP GOES
THE WEASEL

1

The fog crept in from the sea, suffocating the city. It descended like an invading army, consuming landmarks, choking out the moonlight, rendering Southampton a strange and unnerving place.

Empress Road industrial estate was quiet as the grave. The body shops had shut for the day, the mechanics and supermarket workers had departed and the streetwalkers were now making their presence felt. Dressed in short skirts and bra tops, they pulled hard on their cigarettes, gleaning what little warmth they could to ward off the bone-chilling cold. Pacing up and down, they worked hard to sell their sex, but in the gloom they appeared more like skeletal wraiths than objects of desire.

The man drove slowly, his eyes raking the line of half-naked junkies. He sized them up—a sharp snap of recognition occasionally punching through—then dismissed them. They weren't what he was looking for. Tonight he was looking for something special.

Hope jostled with fear and frustration. He had thought of nothing else for days. He was so close now, but what if it was all a lie? An urban myth? He slammed the steering wheel hard. She *had* to be here.

Nothing. Nothing. Noth—

There she was. Standing alone, leaning against the graffiti-embossed wall. The man felt a sudden surge of excitement. There *was* something different about this one. She wasn't checking her nails or smoking or gossiping. She was simply waiting. Waiting for something to happen.

He pulled his car off the road, parking out of sight by a chain-link fence. He had to be careful, mustn't leave anything to chance. He scanned the streetscape for signs of life, but the fog had cut them off completely. It was as if they were the only two people left in the world.

He marched across the road toward her, then checked himself, slowing his pace. He mustn't rush this—this was something to be savored and enjoyed. The anticipation was sometimes more enjoyable than the act—experience had taught him that. He must linger over this one. In the days ahead, he would want to replay these memories as accurately as he could.

She was framed by a row of abandoned houses. Nobody wanted to live round here anymore and these homes were now hollow and dirty. They were crack dens and flophouses, strewn with dirty needles and dirtier mattresses. As he crossed the street toward her, the girl looked up, peering through her thick fringe. Hauling herself off the wall, she said nothing, simply nodding toward the nearest shell of a house before stepping inside. There was no negotiation, no preamble. It was as if she was resigned to her fate. As if she *knew*.

Hurrying to catch up with her, the man drank in her backside, her legs, her heels, his arousal growing all the time. As she disappeared into the darkness, he picked up the pace. He couldn't wait any longer.

The floorboards creaked noisily as he stepped inside. The derelict house was just how he had pictured it in his fantasies. An overpowering smell of damp filled his nostrils—everything was rotten here. He hurried into the sitting room, now a repository for abandoned G-strings and condoms. No sign of her. So they were going to play "Chase me," were they?

Into the kitchen. No sign. Turning, he stalked out and climbed the stairs to the second floor. With each step, his eyes darted this way and that, searching for his prey.

He marched into the front bedroom. A mildewed bed, a broken window, a dead pigeon. But no sign of the girl.

Fury now wrestled with his desire. Who was she to mess with him like this? She was a common whore. Dog shit on his shoe. He was going to make her suffer for treating him like this.

He pushed the bathroom door open—nothing—then turned and marched into the second bedroom. He would smash her stupid fa—

Suddenly his head snapped back. Pain raged through him—they were pulling his hair so tight, dragging him back, back, back. Now he couldn't breathe—a rag was being forced over his mouth and nose. A sharp, biting odor flared up his nostrils and, too late, instinct kicked in. He struggled for his life, but already he was losing consciousness. Then everything went black.

2

They were watching her every move. Hanging on her every word.

"The body is that of a white female, aged between twenty and twenty-five. She was found by a Community Support officer yesterday morning in the boot of an abandoned car on the Greenwood estate."

Detective Inspector Helen Grace's voice was clear and strong, despite the tension that knotted her stomach. She was briefing the Major Incident Team on the seventh floor of Southampton Central Police Station.

"As you can see from the pictures, her teeth were caved in, probably with a hammer, and both her hands have been cut off. She is heavily tattooed, which might help with IDing, and you should concentrate your efforts on drugs and prostitution to begin with. This looks like a gang-related killing rather than a common or garden-variety murder. DS Bridges is going to lead on this one and he'll fill you in on particular persons of interest. Tony?"

"Thank you, ma'am. First things first: I want to check precedents . . ."

As DS Bridges hit his stride, Helen slipped away. Even after all this time, she couldn't bear being the center of everyone's attention, gossip and intrigue. It had been nearly a year since she'd brought Marianne's terrible killing spree to an end, but the interest in Helen was as strong as ever. Bringing in a serial killer was impressive enough; shooting your own sister to do so was something else. In the immediate aftermath, friends, colleagues, journalists and strangers had rushed to offer sympathy and support. But it was all largely fake—what they wanted were *details*. They wanted to open Helen up and pick over her insides— what was it like to shoot your sister? Were you abused by your father? Do you feel guilty for all those deaths? Do you feel *responsible*?

Helen had spent her entire adult life building a high wall around herself—even the name Helen Grace was a fiction—but thanks to Marianne that wall had been destroyed forever. Initially Helen had been tempted to run—she'd been offered leave, a transfer, even a retirement package—but somehow she had caught hold of herself, returning to work at Southampton Central as soon as they would allow her to do so. She knew that wherever she went the eyes of the world would be on her. Better to face the examination on home turf, where for many years life had been good to her.

That was the theory, but it had proved far from easy. There were so many memories here—of Mark, of Charlie—and so many people who were willing to probe, speculate or even joke about her ordeal. Even now, months after she'd returned to work, there were times when she just had to get away.

"Good night, ma'am."

Helen snapped to, oblivious to the desk sergeant she was walking straight past.

"Good night, Harry. Hope the Saints remember how to win for you tonight."

Her tone was bright, but the words sounded strange, as if the effort of being perky was too much for her. Hurrying outside, she picked up her Kawasaki and, opening the throttle, sped away down West Quay Road. The sea fog that had rolled in earlier clung to the city and Helen vanished inside it.

Keeping her speed strong but steady, she glided past the traffic crawling its way to St. Mary's Stadium. Reaching the outskirts of town, she diverted onto the motorway. Force of habit made her check her mirrors, but there was no one following her. As the traffic eased, she raised her speed. Hitting eighty miles per hour, she paused for a second before pushing it to ninety. She never felt so at ease as when she was traveling at speed.

The towns flicked by. Winchester, then Farnborough, before eventually Aldershot loomed into view. Another quick check of the mirrors, then into the city center. Parking her bike, Helen sidestepped a group of drunken cadets and hurried off, hugging the shadows as she went. Nobody knew her here, but even so, she couldn't take any chances.

She walked past the train station and before long she was in Cole Avenue, in the heart of Aldershot's suburbia. She wasn't sure she was doing the right thing, yet she'd felt compelled to return. Settling herself down amid the undergrowth that flanked one side of the street, she took up her usual vantage point.

Time crawled by. Helen's stomach growled and she realized that she hadn't eaten since breakfast. Stupid, really—she was getting thinner by the day. What was she trying to prove to herself? There were better ways of atoning than by starving yourself to death.

Suddenly there was movement. A shouted "bye" and then the door of number 14 slammed shut. Helen crouched lower. Her eyes remained glued to the young man who was now hurrying down the street, tapping numbers into his mobile phone. He passed within ten feet of Helen, never once detecting her presence, before disappearing round the corner. Helen counted to fifteen, then left her hiding place and set off in pursuit.

The man—a boyish twenty-five-year-old—was handsome, with thick dark hair and a full face. Casually dressed, with his jeans hanging around his bum, he looked like so many young men, desperate to appear cool and uninterested. It made Helen smile a little at the studied casualness of it all.

A knot of rowdy lads loomed into view, stationed outside the Railway Tavern. Two pounds a pint, fifty pence a shot and free pool, it was a mecca for the young, the skint and the shady. The elderly owner was happy to serve anyone who'd hit puberty, so it was always packed, the crowds spilling out onto the street. Helen was glad of the cover, slipping in among the bodies to observe undetected. The gaggle of lads greeted the young man with a cheer as he waved a twenty-pound note at them. They entered and Helen followed. Waiting patiently in the queue for the bar, she was invisible to them—anyone over the age of thirty didn't exist in their world.

After a couple of drinks, the gang drifted away from the prying eyes of the pub toward a kids' playground on the outskirts of town. The tatty urban park was deserted and Helen had to tail the boys cautiously. Any woman wandering alone at night through a park is likely to draw attention to herself, so she hung back. She found an aged oak tree, grievously wounded with scores of lovers' carvings, and stationed herself in its shadow. From here, she could watch unmolested as the gang smoked dope, happy and carefree in spite of the cold.

Helen had spent her whole life being watched, but here she was invisible. In the aftermath of Marianne's death, her life had been picked apart, opened up for public consumption. As a result, people thought they knew her inside and out.

But there was one thing they didn't know. One secret that she had kept to herself.

And he was standing not fifty feet away from her now, utterly oblivious to her presence.

3

His eyes blinked open, but he couldn't see.

Liquid oozed down his cheeks as his eyeballs swiveled uselessly in their sockets. Sound was horribly muted, as if his ears were stuffed with cotton wool. Scrambling back to consciousness, the man felt a savage pain ripping through his throat and nostrils. An intense burning sensation, like a flame held steadily to his larynx. He wanted to sneeze, to retch, to spit out whatever it was that was tormenting him. But he was gagged, his mouth bound tightly with duct tape, so he had to swallow down his agony.

Eventually the stream of tears abated and his protesting eyes began to take in their surroundings. He was still in the derelict house, only now he was in the front bedroom, lying prostrate on the filthy bed. His nerves were jangling and he struggled wildly—he had to get away—but his arms and legs were bound tight to the iron bedstead. He yanked, pulled and twisted, but the nylon cords held firm.

Only now did he realize he was naked. A terrible thought pulsed through him—were they going to leave him here like this? To freeze to death? His skin had already raised its defenses—goose bumps erect with cold and terror—and he realized how perishingly cold it was.

He bellowed for all he was worth—but all he produced was a dull, buzzing moan. If he could just talk to them, reason with them . . . he could get them more money, and they would let him go. They couldn't leave him here like *this*. Humiliation seeped into his fear now, as he looked down at his bloated, middle-aged body stretched out on the stained eiderdown.

He strained to hear, hoping against hope that he was not alone. But there was nothing. They had abandoned him. How long would they leave him here? Until they had emptied all his accounts? Until they had got away? The man shuddered, already dreading the prospect of bargaining for his liberty with some junkie or whore. What would he do when he was liberated? What would he say to his family? To the police? He cursed himself bitterly for being so bloody stup—

A creaking floorboard. So he *wasn't* alone. Hope flared through him—perhaps now he could find out what they wanted. He craned round to try to engage his attacker, but they were approaching from behind and remained out of view. It suddenly struck him that the bed he was tied to had been pushed out into the middle of the room, as if center stage at a show. No one could possibly want to sleep with it like that, so why . . . ?

A falling shadow. Before he could react, something was passing over his eyes, his nose, his mouth. Some sort of hood. He could feel the soft fabric on his face, the drawstring being pulled taut. Already he was struggling to breathe, and now thick velvet was resting over his protesting nostrils. He shook his head furiously this way and that, fighting to create some tiny pocket of breathing space. Any moment he expected the string to be pulled still tighter, but to his surprise nothing happened.

What now? All was silent again, apart from his labored breathing. It was getting hot inside the hood. Could oxygen get inside it? He forced himself to breathe slowly. If he panicked now, he would hyperventilate and then . . .

Suddenly he flinched, his nerves pulsing wildly. Something cold had come to rest on his thigh. Something hard. Something metal? A knife? Now it was drifting up his leg, toward . . . The man bucked furiously, tearing his muscles as he wrenched at the cords that held him. He knew now that this was a fight to the death.

He shrieked for all he was worth. But the tape held firm. His bonds wouldn't yield. And there was no one to hear his screams anyway.

4

"Business or pleasure?"

Helen spun round, her heart thumping. Climbing the darkened stairwell to her flat, she had assumed she was alone. Irritation at being surprised mingled with a brief burst of anxiety . . . but it was only James, framed in the doorway of his flat. He had moved into the flat below her three months ago, and being a senior nurse at South Hants Hospital, he kept unsociable hours.

"Business," Helen lied. "You?"

"Business that I thought was going to become pleasure. But . . . she just left in a cab."

"Pity."

James shrugged and smiled his crooked smile. He was in his late thirties, handsome in a scruffy way, with a lazy charm that usually worked on junior nurses.

"No accounting for taste," he continued. "I thought she liked me, but I've always been crap at reading signals."

"Is that right?" Helen responded, not believing a word.

"Anyway, do you fancy company? I've got a bottle of wine that's . . . tea, I've got tea . . . ," he said, correcting himself.

Up until that point Helen could have been tempted. But the correction irritated her. James was like all the others—he knew she didn't drink, knew she preferred tea to coffee, knew that she was a killer. Another voyeur staring at the wreckage of her life.

"Love to," she lied again, "but I've got an armful of files to go through before my next shift."

James smiled and bowed his submission, but he knew what was going on. And he knew not to push it. He watched with undisguised curiosity as Helen skipped up the steps to her flat. Her front door shut behind her with an air of finality.

The clock read five a.m. Nestling on her sofa, Helen took a big swig of tea and fired up her laptop. The first twinges of fatigue were making themselves felt, but before she could sleep, she had work to do. The security on her laptop was elaborate—an impregnable wall surrounding what remained of her private life—and she took her time, enjoying the complex process of entering passwords and unlocking digital padlocks.

She opened her file on Robert Stonehill. The young man she'd been shadowing earlier knew nothing of her existence, but she knew all about his. She began typing, fleshing out her growing portrait of him, adding the small details of his character and personality that she'd picked up on her latest bout of surveillance. The boy was smart—you could tell that right away. He had a good sense of humor and, though he swore every second word, had a ready wit and a winning smile. He was very good at getting people to do what he wanted them to do. He never queued for a drink at the bar, always managing to get some sidekick to do that for him while he larked about with Davey—the thickset one who was obviously the leader of the gang.

Robert always seemed to have money, which was odd given that he worked as a shelf stocker in a supermarket. Where did he get his cash? Theft? Something worse? Or was he just spoiled by his parents? He was Monica and Adam's only child—the center of their world—and Helen knew that he could wrap them around his little finger. Is that where he got his seemingly limitless funds?

There were always girls buzzing round him—he was fit and handsome—but he didn't have a girlfriend as such. This was the area Helen was most interested in. Was he straight or gay? Trusting or suspicious? Who would he allow to get close to him? It was a question Helen didn't know the answer to, but she was confident that she would figure it out. She was slowly, methodically creeping inside every quarter of Robert's life.

Helen yawned. She had to be back at the station shortly, but there was still time for a few hours' sleep if she packed it in now. With practiced ease, she ran her computer's encryption programs, locked down her files, then changed the master password. She changed it every time she used her computer now. She knew it was over the top, that she was being paranoid, but she refused to leave anything to chance. Robert was hers and hers alone. And that was the way she wanted it to stay.

5

Dawn was breaking, so he had to move fast. In an hour or two, the sun would have burned off the thick fog, exposing those who hid within it. His hands were shaking and his joints ached, but he willed himself forward.

He'd stolen the crowbar from a hardware store on Elm Street. The Indian guy who ran it was too busy watching cricket on his tablet to notice him slipping it into his long coat. The rigid, cold metal felt good in his hands and he worked it hard now, back and forth, attacking the rusty bars that protected the windows. The first bar fell away easily; the second required more work, but soon there was enough room for a body to fit through. It would have been easier to go around the front and force his way in there, but he daren't be seen on the streets round here. He owed money to too many people—people who would gladly take him apart for the hell of it. So he moved in the shadows, like all creatures of the night.

He checked again that the coast was clear, then swung the crowbar at the window. It splintered with a satisfying crash. Wrapping his hand in an old towel, he quickly punched out the rest of the glass before levering himself up onto the sill and inside.

Landing softly, he hesitated. You could never be sure what you might find in these places. There were no signs of life, but it pays to be careful and he held his crowbar tightly as he ventured forward. There was nothing of use in the kitchen, so he quickly scurried into the front room.

This was more promising. Abandoned mattresses, discarded condoms and near them their natural bedfellows, used syringes. He felt his hope and anxiety rising in equal measure. Please, God, let there be enough residue inside to harvest a proper fix. Suddenly he was on his hands and knees, pulling out the plungers, thrusting his little finger inside, desperately grubbing around for a little bit of brown to ease his suffering. Nothing in the first, nothing in the second—goddammit—and a fingerful in the third. All this bloody effort for a fingerful. He greedily rubbed it round his gums—it would have to do for now.

He sank back on the soiled mattress and waited for the numbness to kick in. His nerves had been jangling for hours now, his head pounding. He wanted—needed—some peace. He closed his eyes and exhaled slowly, willing his body to relax.

But something wasn't right. Something wouldn't let him relax. Something was . . .

Drip. There it was. A sound. A slow but steady sound, disturbing the quiet, drumming out an insistent warning.

Drip. Where was it coming from? His eyes flicked nervously this way and that.

Something was dripping in the far corner of the room. Was it a leak? Shrugging off his irritation, he dragged himself to his feet. It was worth checking out—might be some copper piping in it for him.

He hurried over, then stopped in his tracks. It wasn't a leak. It wasn't water. It was blood. Drip, drip, dripping through the ceiling. Spinning, he hurried away—none of my fucking business—but as he reached the kitchen, he slowed. Perhaps he was being too hasty. He was armed, after all, and there was no sign of movement upstairs. Anything could have happened. Someone could have topped themselves, could have been mugged, killed, whatever. But there might be spoils in it for a scavenger, and that was something that couldn't be ignored.

A moment's hesitation, then the thief turned and crossed the room, edging past the thick pool of congealing blood into the hallway. He darted his head out, crowbar raised to strike at the first sign of danger.

But no one was there. Cautiously, he stepped out and began to climb the stairs.

Creak. Creak. Creak.

Every step announced his presence, as he swore quietly under his breath. If there *was* anyone up there, they would know he was coming. He gripped the crowbar a little tighter as he crested the staircase. Better to be safe than sorry, so he darted his head into the bathroom and the back bedroom—only an amateur gets attacked from behind.

Satisfied that he was safe from ambush, he turned to face the front bedroom. Whatever had happened, whatever *it* was, it was in there. The thief took a deep breath, then stepped inside the darkened room.

6

She dived farther and farther down, the brackish water filling her ears and nostrils. She was far below the surface now and already running out of breath, but she didn't waver. Strange lights illuminated the lake bed, rendering it diaphanous and beautiful, tempting her deeper still.

Now she was clawing her way through the thick weeds that clung to the bottom. Visibility was poor, the going hard, her lungs bursting. They said he was here, so where was he? There was a rusting pram, an old shopping trolley, even an oil drum, but no sign of . . .

Suddenly she knew she'd been tricked. He wasn't here. She turned to make for the surface. But she didn't move. She craned her head round to see that her left leg was stuck in the weeds. She kicked with all her might, but the weeds wouldn't yield. She was beginning to feel faint now, couldn't hold out much longer, but she forced herself to relax, letting her body drift to the bottom. Better to try to disentangle herself calmly than kick herself into an even bigger mess. Forcing her head down, she dug through the offending weeds, tugging hard. Then she stopped. And screamed—her last ounce of breath escaping from her mouth. It wasn't weeds holding her under. It was a human hand.

Gasping, Charlie sat bolt upright in bed. She cast about her wildly, trying to process the weird disjunction between the weeds she'd been swallowed by and the homely bedroom she now found herself in. She ran her hands over her body, convinced that her pajamas should be wringing wet, but she was bone-dry except for a sheen of sweat on her brow. As her breathing began to slow she realized it was just a nightmare, just a stupid bloody nightmare.

Forcing herself to keep calm, she turned to look at Steve. He'd always been a heavy sleeper and she was pleased to see him snoring softly beside her. Slipping quietly off her side of the bed, she picked up her dressing gown and tiptoed out of the room.

She crossed the landing and headed for the stairs. She hurried past the door to the second bedroom, then scolded herself for doing so. When they'd first learned they were expecting, Steve and Charlie had discussed the changes they'd make to that room—replacing the double bed with a cot and nursing chair, covering the white walls with cheery yellow wallpaper, putting thick rugs on the hardwood floor—but of course all that excitement had come to nothing.

Their baby had died inside Charlie during her incarceration with Mark. By the time they got her to the hospital, she already knew, but had still hoped that the doctors would confound her worst fears. They hadn't. Steve had cried when she'd told him. The first time Charlie had ever seen him cry, though not the last. There were times in the intervening months when Charlie thought she was on top of things, that she could somehow process the awfulness of it all, but then she would find herself hesitating to go into the second bedroom, scared to see the imprint of the nursery they had imagined together, and then she knew that the wounds were still raw.

She headed downstairs to the kitchen and flipped the kettle on. Recently she'd been dreaming a lot. As her return to work had drawn closer, her anxiety had found its release in nightmares. She had kept these to herself, keen not to give Steve further ammunition.

"Couldn't sleep?"

Steve had snuck into the kitchen and was looking at her. Charlie shook her head.

"Nervous?"

"What do you think?" Charlie replied, trying to keep her tone light.

"Come here."

He opened his arms and she gratefully snuggled inside.

"We'll take it a day at a time," he continued. "I know you're going to be great, that you're going to get there . . . but if you ever feel it's too much, or it's not the right thing, then we can think again. No one will think any the less of you. Right?"

Charlie nodded. She was so grateful for his support, for his ability to *forgive* her, but his determination to get her to leave her job riled her. She understood why he hated the police force now, hated her job, hated the awful people out there in the world, and many times she'd thought about heeding his advice and just walking away. But then what? A lifetime spent knowing she'd been beaten. Forced out. Broken. The fact that Helen Grace had returned to work a month after Marianne's death only poured fuel on the fire.

So Charlie had dug in, insisting she would return to work when her sick leave was up. Hampshire Police had been generous to her, had given her every ounce of support they could, and now it was her turn to give something back.

Breaking away, she made them both coffee—there was no point in going back to bed now. The boiling water fell into the mugs erratically, splashing over the sides. Irritated, Charlie stared at the kettle accusingly, but it was her right hand that was to blame. She was shocked to see how much it was shaking. She swiftly put the kettle back on the mount, praying that Steve hadn't seen.

"I'm going to skip coffee. Just shower and run today, I think."

She turned to leave, but Steve stopped her, once more folding her into his big arms.

"Are you *sure* about this, Charlie?" he asked, his eyes boring into her.

A brief pause, then Charlie said:

"Yes, absolutely."

And with that she was gone. As she tripped up the staircase to the shower, however, she was well aware that her brave optimism was fooling no one, least of all herself.

7

"I don't want her."

"We've had this discussion, Helen. The decision's been made."

"Then unmake it. I can't say it any more clearly: I don't want her back."

Helen's tone was flinty and unyielding. She wouldn't normally be so aggressive to her superior, but she felt too much passion on this point to back down.

"There are lots of good DCs out there. Choose one of them. I'll have a full team and Charlie can go to Portsmouth, Bournemouth, wherever. A change of scene might do her good."

"I know it's hard for you and I do understand, but Charlie's got just as much right to be here as you. Work with her—she's a good police-woman."

Helen swallowed down her knee-jerk response—getting abducted by Marianne hadn't been Charlie's finest hour—and considered her next move. Detective Superintendent Ceri Harwood had replaced the disgraced Michael Whittaker and was already making her presence felt. She was a different sort of station chief to Whittaker—where he had been irascible, aggressive but often good-humored, she was smooth, a born communicator and largely humorless. Tall, elegant and handsome, she was known to be a safe pair of hands and had excelled wherever she'd been stationed. She seemed to be popular, but Helen found it hard to get any purchase on her, not just because they had so little in common—Harwood was married with kids—but because they had no history. Whittaker had been at Southampton a long time and had always regarded Helen as his protégée, helping her to rise through the ranks. There was no such indulgence from Harwood. She generally didn't stay anywhere too long and was not the kind to have favorites anyway. Her forte was keeping things nice and steady. Helen knew this was why she'd been drafted in here. A disgraced detective superintendent, a DI who'd shot and killed the prime suspect, a DS who'd killed himself to save his colleague from starvation—it was a sorry mess, and predictably the press had gone to town on it. Emilia Garanita at the *Southampton Evening News* had fed off it for weeks, as had the national press. It was never likely in these circumstances that Helen was going to be promoted into Whittaker's vacant shoes. She had been allowed to keep her job, which the police commissioner had apparently felt was more than generous. Helen knew all this and she understood it, but it still made her blood boil. These people *knew* what she'd had to do. They knew she'd killed her own sister to stop the killings and yet they still treated her like a naughty schoolgirl.

"Let me talk to her at least," Helen resumed. "If I feel we can work together, then maybe we can fi—"

"Helen, I really do want us to be friends," Harwood interrupted deftly, "and it's a little early in our relationship for me to be issuing you an order, so I am going to ask you nicely to step back from this one. I know there are issues that you and Charlie have to resolve—I know that you were close to DS Fuller—but you have to see the bigger picture. The man on the street thinks you and Charlie are *heroes* for stopping Marianne. Rightly so, in my view, and I don't want to do anything to undermine that perception. We could have suspended, transferred or dismissed either of you in the aftermath of the shooting, but that wouldn't have been right. Nor would it be right now to split up this successful team just when Charlie's ready to return to work—it would send out completely the wrong message. No, the best thing to do is to welcome Charlie back, applaud you both for what you did together and let you get on with your jobs."

Helen knew there was no point fighting this one any further. In her artfully worded way, Harwood had reminded Helen just how close she *had* come to dismissal. During the public inquiry that followed the Independent Police Complaints Commission's initial investigation into Marianne's shooting, there had been many who'd called for her to be stripped of her badge. For acting alone in her pursuit of Marianne, for deliberately misleading fellow officers, for shooting a suspect without issuing a formal warning—the list went on and on. They could have killed her career if they'd wanted to— and she was surprised and grateful that they hadn't—but she knew she was only back on probation. Her "charges" were still on file. From now on, she would have to choose her battles carefully.

Helen relented as gracefully as she could and left Harwood's office. She knew she was being unfair to Charlie, that she should be more supportive, but the truth was that she didn't want to see Charlie again. It would be like standing in front of Mark Fuller. Or Marianne. And for all her strength over the last few months, Helen couldn't face that.

. . .

Heading back to the Major Incident Team, Helen immediately picked up on the buzz of excitement. It was early morning, but already the place was busier than usual. The team had been waiting for her, and DC Lloyd Fortune hurried over to bring her up to speed.

"You're needed down at Empress Road, ma'am."

Helen was already picking up her coat.

"What is it?"

"A murder—called in by one of the local junkies about an hour ago. Uniform have been in, but I think you'd better take a look at it."

Already Helen's nerves were jangling. There was something in the DC's voice that she hadn't heard since Marianne.

Fear.

8

Eschewing her bike, Helen drove to the scene with DS Tony Bridges. She liked him—he was a diligent, committed copper whom she had come to trust. Whoever replaced Mark as the new DS was always going to have to work hard to win the team round, but Tony had managed it. He'd played it very straight, never ducking the awkwardness of appearing to profit from Mark's death. His humility and sensitivity had raised him in everyone's estimation, and he now inhabited the role pretty comfortably.

His relationship with Helen was more complex. Not just because of her feelings for Mark, but because Bridges had been there when Helen had pulled the trigger on her sister. He had seen it all—Marianne collapsing to the floor, Helen's futile attempts to revive her. Tony had seen his boss at her most naked and vulnerable—and that would always be a source of discomfort between them. On the other hand, Tony's testimony to the IPCC, during which he had insisted that Helen had no option but to shoot Marianne—had gone a long way toward saving her from demotion or dismissal. Helen had thanked him at the time, but the debt she owed him would never be mentioned again. You had to forget it and move on; otherwise the chain of command would be compromised. For all intents and purposes they now operated as any normal DI and DS would, but in truth they would always have a bond forged in battle.

They sped past the hospital, blue lights flashing, before cutting down a narrow side street and onto the Empress Road industrial estate. It wasn't hard to see where they were headed. The entrance to the derelict house was taped off and already a gaggle of curious onlookers was idling by it. Helen hustled her way through, warrant card raised, Tony following behind her. A quick word with uniform while they suited up, and then they were in.

Helen took the stairs two at a time. Whatever you've been through, you never get inured to violence. Helen didn't like the looks on the faces of the attending uniforms—as if their eyes had been brutally opened—and she wanted to get this over with as quickly as possible.

The small front bedroom was busy with the Scene of Crime Team, and Helen immediately asked them to take a break so she and Tony could get a clear view of the victim. You steel yourself on these occasions, swallowing down your disgust in advance; otherwise you'd never be able to take it in, to form valuable first impressions. The victim was male, white, probably in his late forties or early fifties. He was naked and there was no sign of any clothes or possessions. His arms and legs were tied tight to the iron bedstead with what looked like nylon climbing cord and he had some sort of hood over his head.

It hadn't been designed for the purpose—it looked like the kind of felt bag you get with expensive shoes or luxury gifts—but it was there for a reason. Was it to suffocate him? Or conceal his identity? Either way, it was devastatingly clear that this wasn't what had killed him.

His upper torso had been split up the middle from his belly button to his throat, then forcibly peeled back to reveal his internal organs. Or what remained of them. Helen swallowed hard, as she realized that at least one of his organs had been removed. She turned to Tony—he was ashen and staring at the bloody pit that had once been this man's chest. The victim had not just been killed; he had been destroyed. Helen fought to suppress a spike of panic. Taking a pen from her pocket, she crouched over the victim, gently lifting the rim of the hood to get a look at the man's face.

Mercifully it was untouched and looked oddly peaceful, despite the blank eyes that stared hopelessly at the interior of the bag. Helen didn't recognize him; she removed her pen, letting the fabric fall back into position. Returning her attention to the body, she took in the stained eiderdown, the congealing pool of blood on the floor, the path to the door. The man's injuries looked recent—less than a day old—so if there were traces of the killer to be found here, they would be fresh. But there was nothing—nothing obvious at least.

Padding round the bed, she stepped over a dead pigeon and walked to the far side of the room. There was one window, which was boarded up. It had been that way for some time by the look of the rusty nails. An abandoned house in a forgotten part of Southampton, with no accessible windows—it was the perfect spot to kill someone. Was he tortured first? That was what was concerning Helen. The victim's injuries were so unusual, so extensive, that it seemed clear someone was making a point here. Or worse, simply enjoying himself. What had driven them to do this? What had *possessed* them?

That would have to wait. The most important thing now was to give the victim a name, to let him recover a modicum of his dignity. Helen called Forensics back in. It was time to take the photos and set the investigation in motion.

It was time to find out who this poor man was.

9

It was business as usual in the Matthews household. The porridge bowls had been emptied and cleaned, school bags were lined up in the hall and the twins were putting on their school uniforms. Their mother, Eileen, chided them as she always did—it was amazing how long these boys could spin out getting dressed. When they were little they'd loved the status that their smart school uniforms had bestowed upon them and they'd hurried to put them on, desperate to appear as grown-up and important as their elder sisters. But now that the girls had left home and the twins were teenagers, they viewed the whole thing as an awful drag, delaying the inevitable for as long as possible. If their father was around, they'd snap to it, but when it was just Eileen, they took the mickey—it was only by threatening to stop their pocket money that she got them to do anything these days.

"Five minutes, boys. Five minutes and we *must* be out of the house."

Time was ticking by. The register would soon be called at Kingswood Secondary, the independent school that the boys attended, and it wouldn't do to be late. The school was very hot on discipline, sending terse letters to parents they perceived to be tardy or lax. Eileen lived in fear of these missives, despite the fact that she had never received one. As a result, the morning routine was rigidly mapped out, and usually they would have been out of the door by now, but today she was at sixes and sevens. Her chivvying of the boys was more out of habit than conviction this morning.

Alan hadn't come home last night. Eileen always worried about his being out after dark. She knew it was for a good cause and that he felt a duty to help those less fortunate than himself, but you never knew who—or what—you might run into. There were bad people out there—you only had to read the newspapers to see that.

Normally he would return around four a.m. Eileen would feign sleep, as she knew Alan didn't like the idea of her waiting up for him, but in reality she never slept a wink until he was home safe and sound. By six a.m., she couldn't hold off any longer, so she got up and rang Alan's mobile phone—but it went straight to voice mail. She'd thought about leaving a message, then decided against it. He'd be back soon enough and would accuse her of fussing. She made herself breakfast but couldn't face eating it, so it sat on the breakfast bar untouched. Where *was* he?

The boys were ready now and staring at her. They could tell she was anxious and they weren't sure whether to be amused or worried. At fourteen, they were the classic mixture of man and child, wanting to be independent, grown-up, even cynical, yet cleaving to the familiar routines and discipline that their parents provided. They were waiting to go, but still Eileen hesitated. A strong instinct was telling her to stay put, to wait for her husband to return.

The doorbell rang and Eileen bolted into the hallway. The silly so-and-so had forgotten his key. Perhaps he had been robbed. It would be just like him to help some ne'er-do-well and get his wallet pinched in the bargain. Composing herself, Eileen opened the door calmly, her brightest smile painted on her face.

But no one was there. She cast about for Alan—for anyone— but the street was quiet. Was it kids playing silly beggars?

"I'm surprised you haven't got better things to do," she called out, silently cursing the unruly children who lived at the cheaper end of the street. She was about to slam the door shut, when she noticed the box. A courier's cardboard box left on her doorstep. A white label adorned the top and on it was written *The Matthews family* and then their address—misspelled in spidery, crabbed handwriting. It looked like a present of some sort—but it wasn't anybody's birthday. Eileen stuck her head out once more, expecting to see Simon the postman or a courier's van parked up on the double yellow lines—but there was no one in sight.

The boys were onto her immediately, asking her if they could open it, but Eileen held firm. *She* would open it, and if it was appropriate, she would share it with them. They didn't really have time—it was eight forty already, for goodness' sake—but better to open it now, put the boys out of their misery and then get on with their morning. Suddenly Eileen felt cross with herself for dawdling and she resolved to get on with things—if they hurried they might just make it to school on time.

Pulling a pair of scissors from the kitchen drawer, she sliced a line down the duct tape that bound the box together. As she did so, her nose wrinkled—a strong odor emanated from inside. She couldn't put her finger on what it was, but she didn't like it. Was it something industrial? Something animal? Her instinct was to reseal the package and wait for Alan's return, but the boys were nagging her to get on with it . . . so gritting her teeth, she threw open the box.

And screamed. Suddenly she couldn't stop screaming, despite the fact that the boys were clearly terrified by the noise. Tearful, they hurried to her, but she pushed them angrily away. When they fought back, begging her to tell them what was going on, she grabbed them by their collars and hauled them roughly out of the room, screaming all the while for someone—anyone—to help.

The offending box was left alone in the room. The top lolled lazily backward, revealing the legend *Evill* written in dark crimson on the underside. It was the perfect introduction to the box's awful contents. Lying within, in a nest of dirty newspaper, was a human heart.

10

"Where are the others?"

Clutching her case file, Charlie surveyed the Major Incident Team's office. It felt extremely odd to be back, but the situation was made stranger still by the fact that the office seemed to be completely deserted.

"Murder on Empress Road. DI Grace has got most of the team down there," replied DC Fortune, just about managing to contain his disgruntlement at being left behind. He was a smart, conscientious policeman and one of the few black officers based at Southampton Central. He was tipped for higher things, and Charlie knew that he would be deeply pissed off to be stuck here, chaperoning her on her return to action. Charlie had felt shaky as she'd entered the building half an hour earlier, and the lack of a welcoming committee was making things worse. Was this a deliberate snub? A way of letting her know she wasn't wanted?

"What do we know about this?" Charlie replied, mustering as much professional poise as she could.

"Sex worker found in the boot of a car. The killers had gone to town on her, which made the ID a bit tricky initially, but her DNA did the job. She was on the database—you'll find her charge sheet on page three."

Charlie flicked through the file. The dead girl—a Polish woman called Alexia Louszko—had been striking in life, with dark auburn hair, multiple piercings and tattoos and plump, pillow lips. If you liked it gothic, then she was the one. Even in her police photo she looked aggressively sexual. Her tattoos were all of mythological beasts, giving her a primal, animalistic quality.

"Last known address is a flat near Bedford Place," DC Fortune offered helpfully.

"Let's get going, then," replied Charlie, ignoring her colleague's obvious eagerness to get the whole thing over with.

"Are you going to drive, or am I?"

Most of Southampton's sex workers lived in St. Mary's or Portswood, mixing in with the students, junkies and illegal immigrants. So the fact that Alexia lived on Bedford Place, near the smarter clubs and bars, was interesting in itself. She had been arrested for streetwalking a year ago, but must have been pulling in good money to live in this desirable area.

The interior of her flat only served to reinforce this feeling. Faced by a police warrant, the block's concierge reluctantly let the officers inside, and while DC Fortune questioned him, Charlie took a detailed look at the place. It was a recently decorated, open-plan setup with affordable but fashionable furniture. In addition to the wraparound sofa and large plasma TV, there were a glass table, espresso machine, retro jukebox. Hell, it was nicer than Charlie's house. Was this girl earning enough for all these middle-class trappings or was she being kept by someone? A lover? Her pimp? Someone she was blackmailing?

Ignoring the kitchen, Charlie headed straight for the bedroom. It was exceptionally neat and clean. Donning her latex gloves, she began to search. The wardrobes were full of clothes, the drawers of underwear and bondage gear, and the bed was neatly made. A single paperback—by a Polish author Charlie hadn't heard of—rested on the bedside table. And that was it. Was that all there was to her?

The bathroom yielded little of any interest, so Charlie moved on to the box room, which served as a space for drying laundry and a mini office. A phone and cheap laptop sat on a battered desk. Charlie pressed the power button on the computer. It buzzed aggressively, as if coming to life, but the screen remained resolutely blank. Charlie pressed a few keys. Still nothing.

"You got your penknife?" she asked DC Fortune. She knew he would have it (even though he wasn't supposed to); he was that kind of guy. Nothing pleased him more than fixing a broken machine in front of his female colleagues. He was a modern kind of caveman.

Taking it from him, Charlie flipped out the screwdriver extension and undid the panels on the back of the computer. As she expected, the battery was still in place, but the hard drive had been removed.

So the flat *had* been swept. From the moment she'd stepped into the place Charlie had had a suspicion that it had been tidied up. Nobody's life was this ordered. Someone who knew that the police would be coming had trawled the flat, divesting it of any trace of

Alexia, either physical or digital. What had she been doing to earn all this money? And why was someone so keen to conceal it?

There was no point in looking for anything in the usual places anymore. It was now a question of lifting wardrobes and tables, pulling up mattresses and rifling through pockets. Looking under, behind, above. It felt very much like a wild-goose chase, and Charlie had to put up with a lot of unsubtle sighing by her colleague—who was probably imagining himself busting heads on the Empress Road—but finally after two and a half hours of diligent searching the pair got a break.

The kitchen had an island in it with a pull-out bin. The bin had been lifted out and emptied, but whoever had done so hadn't spotted a piece of paper on the bottom of the pull-out drawer. It must have slipped between the bin edge and the drawer wall when tossed inside and lain there undetected ever since. Charlie pulled it out.

To her surprise it was a payslip. For a woman called Agneska Suriav, who was employed by a health club in Banister Park. It looked official—with National Insurance deductions, a PAYE Employee number—and was for a healthy monthly wage. But it didn't make a lot of sense. Who was Agneska? A friend of Alexia's? An alias of hers? It raised more questions than it answered, but it was a start. For the first time in ages, Charlie felt good about herself. Perhaps there was life after Marianne after all.

11

"I want an absolute information lockdown on this until we know more. Nothing leaves these four walls without my say-so, okay?"

The team nodded obediently as Helen spoke. DS Bridges, DCs Sanderson, McAndrew and Grounds, junior officers, data processors and Media Liaison were all crammed into the hastily requisitioned incident room. The investigation was coming to life and there was a suppressed hum of excitement in the room.

"We are obviously looking for a highly dangerous individual, or individuals, and it is imperative that we move swiftly to bring them in. First priority is to ID our victim. Sanderson, I want you to liaise with Forensics but also uniform—they are out canvassing witnesses in the area and checking for vehicles that might have belonged to the victim. I doubt there'll be cameras on that street, but ask the supermarkets and businesses nearby. They may have something that can help us."

"On it," DC Sanderson replied. It was dull work, but often it was the obvious things that opened up a case. There was always the possibility of glory in the drudgery.

"McAndrew, I want you to talk to the street girls. There must have been a dozen or more out in the area last night. They might have seen or heard something. They won't want to talk to us, but things like this are bad for business, so impress upon them that it's in their interest to help us. They may be happier talking to a plainclothes officer, so use the beat coppers to guide you, but do as many of the one-on-ones as you can yourself."

DC McAndrew nodded, knowing her evening plans had just gone up in smoke. No wonder she was still single.

Helen paused for a second, then slowly and deliberately pinned the crime scene photos—one by one—to the board behind her. As she did so, she heard a faint but audible intake of breath. Few of the officers present had seen a man turned inside out before.

"First question—why?" Helen said, as she turned back to face the team. "What did our victim do to provoke an attack like this?"

She let the question hang in the air, taking in the reaction to the photos, before continuing:

"The derelict houses on this street are used by prostitutes and junkies on a daily basis, so why was this man there? Was he a punter who refused to pay? Was he a pimp who tried to rip off a client? Or a supplier who'd shortchanged his dealers? The level of savagery in this attack denotes real anger or the desire to make a very public statement. This is *not* a crime of passion. Our killer was well prepared—with nylon cords, duct tape, a weapon—and they took their time. Forensics will confirm this later, but given the level of blood saturation on the body and floor, it looks like the victim bled to death. The killer didn't panic, didn't run. They had no fear of detection, calmly going about their business, cutting the victim open before . . ."

Helen paused momentarily before completing her sentence:

". . . before removing his heart."

One of the data processors was beginning to look a little green, so Helen pressed on.

"It looks to me like an ambush. Like punishment. But what for? Is this part of a turf war? A warning to a rival gang? Did the victim owe someone money? Was it robbery? Hookers and pimps have tortured their punters for PIN numbers and got carried away before. Or was it something else?"

It was the something else that Helen was afraid of. Was the heart some sort of trophy? Helen batted the thought away and returned to the briefing. There was no point getting ahead of herself, imagining crazy things that might have a violently mundane explanation.

"We need to cast our net as wide as possible. Prostitution, gang crime, drugs, criminal grudges. It's highly likely the killer or killers will give themselves away in the next twenty-four hours. They may be shitting themselves or they may be exhilarated—it's hard to behave calmly after doing something like this. So eyes and ears open—any sources, any leads. From now on this case is your top priority. Everything else can be handled by others."

Which everyone knew meant Charlie. Helen hadn't seen her yet, but their reunion wouldn't be long in coming. Helen had resolved to be polite and formal, as was her way when nervous, but would she be able to carry it off? In the past her mask had been impenetrable, but not now. Too much had happened—too much of her past had been exposed for people to buy that persona anymore.

The room had emptied as officers rushed off to cancel plans, assuage loved ones and grab some food in expectation of a long night ahead. So Helen was standing alone, wrapped up in her own thoughts, when Tony Bridges hurried back in.

"Looks like we've found our man."

Helen snapped out of her reverie.

"Front desk took a call from a highly distressed woman who'd just had a human heart left on her doorstep. Her husband didn't come home last night."

"Name?"

"Alan Matthews. Married, father of four, lives in Banister Park. He's a businessman, charity fund-raiser and an active member of the local Baptist church."

Tony had tried to say the last bit without wincing, but he'd failed. Helen closed her eyes, aware that the next few hours would be deeply unpleasant for everyone concerned. A family man had died a grim death in a known prostitutes' haunt—there was no nice way to say that. But experience had taught her that prevaricating never helped, so she picked up her bag and nodded at Tony to follow her.

"Let's get this over with."

12

Eileen Matthews was holding it together, but only just. She sat erect on the plump sofa, her eyes fixed on the policewoman as she described the awful events of the last few hours. The detective inspector was flanked by a male officer, Tony, and a Family Liaison officer whose name she'd already forgotten—but Eileen had eyes only for the inspector.

The twins were now safely installed with friends. This was the right thing to do, but Eileen was already regretting it. What must they be thinking and feeling? She had to be here, answering questions, but every instinct told her to run from this room, find her boys, hug them tight and never let them go. Nevertheless, she stayed where she was, pinned down by the policewoman's questions, paralyzed by her experiences.

"Is this your husband?"

Helen handed Eileen a close-up of the victim's face. She took one look at it, then dropped her eyes to the floor.

"Yes."

Her answer was muted, lifeless. Shock still gripped her, keeping tears at bay. Her brain was struggling to process these strange events.

"Is he . . . ?" she managed.

"Yes, I'm afraid he is. And I'm very sorry for your loss."

Eileen nodded as if Helen had confirmed something obvious, something mundane, but she was only half listening. She wanted to push this whole thing away, pretend none of it was happening. Her gaze was fixed on the many family photos that plastered the sitting room wall—scenes of happy family life.

"Is there someone we can call to be with you?"

"How did he die?" Eileen replied, ignoring Helen's question.

"We're not sure yet. But you should know straightaway that this wasn't an accident. Or suicide. This is a murder inquiry, Eileen."

Another hammer blow.

"Who would do such a thing?" For the first time, Eileen looked Helen in the eye. Her face was a picture of bewilderment.

"Who would do such a thing?" she repeated. "Who could . . ."

Her words petered out as she gestured toward the kitchen, where a couple of Forensics officers were photographing the heart prior to bagging it.

"We don't know," Helen replied. "But we're going to find out. Can you tell me where your husband was last night?"

"He was where he always is on Tuesday nights. Helping out at the soup kitchen on Southbrook Road."

Tony scribbled a note in his notebook.

"So this is a regular commitment?"

"Yes, Alan is very active in the church—we both are—and our faith puts great emphasis on helping those less fortunate than ourselves."

Eileen caught herself referring to her husband in the present tense.

Once again the sudden awfulness of it all overwhelmed her. He couldn't be dead, could he? A sound from upstairs made her jump. But it wasn't Alan padding around his study; it was those other officers leafing through his things, removing his computer, robbing the house of his presence.

"Is there any reason why he would have been in the Bevois Valley area last night? Empress Road in particular."

"No. He would have been at Southbrook Road from eight p.m. until . . . well, until they ran out of soup. There are always too many people for their limited resources, but they do their best. Why?"

Eileen didn't want to know the answer but felt compelled to ask.

"Alan was found in a derelict house on the Empress Road industrial estate."

"That doesn't make sense."

Helen said nothing.

"If he was attacked by one of the people at the soup kitchen, surely they wouldn't have dragged him halfway across Southampton . . ."

"His car was found a stone's throw from the house. It was neatly parked and had been locked with the key fob. Is there any reason why he might have gone there of his own free will?"

Eileen eyed her—what was she getting at?

"Asking hard questions is part of my job, Eileen. I need to ask them if we're to get to the truth of what happened. Empress Road is often used by prostitutes to pick up clients and occasionally by drug dealers to peddle drugs. To your knowledge has Alan ever used prostitutes or taken drugs?"

Eileen was too stunned to answer for a second; then, without warning, she exploded:

"Have you not been listening to a word I've been saying? We are a religious family. Alan is a church elder."

She said each word slowly, enunciating every syllable as if talking to someone simple.

"He was a good man who cared about others. He had a sense of his mission in life. If he came into contact with prostitutes or drug dealers it was purely to help them. He would never use prostitutes in *that* way."

Helen was about to interject, but Eileen wasn't finished.

"Something *awful* happened last night. A kind, honorable man offered to help someone and they robbed and killed him in return. So instead of insinuating these . . . disgusting things, why don't you get out of my house and find the *man* who did this to him?"

And now the tears did come. Eileen pulled herself up off the sofa abruptly and ran from the room—she wouldn't cry in front of these people, wouldn't give them the satisfaction. Heading into the bedroom, she threw herself on the bed she'd shared with her husband for thirty years and cried her heart out.

13

The man crept up the stairs, careful to avoid the creaky board on the fifth step.

Crossing the landing, he avoided Sally's room and headed straight to his wife's bedroom. Strange how he always thought of it as her room. A moment's hesitation, then he placed his fingers on the wooden door and pushed it open. It protested loudly, the hinges groaning as the door swung round.

The man held his breath.

But there was no sound, no sense that he'd disturbed her. So he quietly stepped inside.

She was fast asleep. For a moment a pulse of love shot through him, swiftly followed by a spasm of shame. She looked so innocent and peaceful lying there. So happy. How had it come to this?

He walked out quickly, heading for the stairs. Dwelling on it would only weaken his resolve. Now was the time, so there was no point hesitating. Opening the front door soundlessly, he shot one more cautious glance upstairs, then slipped out into the night.

14

The sign was discreet—if you didn't know it was there, you'd miss it.

Brookmire Health and Wellbeing. Strange that a commercial enterprise should be so bashful about announcing its presence. Charlie pressed the buzzer—it was swiftly answered.

"Police," Charlie shouted, struggling to be heard above the traffic. There was a pause, longer perhaps than was necessary, then she was buzzed in. Already she had the feeling she wasn't welcome.

Charlie climbed the stairs to the top floor. The smile that greeted her was wide but fake. A neat, attractive young woman in a crisp white uniform, hair tied back in a ponytail, asked how she could be of assistance—clearly intending to be no help at all. Charlie said nothing, casing the place—it looked like an upmarket Champneys and had that perfumed smell that all spas have. Eventually Charlie's eyes returned to the receptionist, whose name badge revealed she was called Edina. Her accent was Polish.

"I'd like to speak to the manager," Charlie said, presenting her warrant card to underline her request.

"He's not here. May I be of assistance?"

Still the same forced smile. Irritated, Charlie walked round the desk and down the corridor that led to more rooms at the back.

"You can't go down there—"

But Charlie carried on. It was pleasant enough—a series of treatment rooms and off them a communal kitchen. A young mixed-race boy was sitting at the table playing with a train. He looked up, saw Charlie and grinned a huge grin. Charlie couldn't help smiling back.

"The manager will be back tomorrow. Perhaps you can come back then?" Edina had caught up with Charlie.

"Maybe. In the meantime, I'd like to ask you some questions about an employee. A woman by the name of Agneska Suriav."

Edina looked blank, so Charlie handed her a photocopy of Agneska's payslip.

"Yes, yes. Agneska is one of our therapists. She is on holiday at the moment."

"Actually she's dead. She was murdered two days ago."

For the first time, Charlie saw a genuine reaction—shock. There was a long pause as Edina processed this, and then she muttered:

"How did she die?"

"She was strangled, then mutilated."

Charlie waited for that to land before continuing:

"When did you last see her?"

"Three or four days ago."

"Friend of yours?"

Edina shrugged, clearly not wanting to commit either way.

"What did she do here?"

"She was a dietitian."

"Popular?"

"Yes," Edina replied, though she looked bemused by the question.

"How much did she charge?"

"We have a price list here. I can show—"

"Did she give the full service or did she specialize in certain areas?"

"I don't understand what you mean."

"I've checked out Agneska and I don't see too many diplomas in dietary science. Her real name was Alexia Louszko and she was a prostitute—a good one by all accounts. She was also Polish. Like you."

Edina said nothing, clearly not liking where this was going.

"Let's start again, shall we?" Charlie resumed. "Why don't you tell me what Alexia did here?"

There was a long, long silence. Then, finally, Edina said:

"Like I said, the manager will be back tomorrow."

Charlie laughed.

"You're good, Edina, I'll give you that."

Her eyes flitted to the corridor of treatment rooms.

"What would happen if I walked into one of those treatment rooms right now? Room 3 is in use. If I were to kick it open right now, what would I find? Shall we go and see?"

"Be my guest. If you have a warrant."

Edina was no longer even pretending to be friendly. Charlie paused to reconsider her line of attack—this girl was no amateur.

"Whose boy is that?" Charlie said, gesturing toward the kitchen.

"A client's."

"What's his name?"

A tiny pause, then:

"Billy."

"His real name, Edina. And if you lie to me again, I'm going to arrest you."

"Richie."

"Call him."

"You don't have to inv—"

"Call him."

She hesitated, then:

"RICHIE."

"Yes, mama," came the call from the kitchen.

Edina's eyes fell to the floor.

"Who's his father?" Charlie continued her attack.

Suddenly there were tears in Edina's eyes.

"Please don't involve him or the boy. This has nothing to do with—"

"Do they have papers?"

Nothing in response.

"Are they in this country illegally?"

A long pause. Then finally Edina nodded.

"Please" was all she could say by way of entreaty.

"I'm not here to cause you or your boy trouble, but I need to know what Alexia did here. And what happened to her. So either you start talking or I make a phone call. Your choice, Edina."

There was no choice, of course. And Charlie wasn't surprised by Edina's answer.

"Not here. Meet me in the café round the corner in five minutes."

She hurried off to her son. Charlie breathed a sigh of relief. It was strange to be doing battle once more and suddenly she felt exhausted. She hadn't expected her first day back to be so grueling. But she knew that worse was to come. Tonight was her welcome-back drinks. Time to face Helen Grace.

15

For the first time in years, Helen craved a drink. She had seen what it had done to her parents and that had put her off for life, but sometimes she still craved the hit. She was wound tight tonight. The interview with Eileen Matthews had gone badly, as the disgruntled Family Liaison officer had been quick to point out. There was little Helen could have done differently—she had to ask the tough questions—but still she berated herself for upsetting someone who was blameless and distraught. In the end, they had had no choice but to leave, having learned nothing of use along the way.

Helen had biked straight from Eileen's house to the Parrot and Two Chairmen pub, Tony following behind. Situated a couple of blocks from Southampton Central, it was the traditional venue for leaving dos and the like. Tonight they were wetting Charlie's head on her return to work—another stupid tradition. Helen had steeled herself and walked in, Tony trying a bit too hard to be jaunty and relaxed beside her . . . only to find that Charlie wasn't there. She was still out on the job and was expected shortly.

The team made small talk, but no one knew quite how to play it. Furtive eyes were cast toward the pub entrance; then suddenly there she was. Charlie bounded over toward the group—keen to get this over with?—and as if by magic the crowd seemed to part, allowing Charlie a clean run at her superior.

"Hello, Charlie," Helen said. Not exactly inspired, but it would have to do.

"Boss."

"How's your first day been?"

"Good. It's been good."

"Good."

Silence. Mercifully Tony leaped to Helen's aid:

"Nicked anyone yet?"

Charlie laughed and shook her head.

"You're losing your touch, girl," Tony continued. "Sanderson, you owe me a fiver."

The team laughed and slowly they crowded round, patting Charlie on the back, buying her drinks, peppering her with questions. Helen did her best to join in—asking after Steve, her parents—but her heart wasn't in it. Seizing a suitable moment, she nipped off to the toilets. She needed solitude.

She entered the cubicle and sat down. She felt light-headed and rested her head in her hands. Her temples throbbed; her throat was dry. Charlie had looked surprisingly well—nothing like the broken woman who'd stumbled free from her terrible captivity—but seeing her had been harder than Helen had anticipated. Without her around as a reminder, Helen had settled back into life at the station. With Tony promoted to DS and new blood introduced, it had almost been like engaging with a new team. Charlie's return took her straight back to that time, reminding her of all that she'd lost.

Helen exited the cubicle and gave her hands a long, thorough cleaning. In the background a toilet flushed and a cubicle door opened. Helen flicked a glance into the mirror and her face fell.

Walking toward her was Emilia Garanita, chief crime reporter for the *Southampton Evening News.*

"Fancy meeting you here," said Emilia, smiling the broadest of grins.

"I would have thought this was your natural habitat, Emilia."

It was cheap, but Helen couldn't resist. She disliked this woman both professionally and personally. The fact that she had suffered— one side of Emilia's face was still heavily disfigured following a historic acid attack—cut no ice with Helen. Everyone suffered. It didn't have to make you a merciless shit.

Emilia's smile didn't waver; she liked dueling, as Helen knew to her cost.

"I was rather hoping we'd run into each other, *Inspector*," she continued. Helen wondered if the stress on the last word was Emilia's way of emphasizing how Helen's career had stalled. "I hear you had yourself a nasty little murder on the Empress Road."

Helen had given up asking how she came by her information. There was always some newbie in uniform who would cough up information when caught in Emilia's tractor beam. Whether intimidated by her or just keen to be rid of her, they gave her what she wanted in the end.

Helen looked at her, then walked off, pushing through the door back into the pub. Emilia fell into stride next to her.

"Any working theories? I heard it was pretty savage."

No mention of the heart. Was she ignorant of this little detail or teasing Helen with its omission?

"Any idea who the victim is yet?"

"Nothing confirmed, but as soon as it is you'll be the first to know." Emilia grinned, but didn't get a chance to respond.

"Emilia, how nice to see you. Come to buy me a drink?" Ceri Harwood was now hurrying over. Where had she sprung from?

"On a journalist's wage?" Emilia countered good-humoredly.

"Then allow me," Harwood replied, steering her toward the bar.

Helen watched them go, unsure whether Harwood had rescued her from Emilia or stepped in to prevent Helen from irritating the fourth estate. Either way she was glad of the intervention. She shot a glance at her team. Happy, relaxed and already a few drinks to the good, they chatted animatedly, clearly pleased to have Charlie back.

Helen felt like the bad fairy at the christening. The one person unable to welcome Charlie back with an open heart. The team was oblivious to her, which provided Helen with the perfect opportunity.

There was somewhere she needed to be.

Helen climbed onto her bike and pulled her helmet on, rendering her temporarily anonymous. Turning the ignition, she tested the throttle, then kicked off the brake and roared down the darkened street. She was glad to see the back of Emilia and Charlie. She had had enough for one day—more than enough.

Rush hour was long gone and Helen cut easily through the empty streets. At times like this she really did feel at home in South-ampton. It was as if the streets had been cleared for her, as if it were her city, a place where she could exist unmolested and undisturbed. Slowly her mood lifted. Not simply because of where she was, but because of where she was going.

Having parked up, she rang the bell three times and waited. The buzzer sounded—like a warm welcome—and she stepped inside.

Jake was waiting for her, the door wide-open. Helen knew he didn't do this for other clients—the dangers inherent in his business meant he always verified a client's identity through the spyhole before opening the reinforced door. But he knew it was her—the three rings being their code—and, besides, he knew now what she did for a profession.

It hadn't always been that way, of course. For the first year of their association, she had told him nothing, despite his numerous attempts to open up a conversation. But recent events had changed all that—dominators read the papers too. Thankfully, he was too professional to mention it. He was tempted to—she sensed that—but he knew how much she had suffered, how much she loathed the exposure. So he kept his counsel.

This was Helen's space. A place where she could be the closed book she used to be. A throwback to a time when her life was under control. If she hadn't been happy then, she had nevertheless been at peace. And peace was what she craved now. It was a risk coming here, for sure—many other coppers had been driven out of the force in disgrace because of their "unconventional" lifestyles—but it was a risk Helen was prepared to take.

She stripped off her biking leathers, then removed her suit and blouse, hanging them up on the expensive hangers in Jake's wardrobe. Slipping off her shoes, she was now just in her underwear. Already she could feel her body relaxing. Jake had his back to her—his usual, discreet self—but Helen knew he wanted to look at her. She liked that—it made her feel good; she wanted him to look at her. But you can't have it both ways. Privacy and intimacy are mutually exclusive.

Closing her eyes, Helen waited for him to strike. Finally, on the cusp of release, dark thoughts suddenly reared up unbidden, surprising and unsettling her. Thoughts of Marianne and Charlie, of the people she'd hurt and betrayed, the damage she'd done—the damage she was *still* doing.

Jake brought the crop firmly down on her back. Then again, harder. He paused as Helen's body reacted to the blows; then, just as she began to relax, he whipped her again. Helen felt the sharp spasm of pain dissipate into an all-over tingling. Her heart was pumping, her headache receding, the endorphins pulsing round her brain. Her dark thoughts were in full flight now—punishment, as always, her savior. As Jake brought the crop down for the fourth time, Helen realized that for the first time in days, she felt truly relaxed. And more than that, she felt happy.

16

He had left his wedding ring on. As he turned the steering wheel, maneuvering the car over Redbridge Causeway, he caught sight of the gold band nestling on his fourth finger. He cursed himself—he was still bloody green at this. Looking up, he noticed that she had clocked his discomfort.

"Don't worry, love. Most of my punters are married. Nobody's judging you here."

She smiled at him, then turned to look out the window. He chanced another, longer look at her. She was just how he'd hoped she'd be. Young, fit, her long legs clad in thigh-high plastic boots. A short skirt, a loose top that revealed her large breasts, and elbow-length gloves— were they to arouse or simply to ward off the perishing cold? A pale face with high cheekbones and then that striking hair—long, black and straight.

He had picked her up on Cemetery Road, just south of the Common. There was no one around at that time of night, which suited them both. They headed west, crossed the river and, on her instructions, cut off down a narrow side road. They were approaching Eling Great Marsh, a lonely strip of land that looks back toward the docks. During daylight hours, nature lovers came here searching for wildlife, but at night it was used by a very different clientele.

They parked and for a moment sat in silence. She delved in her bag for a condom, placing it on the dashboard.

"You're going to have to tip your seat back or I'm not going to be able to do anything," she said gently.

Smiling, he shunted his chair back abruptly, then slowly lowered it to allow them more wriggle room. Already her gloved hand was casually brushing over his groin, provoking an erection.

"Mind if I keep these on?" she asked. "It's more fun that way."

He nodded, desire rendering him mute. She began to unzip his trousers.

"Close your eyes, honey, and let me take care of you."

He did as he was told. She was in command and he liked it that way. It was nice to be taken care of for once, to be free of responsibility, to please oneself. When did he ever get the chance to do that?

Unbidden, an image of Jessica popped into his mind. His loving wife of two years, the mother of his child, unsuspecting, betrayed . . . He pushed the thought away, swallowing this sudden intrusion of real life. It had no place here. This was his fantasy made flesh. This was his moment. And despite the feelings of guilt that now circled him, he was going to enjoy it.

17

It was nearly midnight when he returned home. The house was dark and still, as it always seemed to be. Nicola would be sleeping peacefully upstairs, her caregiver camped by her side, reading a book by torchlight. Usually this was an image that cheered him—a cozy cocoon for his wife—but tonight the thought of it saddened him. A fierce sense of loss ripped through him, sudden and hard.

Dropping his keys on the table, Tony Bridges hurried upstairs to relieve Anna, who'd been helping look after Nicola for nearly eighteen months now. Tony was suddenly aware that he'd had too much to drink. He'd left the car by the pub and cabbed it home, allowing him the luxury of drinking. Caught up in the emotion of Charlie's return, he'd ended up having four or five pints and he swayed slightly on the stairs. He was allowed to have a life, of course, but still he always felt ashamed when Anna—or, worse, Nicola's mother—caught him drinking. Would his speech give him away? The smell of alcohol on his breath? He tried his best to look sober and walked into Nicola's bedroom.

"How's she been?"

"Very good," replied Anna, smiling. She was always smiling, thank goodness. "She had her dinner and then I read her a few chapters."

She held up *Bleak House*. Nicola had always loved Dickens— *David Copperfield* being her particular favorite—so they were working through his back catalog. It was a project, something for Nicola to achieve, and she seemed to enjoy the stories with their plucky heroes and diabolical villains.

"We're just getting to the exciting bit," Anna continued, "and she wanted to read on, so I gave her a couple of bonus chapters. But she'd pretty much nodded off by the end of it—you might have to recap a bit tomorrow. Make sure she doesn't miss anything."

Tony suddenly felt very emotional, moved by the tender care Anna lavished on his wife. Fearing his voice would falter, he patted Anna's arm, thanked her quickly and sent her on her way.

Nicola was his childhood sweetheart and they had married young. Their life was set fair, but two days before her twenty-ninth birthday, Nicola had suffered a massive stroke. She survived it, but the resulting brain damage was extensive, and she was now a prisoner of locked-in syndrome. She could see and was aware, but was able only to move her eyes due to the paralysis that gripped her body. Tony looked after her lovingly, patiently teaching her to communicate with her eyes, dragooning in family or hiring caregivers when he had to work, but still he often felt he was a bad husband to her. Impatient, frustrated, selfish. In reality, he did everything he could for her, but that didn't stop him from castigating himself. Especially when he'd been out having a good time. Then he felt callous and unworthy.

He stroked her hair, kissed her forehead and then retreated to his bedroom. Even now, two years after her stroke, the fact that they had separate bedrooms still hurt. Separate bedrooms were for couples who'd fallen out of love, for show marriages, not for him and Nicola. They were better than that.

He couldn't be bothered to get undressed, so he sat down on the bed and flicked through *Bleak House*. In the early days, when they were still dating, Nicola had read passages from Dickens aloud to him. He'd been uncomfortable with it at first—he'd never been much of a reader and it felt pretentious—but in time he'd come to love it. He would close his eyes and listen to her soft Home Counties voice playing with the words. He was never happier and he would have killed now to have a recording—just one—of her reading to him.

But he never would have that, and pipe dreams get you nowhere, so he settled down with the book instead. It wasn't much, but it would have to do.

18

The lights of Southampton docks glittered in the distance. The port was used twenty-four/seven and would be a hive of activity even now, giant cranes unloading the containers that arrived from Europe, the Caribbean and beyond. Forklifts would be racing up and down the quay as men shouted insults at one another, enjoying the camaraderie of the night shift.

On Eling Great Marsh all was still. It was a cold night, an arctic wind blasting up the river channel, buffeting the car that stood alone in the bleak emptiness. The driver's door hung wide-open and the interior lights were on, casting a weak glow over the lonely scene.

Holding his ankles firmly, she began to pull. He was heavier than he looked and she had to use all her strength to maneuver him over the uneven ground. The going was soft, rendering progress slow, and they left a snail-like trail behind them. His head caught on a rock as she pushed him over the lip of a small ditch. He stirred, but not enough—he was too far gone for that.

She cast around quickly, checking once again that they were alone. Satisfied, she placed her bag on the ground, unzipping it to reveal its contents. She pulled out a roll of duct tape and broke off a stretch. Pushing it down firmly on his mouth, she smoothed her gloved hand over and over it to make sure there was no breathing room. Her heart was beginning to beat faster now, her adrenaline spiking, so she didn't delay. Grasping his hair, she pulled his lolling head back to reveal his throat. Retrieving the long blade from the bag, she cut deep into his throat. Instantly his body writhed, as his mind desperately tried to regain some form of consciousness, but it was all too late. Blood spurted up, splattering her chest and face, binding them together. She let his warm blood settle and cloy on her—plenty of time to clean up later.

Driving the blade deep into his stomach, she set about her business. Within ten minutes, she had what she wanted, placing the bloody organ in a zippered bag. Straightening up, she surveyed her work. Whereas her first effort had been imprecise and labored, this was smooth and efficient.

She was getting better at this.

19

"So, how did it go?"

Steve had been waiting up for Charlie and was walking toward her. The TV burbled in the background. Four empty cans of lager on the coffee table revealed that, like Charlie, he'd felt the need for a few drinks.

"The day or my welcome back?"

"Both."

"Okay, actually. I made some decent progress on a case and the gang were pleased to see me. Helen was pretty much how I expected, but there's nothing I can do about that, so . . ."

Charlie was relieved to see that Steve looked genuinely pleased for her. He had been so against the idea of her returning to work that she was grateful now that he was trying his best to be positive and supportive.

"Well done, you. I told you you'd be great," he said, slipping his arm round her waist and giving her a congratulatory kiss.

"First day back," Charlie replied, shrugging. "Long way to go yet."

"One step at a time, eh?"

Charlie nodded and they kissed again, a little deeper this time.

"How much have you had?" Steve continued, a little glint in his eye now.

"Enough," replied Charlie, smiling. "You?"

"Definitely enough," said Steve, suddenly sweeping her off the floor and into his arms. "Keep your head up. That banister's a bastard."

Smiling, Charlie let Steve carry her upstairs to the bedroom. They had always been a loving couple, but recently genuine intimacy had been absent from their relationship. Charlie was both exhilarated and relieved that they seemed to be recovering their old spontaneity and desire.

Perhaps everything was going to be all right after all.

20

"You're looking at a DIY thoracotomy."

Jim Grieves savored the last word, aware that it would mean little to Helen. It was seven a.m. and they were alone in the police mortuary. Alan Matthews lay naked on the slab before them. They had already established that he had bled to death and they had now moved on to examining the removal of his heart.

"This particular operation is not exactly textbook, but, then again, he or she was operating in less than optimum conditions. Their adrenaline would have been pumping, they would have been fearful of discovery, and we shouldn't forget that the victim was still alive when they started. Not exactly standard practice, so given that, it's not a bad job."

There was almost a note of admiration in his voice. Many would have chided him for this, but Helen let it go. Too much time in a mortuary does strange things to you and Jim was saner than most.

He was also fiercely bright, so Helen always paid attention to what he had to say.

"First incision was made just below the sternum. A big blade, perhaps twenty centimeters in length. Then they cut through the ribs and breastbone. After that you'd usually use muscle retractors—rib spreaders—to peel open the chest. But our killer used something more interesting. See those two puncture holes there?"

Helen craned over the body to look inside the chest cavity. There were two holes about fifty centimeters apart in the right flap of what had once been his chest.

"They were made by some sort of hook. A butcher's hook maybe? Two hooks embedded to the side of the main incision, then you just use brute force. They ripped open the right half first, then did the same again with the left side. Once the chest is open and the heart revealed, it's simply a matter of cutting around the surrounding tissue and lifting it out. Bit of a hatchet job, but effective."

Helen digested these macabre details.

"So what are we talking? A butcher's knife and a meat hook?"

"Could be," Grieves replied, shrugging.

"How long would it take?"

"Ten to fifteen minutes depending on how experienced you are and how much care you take."

"Anything else?"

"Your victim was immobilized with chloroform—found it in his nostrils and his mouth. Forensics are doing their work on it now, but I'd hazard that it was homemade. Any fool can make it with bleach, acetone and Internet access."

"Any traces of our killer?"

Jim shook his head.

"Looks like there was minimal contact between them. That said, your man has had a good deal of contact with others over the years."

Jim paused, as he always did when he had something good up his sleeve. Helen tensed slightly, eager to be put out of her misery.

"There is plenty of evidence of STDs. Mr. Matthews certainly suffered from gonorrhea—recently, I would suggest. There's also evidence of *Mycoplasma genitalium*, which sounds weird but actually is very common, and possibly pubic lice too. I wish I'd been a member of his church—sounds like a riot."

He walked off to clean up. Helen let this latest development settle—the first little clue in an otherwise bewildering murder.

Back at Southampton Central, Helen continued her dissection of Alan Matthews. The team had assembled in the incident room and were pooling what they'd learned.

"Forensics have pretty much come up with a complete blank," Tony Bridges announced bleakly. "They've been all over the car, but it hadn't been moved or touched—the only DNA belonged to members of the Matthews family. As to the house, there are so many DNA traces at the murder scene, it's easier to pinpoint who *hasn't* been there. Semen, saliva, blood, skin cells—we've got the lot. This house was used regularly by sex workers and their clients, as well as by drug users. We'll check them all out, see if there're any interesting matches, but there's nothing there that would be useful in court."

"Why use a house with such heavy footfall? Wouldn't they have been scared of being discovered?" interjected DC Sanderson.

"It's possible they weren't aware of how frequently it was used," countered Tony, "though given the level of care and planning that went into this murder, that seems unlikely. In many ways it was a perfect location to choose—the back door was solid and bolted from the inside and the windows were barred, meaning the front door was the only easy means of access. The latch broke long ago, but there was still a solid bolt on the inside. Easy enough for the killer to secure the place once the victim was incapacitated."

"It still seems risky to me . . . ," Sanderson responded, not keen to let her point go.

"It was," said Helen, taking the baton. "Which suggests what? That he or she expected the body to be found quickly perhaps? Or maybe the location was chosen simply to put the victim at his ease. There are no signs that Alan Matthews was dragged into that house against his will. Meaning this was an ambush. He had to be *lured* there. He suffered from STDs indicating widespread sexual activity, so perhaps he spotted a hooker he liked or a pimp he knew, then followed them inside and *bam*! Maybe the house was chosen because they knew he'd feel at ease—"

"We've had a good look at his computer," DC McAndrew broke in, "and there is plenty of evidence that Matthews had an unhealthy interest in pornography and prostitutes. He hasn't been particularly careful at concealing his Internet history, so we can see that he regularly visited porn sites—a lot of the free ones, but also some more extreme pay-per-view setups. He was also active in chat rooms and on message boards. We're still looking into this, but it's basically a lot of sad bastards exchanging anecdotes about their experiences with various prostitutes, marking them out of ten for size of their boobs, what they'd do and so forth—"

"They're reviewing their hookers?" Helen queried, mildly incredulous.

"Basically. It's a bit like TripAdvisor but for prostitutes. He also visited a lot of escort sites," McAndrew continued. "Though there's no evidence yet that he actually used their services. Which might suggest that his tastes were a little more . . . earthy—"

"Let's focus," Helen interrupted. "We're not here to judge Alan Matthews; we just want to find his killer. Whatever else we may think about him, he is a husband and a father and we need to find the person responsible."

Before they kill again. She had almost said it, but choked it down at the last minute.

"Let's look into where he got the money to pay for his hobby. The more exotic his practices, the more money he'd need. The Matthews family don't own their own house, there are four kids to support and Alan is the only breadwinner. He clearly used prostitutes and pay-per-view porn *a lot*, so how was he doing it? Did he owe money to a pimp? Is that what this is about?"

For once, there was no comeback from the team—they were all staring over her head to the doorway of the incident room. Helen turned quickly to see a very nervous-looking uniform hovering. From the look on his face, she knew what was coming. Still, it sent a shiver through her when he finally said:

"They've found another body, ma'am."

21

She was back home, safe and sound. Donning latex gloves, she began to investigate her haul. Two hundred pounds in cash—she put that straight into her purse, then moved on to the credit cards. Snip, snip, snip. Her scissors cut through them deftly, but to make doubly sure she gave them ten minutes on a tray under the grill. It was hard to take your eyes off them as they bubbled into a plasticky pulp—someone's life melting away.

Then to the driving license. She hesitated to look at the name, focusing on the photo instead. Was she scared to see whose life she'd destroyed or was she deliberately holding off the discovery, teasing out every last moment of suspense?

She took a peek. Christopher Reid. Beneath his name, his home address. Her eyes rested on this, calculating. Then she flicked through the rest of the contents of his wallet—his business cards, loyalty cards and dry-cleaning receipts. A thoroughly mundane life.

Satisfied, she rose. Time was of the essence. She would have to move quickly. She opened up the old stove, which was burning nicely now, stoked by a fresh log. She tossed his wallet in and watched it burn. Stripping quickly, she shoved her bloodstained clothes in on top of it. The fire roared and she had to step back to avoid getting burned.

She suddenly felt foolish, standing naked in the room, flecks of blood still on her face and hair. Hurrying to the shower, she cleansed herself, then dressed again. There would be time to scrub the bath and floors properly later. Now she must keep going.

Opening the fridge, she grabbed the half bottle of Lucozade from the shelf and drank it down in one gulp. A half-eaten pie, a couple of chicken nuggets, a Müllerlight; she wolfed them down now, feeling suddenly ravenous and light-headed. Sated, she paused. There on the top shelf was her prize. A human heart sitting snug in a Tupperware box.

She took it out and put it down on the kitchen table. Picking up the box, tape and scissors, she set to work.

She had a delivery to make.

22

The doorbell made her jump. Jessica Reid rose quickly, abandoning the task of feeding her eighteen-month-old daughter and hurrying to the front door. When she'd woken late to find Chris's half of the bed empty, she'd been confused. When she'd found that both he and the car were missing, with no note by way of explanation, she'd become seriously concerned. Where was he?

She'd held off calling the police, hoping that there was a simple explanation for his absence. And now she hurried to the door, imagining her apologetic husband on the other side. But it was only the postman with a letter that had to be signed for.

Flinging it on the table, she returned to Sally, who was demanding more apple puree. She spooned the mush in dutifully, but her mind was elsewhere. Things had been a bit strained between them recently—ever since her discovery—but he was not a callous man. He wouldn't just leave her in the dark like this. Could he have left her? Walked out on them? She shook the thought away. It was impossible— all his stuff was here, and besides, he adored Sally and would never abandon her.

He had been at home when she went to sleep last night. He had always stayed up later than she did, watching action movies that he knew she wouldn't care for, and he had become adept at slipping into bed without waking her. Had he even been to bed last night? His pajamas were neatly folded under his pillow, where she'd put them yesterday afternoon, so she presumed not.

He must have gone out. To work? No, he hated work and had been coasting for months—a sudden burst of enthusiasm seemed unlikely. Would he have gone to his mother's or a friend's on some emergency? No, this didn't wash either. He'd have drafted her in to help at the first sign of trouble.

So where was he? She was probably overreacting, the tension that had characterized their marriage recently no doubt prompting her to imagine dire scenarios that were patently ridiculous. He was fine. Of course he was.

Despite the fear and uncertainty that gripped her, despite all the problems that they'd had recently, Jessica was suddenly sure of one thing. She really wanted their marriage to work; she really wanted Christopher. She knew in that moment that she loved her husband with all her heart.

23

The sun refused to rise. A thick blanket of cloud hung above Eling Great Marsh, framing the figures crawling over it. A dozen Forensics officers in crime scene suits were on their hands and knees, scrabbling over the surface of this forgotten outpost, searching each blade of grass for clues.

As Helen surveyed the scene, her mind went back to Marianne. Different locations, different circumstances, but the same awful feeling. A brutal, senseless murder. A man dead in a ditch, his beating heart ripped from him. A concerned wife out there somewhere, waiting and hoping for his safe return . . . Helen closed her eyes and tried to picture a world in which this wasn't happening. The salty tang of the marsh momentarily took her away to happier times, to family holidays on the Isle of Sheppey. Brief interludes of joy amid the darkness. Helen snapped her eyes open, irritated with herself for indulging in maudlin reverie when there was work to do.

As soon as she'd heard the news, Helen had pulled everyone off what they were doing. Every CID officer, every forensic specialist, every spare uniform had been ordered to this godforsaken sod of wet grass. It would alert the press, but that couldn't be helped. Helen knew they were dealing with something—someone—extraordinary, and she was determined to throw everything at it.

They were still examining the car, but on the ground they'd found their first decent clues. The victim's body had left an impression in the soft earth as it had been dragged from car to ditch, as had the heels of the person dragging him. The indentations were deep, and unless a man was deliberately throwing them off the scent by killing people in six-inch heels, an obvious explanation suggested itself.

A prostitute was killing her punters. Alan Matthews, a serial user of prostitutes, had been killed and mutilated. Twenty-four hours later, another man was killed on a remote promontory that was notorious for dogging and prostitution. It was all pointing one way, and yet already alarm bells were ringing. Prostitutes were the victims, not the killers, well before Jack the Ripper and long afterward. Aileen Wuornos bucked the trend, but that was America. Could something like that happen here?

"We've got a name, ma'am."

DC Sanderson was hurrying over, exaggeratedly avoiding treading on anything significant.

"The car is owned by a Christopher Reid. He lives in Woolston with a Jessica Reid and daughter, Sally Reid."

"How old is the daughter?"

"She's a baby," Sanderson replied, wrong-footed by the question. "Eighteen months, I think."

Helen's heart sank further. This was her duty now—to inform the living of the dead. If the victim *was* Christopher Reid, she hoped against hope that he had been brought here against his will. She knew this was unlikely, but still, the idea that a guy with a young wife and child would abandon them for a sweaty tussle with a prostitute in a car seemed ridiculous to Helen. Could there have been another reason why he was lured here?

"See if you can get a picture of Christopher Reid that we can compare with our victim. If this is Christopher, we need to tell his family before the press do it for us."

Sanderson hurried off to do Helen's bidding. Helen's gaze flitted beyond her to the police tape fluttering in the breeze. As yet they had avoided detection, the scene undisturbed by press. Helen was surprised, particularly by the absence of Emilia Garanita. She seemed to have half the uniformed officers in her pocket and was always excited by a juicy murder. But not in this case. Helen afforded herself a small smile—Emilia must be losing her touch.

24

"I had my head ripped off the last time I was in here."

Emilia Garanita leaned back in her chair, enjoying the rare luxury of being in the nerve center of Southampton Central. It wasn't often you were personally summoned to the detective superintendent's office.

"I don't think I was Detective Superintendent Whittaker's favorite person. How *is* he doing these days?" she continued, failing to hide the gleeful malice that lay behind her inquiry.

"You'll find I'm a rather different character," Ceri Harwood responded. "In fact that's why I asked you to come here."

"A girl-to-girl chat?"

"I wanted to put things on a different footing. I know in the past the relationship between the press and some of my officers has been combustible. And that you have often felt cut out of things. That doesn't help anyone, so I wanted to tell you face-to-face that things will be different now. We can help each other to help ourselves."

Emilia said nothing, trying to work out if she was for real. New bosses always said this when they arrived, then got on with the job of frustrating the local press at every turn.

"How different?" she demanded.

"I want to keep you informed of major developments and harness your reach to help us further our investigations. Starting with the Empress Road murder."

Emilia raised an eyebrow—so this wasn't going to be hot air after all.

"I'll have a name for you soon. And you will be given all pertinent details of the crime. Plus we are setting up a dedicated help line, which I would like you to major on in your next edition. It's imperative that we get any potential witnesses to come forward as soon as possible."

"What's so special about this murder?"

Harwood paused a moment before answering.

"It was a particularly brutal killing. The person who did this is highly dangerous, possibly with mental health problems. As yet we don't have a physical description, which is why we need your eyes and ears. It could make all the difference, Emilia."

Harwood smiled as she said her name, appearing every inch the confidential friend.

"Have you spoken to DI Grace about this?" Emilia countered.

"DI Grace is on board. She knows we're running a different ship now."

"No more diversions? No more lies?"

"Absolutely not," Harwood replied, her broad smile breaking out once again. "I've got a feeling you and I can do business together, Emilia. I do hope I won't be disappointed."

The meeting was over. Emilia rose without having to be asked, impressed by what she'd seen. Harwood was a smart operator and seemed to have Grace's measure. It felt like a sea change and perhaps it was.

Emilia had the distinct impression that she was going to have fun with this one.

25

"So, what are we looking at?"

DC Fortune yawned as he spoke, the noise echoing round the Major Investigative Team office. He and Charlie were an island in the empty room, two lonely figures surrounded by a mass of papers.

"Well, Brookmire Health and Wellbeing Center is obviously a knocking shop, but it's a classy one," Charlie replied. "I've never seen one that's so well run and discreet before. It has a roster of attractive, experienced girls, all of whom are regularly health-checked. You can book an appointment online and they already have some sort of link-up with the cruise companies. They send shuttle busses down there to pick up clients the minute the boats come in. They describe the services they offer as holistic health services, but here's the real beauty: if you pay with a credit card, it appears on your statement as stationery. So the wife will never find out, and even better, you can put it through on expenses. You don't even have to pay for the girls yourself."

"And you found all this out from one interview?" replied Fortune, impressed in spite of himself.

"If you know the questions to ask, people can be surprisingly helpful."

Charlie couldn't help a note of smugness—the smugness of superior experience—creeping into her voice.

Charlie continued. "Have you got anywhere on the list I gave you?"

Edina, Charlie's reluctant snitch at Brookmire, had furnished her with the names of all the girls currently working there.

"Getting there. A lot of them have been bussed straight from Poland via the docks; some are students from the local universities, but several others—including our victim—seem to have been poached off the streets."

"Tarted up and relaunched at Brookmire?"

"Why not? It's safer, and by the look of Alexia's flat well paid too."

"Edina suggested that Alexia was walking the streets for the Campbell family before joining Brookmire. Any of the other girls?"

"Yup, the Campbells had lost a few to Brookmire. Anderson's lot too."

Charlie had a sinking feeling. Prostitution wars were never pretty and it was always the girls that suffered, not the people who ran them.

"So did the Campbells kill Alexia to make a point?"

"Makes sense. Not that we can prove it."

"Anything else?"

DC Fortune had been waiting for this, keeping his trump card up his sleeve until the appropriate moment.

"Well, I chased Brookmire through Companies House and

HMRC. Took a bit of doing, lots of shell companies and foreign-based holdings, but in the end I traced it back to Top Line Management, an 'events company' owned by a certain Sandra McEwan."

Charlie should have known. Sandra McEwan—or Lady Macbeth as she was affectionately known—had been involved in prostitution and racketeering in Southampton for more than thirty years—ever since she'd allegedly killed her own husband to take over his crime empire. She was driven and fearless—she'd already survived three stabbings—but she was also smart and imaginative. Had she taken prostitution to the next stage with Brookmire, provoking her rivals into a deadly response?

"Well done, Lloyd. Good work."

It was the first time she'd used his Christian name and it had the desired effect. He muttered a shy thank-you and Charlie smiled. Perhaps they were going to make a good team after all.

"Let's keep on it. See if you can find out what rock Sandra's hiding under these days, eh?"

DC Fortune scurried off. Charlie was pleased. It was good to be back in the groove and she sincerely hoped that she could now get justice for Alexia and put one more violent lowlife behind bars. It would be quite a feather in her cap. And one in the eye for Helen Grace.

26

People never take any notice of couriers. In their uniform of biking helmet and leathers they are viewed as robots, programmed to come, drop and go without personality or impact. Cogs in the wheels of everyday business.

People thought it was okay to be rude to them, as if they were somehow less human than real people. This was certainly the case now. She stood by the front desk ignored, waiting patiently for the two receptionists to finish their private conversation. Typical—underlining their own sense of self-importance, in the process betraying how utterly worthless they were. Still, they would get their comeuppance.

She coughed and was rewarded with an irritated glance from the fat one. Reluctantly she dragged her carcass over.

"Who?"

Not even the dignity of a whole sentence.

"Stephen McPhail."

She kept her voice neutral.

"Company?"

"Zenith Solutions."

"Third floor."

She paused, momentarily unnerved at having to go inside the building with her precious cargo, then regaining her composure, she walked to the lifts.

The receptionist at Zenith was no more polite than the others.

"Need a signature?"

The courier shook her head and handed over the package. A plain brown cardboard box, bound shut with duct tape. The receptionist turned away without saying thank you and placed it on her desk, before resuming her conversation.

The courier left, slipping away as anonymously as she'd arrived. She wondered how long the receptionist would gossip before actually doing her job and alerting the chief executive to his unexpected package. She hoped they wouldn't wait too long. These things begin to smell after a while.

27

"What I'm asking you to do is potentially very dangerous and if you say no, I will respect that decision."

Tony had suspected something was up the minute Helen had asked to meet him in the Old White Bear. It was a grotty pub round the corner from the station—it was where you went if you didn't want to be overheard.

"I know you've done undercover work before and know the drill," Helen continued, "but your circumstances are different now. That said, you're the best male officer I've got, so . . ."

"What exactly do you want?" replied Tony, blushing slightly at the compliment.

"It looks like our killer is targeting men cruising for sex," Helen went on. "We could put an ad in the *Evening News* asking for punters to come forward and help, but I can't see that working. The girls on the street aren't telling McAndrew a single thing . . ."

"So we have to put someone in the line of fire."

"Exactly."

Tony said nothing. His expression was neutral, but he was excited by the prospect. His life had been so regimented for so long that a chance to be on the front line again was tempting.

"We can only do so much working with motive and MO—this killer is scrupulously careful about forensics and uses out-of-the-way locations. So we need someone on the ground, posing as a punter, sniffing around. I know you'll need time to process this. And I'm sure there'll be loads of questions you want to ask, but I need an answer fast. This could be . . ."

Helen paused, choosing her words carefully.

". . . This could be something big. And I want to nip it in the bud."

Tony promised to think about it overnight, but he knew already that he was going to say yes. It was dangerous for sure, but if it wasn't him, it would be someone else. Someone less experienced. He was a DS now and it was right for him to step up. Mark Fuller wouldn't have ducked something like this and he had had a kid, for God's sake.

Helen headed back to the incident room, leaving Tony to his thoughts. He allowed himself a pint, as he mentally scrolled through the challenges that lay ahead. How to frame it for Nicola? How could he quell her anxiety and reassure her that the risks were minimal?

He sat alone, supping his pint, lost in thought. A last drink for the condemned man.

28

She had snuck up behind her without making a sound. Charlie had been so involved in her work, so excited by her discoveries, that she hadn't noticed Harwood's approach.

"How are you getting on, Charlie?"

Charlie jumped, startled by this sudden intrusion. She turned and blustered a response—it was unnerving to find the station chief looming over you.

"Settling back in okay?" Harwood continued.

"Yes, ma'am. Making good progress and everyone's been very welcoming. Those who are here at least."

"Yes, you've caught us at a busy time. But I'm delighted you're back, Charlie—it would have been a shame to lose such a talented officer."

Charlie said nothing. What was the correct response to this unwarranted compliment? Charlie had been off sick for a year after nearly getting herself killed—it wasn't the greatest recommendation to the new station chief. In the aftermath of her abduction, Charlie had prepared herself for the call suggesting she might be happier elsewhere, but it had never come. Instead she'd been encouraged to return to work and was now being praised by a woman she hardly knew.

"Go at your own pace," Harwood continued. "Do what you're good at. And come to me if you have any problems, okay? My door is always open."

"Yes, ma'am. And thank you. For everything."

Harwood smiled her wide, attractive smile. Charlie was aware she hadn't really said enough, so she continued:

"I know you don't know me from Adam and that you would have been completely justified in washing your hands of me, but I want you to know that I am really, really grateful for this chance you've given me"—Charlie was babbling now but couldn't stop—"and I want to say that I won't let you down. You won't regret giving me a second chance."

Harwood regarded her, clearly unused to such outpourings, then patted her on the arm.

"I don't doubt it for a second."

She turned to go, but Charlie stopped her:

"There was one other thing. A development in the Alexia Louszko case."

Harwood turned, intrigued.

"DC Fortune established that the upmarket brothel Alexia worked for was owned by Sandra McEwan."

Charlie paused, unsure if the name would mean anything to Harwood.

"I know her. Go on."

"Well, I was a bit surprised that she owned the freehold to the Brookmire building. Didn't realize she had that kind of money. So

I did a bit more digging to see if Sandra owned any other properties in Southampton."

"And?"

Charlie paused for a moment. Should she say anything to Harwood without telling Helen first? Too late to be coy now—Harwood was clearly expecting something.

"She owns property on the Empress Road industrial estate."

Now she had Harwood's full attention. Charlie picked up a copy of the street map she'd downloaded from the Land Registry and handed it to her.

"Specifically, she owns this row of derelict houses. Alan Matthews's body was found in the fourth one along."

Harwood processed this. Charlie went on:

"Alexia was killed and mutilated, probably by the Campbells—Alexia used to walk the streets for them before defecting to Brookmire. A day later, a street punter is found murdered and mutilated in a property owned by Sandra McEwan."

"You think that Sandra is sending them a message. That it'll be tit for tat?"

"Could be. History tells us that if you declare war on Sandra McEwan, you'd better be ready for the consequences."

Harwood's brow furrowed. Nobody needed a prostitution war—they tended to be long and bloody and always made it into the papers.

"Bring her in."

Harwood was already heading for the door.

"Should I let DI Grace know before I—"

"Bring her in, DC Brooks."

29

They were huddled together like cattle at an abattoir. It was astonishing how quickly professional poise could disappear. The staff of Zenith Solutions had taken refuge in the atrium, too unnerved to go back into the office, too curious to go home. Helen walked past them and hurried up to the third floor.

Stephen McPhail, the chief executive of Zenith, was trying his best to look composed, but he was clearly perturbed by the morning's events. He was holed up in his office, flanked by his long-serving secretary, Angie. The box remained on Angie's desk where she'd dropped it. It had toppled over on impact, the bloody heart spilling out onto her desk. It lay there still, guarded closely by a pair of uniforms who refused to look at it. The lid flapped down lazily—the single word *SCUM*, daubed in blood, screaming out its simple message.

. . .

"I appreciate that you must be extremely distressed by what's happened, but it's imperative I ask you some questions while events are still fresh in your memory. Is that okay?"

Helen was addressing Angie, who managed a nod between sniffles.

"What firm was the courier from?"

"She didn't say. She didn't have a logo on."

"It was definitely a woman?"

"Yes. She didn't say much . . . but yes."

"Did you see her face?"

"Not really. She had her helmet on. To be honest, I didn't really take much notice of her."

Helen cursed internally.

"Height?"

"Not sure really. Five-eight?"

"Hair color?"

"Couldn't say for sure."

Helen nodded, her fixed smile disguising her exasperation with the unobservant Angie. Had the courier known she could slip in and out without arousing attention or had it just been a lucky break?

"I'm going to ask a police artist to come and sit with you. If you can give her a full description of the courier's clothes, helmet, features, then we can get an accurate picture of who we're looking for. Is that okay?"

Angie nodded heroically, so Helen turned her attention to Stephen McPhail.

"I'm going to need a list of the names and addresses of all your staff—those who were present today, as well as those who were absent."

"Of course," McPhail replied. He tapped some keys and the printer began to whir to life. "We've got twenty permanent staffers—only a couple of them were away today. Helen Baxter is on holiday and Chris Reid—well, I'm not sure where he is."

Helen kept her expression neutral.

"Do you have CCTV in the office?" she continued.

"I'm afraid not, but downstairs reception is covered. I'm sure the management company would let you have whatever you need."

He was so desperate to help, so keen to clear up this mess. Helen wanted to put him out of his misery, but couldn't.

"We have no reason to believe this is specifically aimed at you, but is there anyone you can think of who might have wanted to target you in this way? Someone you've let go recently? A disgruntled client? A family member?"

"We do IT," McPhail replied, as if this explained everything. "It's not the kind of business where you make enemies. All our guys—and girls—have been with us for months, if not years. So, no, I . . . I don't know of anyone who'd do something like this . . ."

He petered out.

"Try not to be too concerned by it. I'm sure it's a prank. We'll have officers here for the next couple of days, talking to staff, but you should try to go about your everyday business. No reason why a sick joke should cost you money."

McPhail nodded, looking a touch more reassured, so Helen hurried down to reception. Charles Holland, the management company rep, had arrived and was waiting for her. He hurriedly sought out the morning's CCTV tapes, desperate to hand over responsibility for this unpleasantness to somebody else. The Forensics Unit had arrived now and were making their way upstairs to recover the heart, exciting the interest of Zenith's exiled staff. It was an interesting development—delivering the victim's heart to his workplace rather than his home. It was riskier, for sure, but was guaranteed to make much more of a splash. Was that the point? What sort of game was this?

And where would it end?

30

She didn't waste any time. Sticking to the back routes, Helen sped across town. She was being overcautious, but it was perfectly possible that one of the startled workers in the Zenith building would alert the press, and Helen was determined not to be followed. She was heading to the Reid household—to destroy happiness and inflict pain—and she wanted to be absolutely sure she was alone.

Jessica Reid's face changed color so quickly when she saw Helen's warrant card that Helen thought she was going to faint. Alison Vaughn, an experienced Family Liaison officer whom Helen had asked to attend, was quick off the mark. A comforting hand on the elbow, then she shepherded the terrified Jessica inside. Helen followed, shutting the front door gently behind her.

Jessica's eighteen-month-old sat in the middle of the front room, grunting benignly at her unexpected visitors. Sally was full of beans, eager to play, and without needing to be told Alison picked her up and took her off to investigate her activity center.

"Is he dead?"

Jessica's question was brutally blunt. Her body was shaking, her eyes just about containing her tears. Helen's eyes flashed across the family photos on the mantelpiece—there was no doubt that Jessica's husband was their latest victim.

"This morning we found the body of a man. We believe it is Chris, yes."

Jessica let her head fall. She started to sob. She was trying to suck them in, to hide her distress from her daughter, but the shock was too great.

"Jessica, the next few days are going to be bewildering, devastating, scary, but I want you to know that we will be supporting you every step of the way. Alison will be here to help with Sally, to provide any assistance you might need and to answer your questions. If you have family who can help, we should call them now. You may even want to think about staying elsewhere for a few days. I can't discount the possibility that the press will try to contact you here."

Jessica looked up, bemused.

"Why would they do that?"

"We believe Chris was murdered. I know that's hard to take in . . . that this all seems like a horrible nightmare, but I can't hide the facts from you. It's important that I tell you as much as we know, so you can help us find who did this."

"How? . . . Where?"

"He was found on Eling Great Marsh. He drove out there in the early hours of this morning."

"Why? Why was he there? We never go there . . . we've never been there."

"We believe he drove there with a companion. A woman."

"Who?" Anger had crept into Jessica's voice now.

"We don't know her identity. But we believe she might be a sex worker."

Jessica closed her eyes in horror. Helen watched her with profound sympathy as another foundation wall of her life collapsed. Helen had had her life smashed to bits more than once and she knew the awful pain that Jessica was experiencing. Nevertheless she had to give her the truth—all of it—without sparing her anything.

"Eling Great Marsh is sometimes used by prostitutes as a discreet place to conduct their business. We think that's why Chris went there. I really am sorry, Jessica."

"The stupid fucking bastard."

Jessica spat out the words with such violence that it silenced the room. Sally looked up from her play, for the first time sensing that something was wrong.

"The stupid, cowardly, selfish, fucking . . . bastard."

She sobbed unreservedly now, deep and long. Helen let her cry. Finally her sobs started to subside.

"To your knowledge had Chris ever used prostitutes before?"

"No! Do you think I'd put up with that? What do you think I am—a fucking doormat?"

Jessica's eyes were burning fiercely.

"Of course not. I know you wouldn't sanction something like that, but sometimes wives have suspicions, fears, things they've locked away deep. Did you ever have any worries about Chris? Anything that upset you?"

Jessica dropped her gaze now, unable to look at Helen. She had struck a nerve, Helen was sure of that, and she had no choice but to pursue it.

"Jessica, if you've anything to tell—"

"I didn't think it would . . ."

Jessica was struggling to find sufficient breath to speak, the shock now taking full effect. Helen gestured to Alison for a glass of water.

"He'd . . . he had . . . He'd promised me."

"Promised you what, Jessica?"

"Since Sally was born, we haven't . . . you know . . . very much."

Helen said nothing. She knew something was coming now and that it was best to let Jessica find her own words.

"We're always so tired," she continued. "There are always so many things that need doing."

She took a big lungful of air before continuing:

"A few months ago, I used Chris's laptop because mine was broken." Another deep breath.

"I opened up Internet Explorer to use Ocado and . . . I found all these sites bookmarked. The stupid bastard hadn't even tried to hide them."

"Pornography?" Helen asked. Jessica nodded.

"I opened one up. I wanted to know. It was . . . disgusting. A young girl—seventeen at the most—and lots of guys . . . they were bloody queuing up to . . ."

"Did you challenge him about it?"

"Yes. I rang him at work. He came straight home."

Her tone softened a little as she continued:

"He was mortified. Ashamed. He hated himself for hurting me. I hated him for looking at that . . . stuff, but he vowed he'd never watch it again. And he meant it. He really meant it."

She looked up imploringly, silently begging Helen not to damn her husband.

"I'm sure he did. I'm sure he was a good husband, a good father . . ."

"He is. He was. He loved Sally. He loved *me . . .*"

At this point Jessica collapsed, the weight of events finally bearing down on her. She had been robbed of her husband and her memory of him would be forever tarnished. His reckless actions had cost him dear, but those left behind had the bitterest legacy. They were staring down a long, dark tunnel.

Suddenly Helen was filled with anger. Whoever was responsible knew what they were doing. They were intent on visiting as much pain on these innocent families as they could. They wanted to take them beyond the limits of human endurance, to destroy them. But Helen wouldn't let them. She would see them destroyed before she let that happen.

Leaving Alison to rally family support, Helen departed. The messenger is never welcome in a house of death, and besides, she had work to do.

31

Helen strode away from the house, confident that Alison would shepherd Jessica slowly, inexorably, toward a semblance of stability. Alison was brilliant at her job—patient, kind and wise. When the time was right she would sit Jessica down and tell her the full details of her husband's murder. Jessica would need to know, would need to understand how her husband would now become public property, the subject of gossip and speculation. But it was too early, the shock too great, and she would leave it to Alison to judge the moment.

"Are you chasing another serial killer, Helen?"

Helen spun round, but she knew that voice.

"You really don't have much luck, do you?"

Emilia Garanita shut the door of her Fiat and walked over. How the hell had she got here so quickly?

"Before you tell me to jump in a lake, I think you should know that I had some face time with your boss today. Ceri Harwood is a breath of fresh air after Whittaker, don't you think? She's promised to be open and honest with us—you scratch my back and all that— and said that you were on board. So let's start off on a new footing, shall we? What can you tell me about this killer and how can the *Evening News* assist the investigation?"

Her pad and pen were poised in anticipation, her face the picture of innocence and enthusiasm. God, Helen wanted to punch her—she had never met anyone who seemed to take such active enjoyment in the unhappiness of ordinary people. She was a ghoul— without a ghoul's redeeming features.

"If Detective Superintendent Harwood has offered to give you the relevant information, then I'm sure she'll do so. She's a woman of her word."

"Don't be cute, Helen. I want details. I want an exclusive."

Helen eyed her up. She could tell Emilia wasn't bullshitting. Somehow she had managed to get Harwood onside—at whose instigation? Helen wondered. More than that, she'd got to the Reid residence almost as quickly as Helen had. She was no longer an adversary who could be crushed. Helen would have to be smarter than that.

"I'll have a name and photo for you by tonight. In time for you to publish. The Empress Road murder was brutal and sustained and involved elements of torture. We're investigating possible links to organized crime, with particular emphasis on drugs and prostitution. We'll be appealing for potential witnesses to contact an anonymous help line with any relevant information. That'll have to do for now."

"That'll do just fine. See, it doesn't hurt, does it?"

Helen returned Emilia's smile. She was surprised that she hadn't asked her about Christopher Reid. Surprised and relieved. But she wasn't going to stick around to be subjected to further interrogation.

Climbing on her Kawasaki, she roared off, Emilia growing smaller and smaller in her rearview mirrors.

She only started to relax when she hit the motorway. Southampton, which for so long had been Helen's happy home, was becoming a hostile and bloody place. She had the distinct feeling that the storm was about to break and she was suddenly unsure of her footing. What was Harwood doing talking to Emilia behind her back? What deal had been struck? Whom could she rely on in the dark days ahead? Previously she'd had Mark and Charlie by her side in the thick of battle; whom did she have now?

Without meaning to, she found herself driving toward Aldershot. Strange how the pull was so strong, even though Robert Stonehill had no concept of her existence. A voice inside her urged her to think twice, to turn around, but she shouted it down, cranking up her speed.

She snuck into town under the cover of darkness. She knew Robert wouldn't be at home today, so she drove straight to the Tesco Metro, where he worked. Parking her bike nearby, she took up a vantage point in the Internet café opposite. Here she had a good view of him as he restocked the fridge with booze in expectation of the evening rush. He wasn't the most diligent worker, getting away with doing the minimum and always finding time to chat with his colleagues. There was one—Alice? Anna?—a pretty nineteen-year-old brunette, who seemed to pass by quite often. Helen made a note to keep an eye on that.

The hours ticked by. Eight p.m., nine p.m., ten p.m. Helen's attention started to wander as her tiredness and hunger grew. Was she wasting her time here? What was she hoping to achieve? Was she going to be a voyeur for the rest of her life, furtively exploiting a connection that didn't really exist?

Robert hurried out of the shop and down the street. As usual

Helen counted to fifteen, then left her hiding place, casually and quietly keeping pace with him. A couple of times Robert shot glances to his left and right, as if expecting or fearing to meet someone, but he never looked directly behind him, so Helen continued her progress undetected.

They had reached the city center now. Without warning, Robert dived into the Red Lion, a cavernous drinking hole that he had visited on previous excursions. Helen waited a moment and then entered, her smartphone clamped to her ear as if she were in conversation. There was no immediate sign of him, so Helen gave up the pretense. She searched the whole of the ground floor, then headed up to the mezzanine level. Still nothing. Had he noticed her and used the pub to shake her off? She hurried down to the basement and predictably he was in the very last place she looked, a booth hidden away in the bowels of the pub. He was packed into it with his mates, and the mood was somber. Helen was intrigued but couldn't get close enough to hear what they were talking about, so she bought a drink and settled down to wait. It was well past eleven o'clock, but the boys showed no signs of moving. The pub had a late license and could serve until two, but the group was oddly restrained in their drinking tonight. They looked tense. Helen wondered what had spooked them.

"Been stood up?"

Helen's daydreaming was abruptly ended by the intrusion of an overweight businessman who had obviously been quenching his thirst since leaving work.

"I'm just waiting for my husband," Helen lied.

"He always this late, is he? I wouldn't be if you were my wife."

"He was competing tonight. The traffic coming out of London is always terrible."

"Competing?"

"Cage fighting. There's a big show on at the Docklands. Stick around and have a chat with him if you like. He always likes to talk to punters and he should be here any second."

"That's very kind . . ."

But he was already retreating. Helen suppressed a smile and returned her attention to Robert. Only to find him staring right at her. Immediately she dropped her gaze, busying herself with her phone. Had he caught her? Better to be safe than sorry, so after a decent pause Helen feigned a phone call and went on her way, decamping to a discreet vantage point on the ground floor.

Twenty minutes later, Robert and his friends brushed past and left the pub, seemingly unaware of her existence. It was pushing midnight now and the streets were empty. As she followed them, Helen was suddenly aware of the stupidity and vulnerability of her position, alone in the darkened streets so late at night. She could handle herself in most situations, but not against a gang of men. What if they spotted her following them and took issue with it?

She hung back now and contemplated giving up altogether, but suddenly the gang came to a stop. They paused, darting looks here and there, then dragged a wheelie bin out from a nearby alleyway. Then Davey, the leader, clambered onto it. It brought him level with a small window at shoulder height. He pulled a crowbar out of his backpack and immediately started working on the window, while the others kept watch.

Helen flattened herself against the wall. She was furious—why had she put herself in this position? Now the window was open and Davey was levering himself inside. Robert was next. Skipping up onto the bin, he swung himself through the window with the practiced grace of a gymnast. The others stayed outside, looking around anxiously for any passersby.

A noise made them look up, but it was just a woman walking away—clearly she hadn't seen them. Helen picked up her pace. Now that it had all gone so wrong, she just wanted to be away from here. With each step, she berated herself. An innocent person was being robbed right now; it was her duty to call it in and stop this thing.

But of course she wouldn't and she hated herself for it. She hurried away, swallowed up by the darkness of the night.

It had been a mistake to come here.

32

The house was an empty shell. A bare, functional space that like most rented properties never received much love. Jason Robins, sitting alone at the IKEA dinner table, felt much the same way. His ex, Samantha, had taken their daughter, Emily, to Disneyland for two weeks—with new man Sean in tow. And though he tried to block it out—by focusing on work, watching football, looking up old mates—in reality he thought about it all the time. The three of them having fun—eating candy floss, screaming on the roller coasters, snuggling up at bedtime after a busy day's fun—fun from which he was utterly excluded. He had never called the shots in his marriage, and now that it was over he was still on the back foot. He had put all his energies into bringing up Emily and providing Samantha with everything she needed, so much so that he had neglected his mates and family. When Samantha admitted her affair and ended the marriage, he had no one to fall back on—no one genuine at least. People looked sympathetic and asked a few questions, but their hearts weren't in it. He could tell no one blamed Samantha for her choice. Jason wasn't much to look at and was hardly a scintillating conversationalist, but even so, he had worked bloody hard to make Samantha happy. And what was his reward? A lonely flat and a custody battle.

Jason scraped the remains of his ready meal into the bin and walked into what the letting agent called the study, but he called a cupboard. There was barely room to swing a cat in here, but it was his favorite room in the house—the only room that didn't seem empty. He liked its warm embrace, and now he settled down into his chair and fired up his computer.

He looked at the BBC News site, then the sports, then checked Facebook. A quick glance, and then he shut it down—he didn't want to see pictures of other people's happy lives. He checked his e-mail—spam, spam and another lawyer's bill. He exhaled, bored. He should go to bed really. He debated whether he could face an early night when he knew he wouldn't sleep, but it was a false debate. He had no intention of going to bed. Opening Safari, he clicked on his bookmarks. Dozens of online porn sites presented themselves. Once they had been exciting; now they were just familiar.

He sat at his desk, bored and disconsolate. Time ticked by slowly, taunting him. God, it was only eleven p.m. Another nine hours at least before he could turn up at work. The night stretched out in front of him, a long blank vista.

He paused, then typed "Escorts" into the search engine. Immediately lots of flash ads popped up in the margins, asking him if he wanted to meet girls in Southampton. He hesitated, weirded out that they knew where he lived, then started to flick through them. They were all thinly disguised invitations to prostitution—girls pretending to be in search of company, but actually touting for business. Should he? He had never done anything like this and if he was honest, he was scared to get involved. What if someone found out?

He flicked through more, his arousal growing. He had the money. So why not? If he got a disease, he could get it fixed—it wasn't like there was anyone else to pass it on to now. Why shouldn't he do something exciting for a change?

His heart was beating faster now, scenarios playing out in his mind. He scanned escort sites, forums, video clips—there was a whole world out there, waiting to be explored. Why not take control? Use his money to get people to do what he wanted for a change. Where would be the harm?

Picking up his wallet, Jason left the room, turning off the light as he went. The night was calling to him and this time he wouldn't resist.

33

He gripped the bullwhip firmly and let fly. It bit into her back with a satisfying snap. Her shoulders arched, then slumped, but she didn't make a sound. Whatever pain she was feeling, she swallowed it down. Raising her shoulders again, she braced herself for more, throwing down a challenge to her dominator. Jake obliged, cracking the whip again. Still she made no sound.

It had now been a couple of months since they'd renewed their relationship. Unquestionably it was different this time—he knew so much more about her and, though he never pried, he tacitly encouraged her to confide further in him by telling her *his* life story. He had shared as much as he was comfortable with—no one else knew that his parents were still alive but refused to talk to him—and yet he received so little in return. He understood that this was her safe space and he would never compromise that, but he wanted to move their relationship on. He had feelings for her—there was no point denying it. This should have prompted him to call time on their arrangement—any professional dominator worth his salt would do so—but he'd tried that before and it hadn't worked.

It wasn't love. At least he didn't think it was. But it was more than he had felt for anyone in a long time. When you've been so unloved, such a castoff in life, you keep your feelings firmly locked down. Since hitting puberty Jake had had many relationships—they had been with men and women, young and old, but one thing had remained constant. His desire to be free. Now, however, he found himself less and less interested in playing the field. Monogamy had never been his thing, but now he could see the attraction. It was crazy, really, given that he and Helen had never even come close to having sex, but then that wasn't what it was really about. There was something about her that he wanted to protect, to save. If she would only let him.

She had been virtually monosyllabic tonight. It felt like a depressing step back to the early days of their acquaintanceship. Something had happened to upset her—Jake was debating whether to say something when, out of the blue, she suddenly said:

"Do you ever feel cursed?"

It was such an unexpected question that he was at first speechless. Then, going too far the other way, he blathered ineffectually, trying to reassure her and at the same time probe without being intrusive. She didn't respond.

He crossed the room and took her hand in his. He was talking all the while, but Helen stared straight ahead, hardly registering his presence. Eventually, she looked down, seemingly noticing for the first time that he had taken her hand. She looked at him, not unkindly, then withdrew it.

She crossed the room, dressed, then headed for the door. Pausing, she whispered:

"Thank you."

And then she was gone. Jake was offended, bemused and worried. What the hell was going on with her? And why did she feel cursed?

There was so much left unsaid, so much bottled up inside her, and Jake was desperate to help her if he could. He was certain she didn't have anyone else to talk to. But in spite of his desperation, he knew he couldn't push it. He was powerless in this relationship and could make none of the running. He would have to wait for Helen to come to him.

34

Lady Macbeth lived in a huge detached house on the outskirts of Upper Shirley, much to her neighbors' chagrin. They were all accountants and lawyers; Sandra McEwan was not. She made thousands of pounds a year selling drugs and sex. Southampton was the nerve center of her business, and she directed operations from her ritzy residence. Sandra was from Fife originally, but had run away from her foster home when she was only fourteen. She was walking the streets before the year was out, working her way down the country before ending up on the south coast, where she was pimped by a fellow Scot—Malcolm Childs. She became his lover, later his wife, and then, according to underworld legend, suffocated him during an S&M session. His body was never found, and she seamlessly took up the reins of his empire, killing or maiming anyone who tried to take it from her. She had walked free from court a dozen times, had survived three attempts on her life and now lived the high life on the south coast. It was a far cry from Fife.

Her maid protested vigorously—it was only seven a.m.—but Charlie had a warrant for Sandra's arrest and wasn't inclined to hang around, in case the lady in question did a bunk. Security cameras covered every inch of her property and it was likely she would see them coming. Fortunately on this occasion she was fast asleep, as Charlie discovered when she opened the doors to Sandra's opulent bedroom.

Her lover—a muscular, athletic man—leaped out of bed the instant the door opened. He was intent on confronting Charlie, but paused when he saw her warrant card.

"Cool it, boy. It's all right."

Sandra's lover was a former boxer, whom she kept by her side at all times. He almost never spoke—Sandra liked to do that for him.

"Climb back in. I can handle this."

"Sandra McEwan, I have a warrant here—"

"Slow down, DC Brooks. It is DC Brooks, isn't it?"

"Yes," Charlie replied tightly.

"I recognize your picture from the papers. How you faring these days? Better, I hope."

"Everything's rosy in my world, Sandra, so cut the crap and get up, will you?"

She handed her a robe. Sandra regarded her.

"How long you been back, DC Brooks?"

"I'm losing my patience."

"Tell me how long and I'll get up."

Charlie paused, then said:

"Two days."

"Two days," Sandra repeated, letting the words hang in the air.

She hauled her generous frame out of the king-sized bed, refusing the robe that Charlie offered her. She made no attempt to hide her nakedness.

"Two days and you're keen to make a name for y'self. Prove all those women-hating doubters wrong, eh?"

Charlie eyeballed her, refusing to acknowledge the truth of Sandra's comments.

"Well, I admire that, Charlie, I do. But don't fucking do it on my time, eh?"

The bonhomie had disappeared now. Sandra's snarl was unmistakable.

"Unless you want my lawyers up your pretty backside night and day for the next week, I'd turn around and scurry back to Ceri Harddick, right?"

Sandra was close now, her naked body inches from Charlie's smart suit. But Charlie didn't blink, refusing to be intimidated.

"You're coming to the station, Sandra. Small matter of a double murder that we need your help with. So what's it going to be? You going to walk out like a lady or be dragged out in cuffs?"

"You don't learn, do you? You lot never learn."

Cursing like a grenadier, Sandra stalked off to source some clothes from her walk-in wardrobe. In Sandra's case crime certainly did pay, as she proved now, subjecting Charlie to an absurd pantomime that involved her choosing, then discarding a number of designer outfits by Prada, Stella McCartney and Diane von Furstenberg . . . before settling on Armani jeans and a jumper.

"Ready?" Charlie said, trying not to show her irritation.

"Ready," replied Sandra, her wide smile revealing two gold teeth. "Let the games begin."

35

"Why wasn't I told about this?"

"Mind your tone, Helen."

"Why wasn't I told about this, ma'am?"

Helen's sarcasm was poorly disguised, her anger overcoming any restraint. Harwood rose and gently closed her office door, shutting out her eavesdropping secretary.

"You weren't told," Harwood continued, "because you weren't here. McEwan is adept at disappearing, so we had to move quickly. I asked DC Brooks to bring her in and told her that I would explain the situation to you. Which I'm doing now."

Harwood's reasonable explanation did nothing to improve Helen's mood. Was she justified in being so furious at being kept out of the loop or was she just pissed off because it was Charlie? If she was honest, she couldn't really tell.

"I understand that, ma'am, but if there is information relating to the Alan Matthews murder, then I should be the first to know."

"You're right, Helen, and it's my fault. If you want to blame somebody, blame me."

Which of course Helen couldn't do, leaving her not a leg to stand on. But she tried one last time nevertheless:

"McEwan may be involved in the Louszko killing, but I can't see her connection to Matthews's murder."

"We have to keep an open mind, Helen. You said yourself that his killing could be part of a turf war. Perhaps he was the collateral damage. Charlie's turned up something genuinely interesting and I'd like us to investigate it fully."

"It doesn't feel right. This is too elaborate, too personal. It has all the hallmarks of an individual who—"

"An individual who has intelligence, ambition and imagination. Someone who's happy to kill without qualm or conscience and who is adept at misleading the police. I'd say that's Sandra McEwan to a T, wouldn't you?"

There was no point fighting it anymore, so Helen conceded the point and departed for the interview room. Charlie was waiting for her, and opposite her, flanked by her lawyer, was Lady Macbeth.

"Lovely to see you, Inspector." Sandra McEwan's grin spread from ear to ear. "How's business?"

"I might ask you the same question, Sandra."

"Never better. Still, you're looking well. Don't tell me you've got a man on the go?"

Helen ignored the taunt.

"DC Brooks is investigating the murder of Alexia Louszko. She worked for you at Brookmire, I believe, under the alias of Agneska Suriav."

Sandra didn't deny it, so Helen continued.

"She was murdered, mutilated and dumped in the open boot of an abandoned car. Her murder was meant to send out a message. Perhaps you could translate it for us?"

"I'd love to help you, but I barely knew the girl. I'd only seen her a handful of times."

"She worked for you—you must have vetted her personally, spoken to her . . ."

"I own the freehold of the building that houses Brookmire. I couldn't say who runs the business."

Her lawyer didn't say a word. He was just window dressing, really. Sandra knew exactly how she wanted to play things.

"You plucked her off the street," said Charlie, keeping up the pressure. "Trained her, polished her. But the Campbells took exception, didn't they? They abducted her. Killed her. Then put her back on the streets where she belonged."

"If you say so."

"Your girl. They took her from under your nose and killed her. How did the rest of your girls feel about that? I bet they were shitting themselves."

Sandra said nothing.

"You knew you had to do something," Charlie continued. "So why not kill two birds with one stone? Tell me about your properties on the Empress Road."

Finally a reaction. It was small, but it was there. Sandra hadn't been expecting that.

"I don't have any . . ."

"Let me show you this, Sandra," Charlie went on. "It's a list of holding companies that have financial relationships with each other. Let's cut the chat and acknowledge that they are all owned by you. This one"—Charlie pointed out a company name—"purchased a row of six derelict houses on the Empress Road nearly two years ago. Why did you buy them, Sandra?"

There was a long pause and then the tiniest of nods from her lawyer. "To redevelop them."

"Why would you want to? They are rotten, derelict, and it's hardly a neighborhood that's ripe for gentrification."

"You don't want to do them up," interrupted Helen, suddenly getting it. "You want to knock them down."

The tiniest flicker from Sandra. The closest thing they would get to an acknowledgment that they were on the right lines.

"Nobody wants the properties in the red-light district—they are used by prostitutes on a nightly basis. But if you bought them, knocked them down and then neglected to rebuild them, what would the girls do? Risk their lives getting into punters' cars every night or look elsewhere for employment? Somewhere safer. Somewhere like Brookmire. I bet if we do some more searching, we'll find a lot of property has changed hands on the Empress Road recently. Am I right?"

A hardness was entering Sandra's eyes now. Charlie pressed home the advantage.

"But what if you wanted to go a step further? The Campbells had struck at you, tried to unsettle your workforce. What if you decided to raise the stakes? You could have killed one of their girls in return, but far more imaginative to kill a punter or two. The press coverage alone would drive the Campbells' clients away in droves. I have to hand it to you, Sandra—it's a smart play."

Sandra smiled and said nothing.

"Did you single out Alan Matthews? Or was he selected at random?"

"My client has no idea what you're talking about and categorically denies involvement in *any* acts of violence."

"Perhaps, then, she could tell me where she was between the hours of nine p.m. and three a.m. on the twenty-eighth of November," Charlie butted in, determined to keep up the pressure.

Sandra looked long and hard at Charlie, then said:

"I was at an exhibition."

"Where?" barked Charlie.

"In a converted warehouse just off Sidney Street. Local artist, a living installation where the punters are part of the art and all that stuff. It's all bollocks, of course, but people say the artist's going to be worth something, so I thought I'd take a look. And here's the funny bit. I'm no good with technology, but the boy knows his stuff and he tells me the whole thing was streamed live on the Internet. You can't fake that kind of thing—you're welcome to check it out. And if you still have doubts, you can confirm my alibi with some of the other guests who were present. The CEO of Southampton City Council was there, as was the Arts editor from BBC South—oh, and I nearly forgot . . . the president of the Association of Chief Police Officers too. What's his name—Anderson? Buck-toothed guy who insists on wearing that awful wig—you can't mistake him."

Sandra sat back in her chair and looked at Charlie, then turned to Helen.

"Now if we're all done here, I'd better be off. I've an evening engagement that I'm very keen to keep."

"What the hell are you playing at, DC Brooks?"

The days when Helen used to call her Charlie seemed a long time ago now.

"What on earth possessed you to pull her in without checking if she was a remotely credible suspect?"

"She still is. She has motive, opportunity—"

"And a cast-iron alibi. She made us look like idiots in there. So stop running errands for Superintendent Harwood and start doing your bloody job. Find out who killed Alexia Louszko."

Helen marched off. They'd have to check Sandra's alibi, but Helen had no doubt that she was telling the truth. It was too good an alibi to be made up. She could have hired others to kill Matthews and Reid, of course, but was it credible that she would give a lone woman the job when she had an army of men to do her bidding? No, it didn't stack up.

The day had started badly and was getting worse. For the first time in her career Helen had the distinct impression that her colleagues were working against her, rather than helping her. This case was weird and difficult enough without Charlie and Harwood leading her down blind alleys and constantly moving the ground beneath her feet.

The truth was that they had got nowhere. Two lives had been destroyed; more would follow. And there was not a thing Helen could do to stop it.

36

Angie had got used to holding court. She had been given a week's leave from Zenith Solutions and had been making the most of it, receiving friends and relatives at home, rehearsing the whole horrid incident over and over again, embellishing it when the mood took her. But even Angie was growing tired of telling her story now, so she ignored the persistent ringing of the doorbell. The curtains were closed, Jeremy Kyle was on and she had a cup of Mellow Bird's on the go.

The doorbell rang again. Angie turned the volume up. Who cared if that confirmed her presence in the house; she didn't have to open the door to anyone she didn't want to. The bell stopped ringing and Angie smiled.

She concentrated on the show—the DNA results were about to be revealed. She had joined the program too late to know what the participants' conflict was about, but there was always a punch-up when DNA results were revealed. She loved this part of the program.

"Hello?"

Angie sat bolt upright. Someone was in the house.

"Are you there, Angie?"

Angie was off the sofa and searching for a weapon. A heavy glass vase was the best she could do. She raised it above her head as the living room door opened.

"Angie?"

Angie froze, her fear dissipating into surprise. The woman's scarred face was instantly recognizable. Emilia Garanita was a minor celebrity in Southampton.

"I am so sorry to intrude, but the back door was unlocked and I am *desperate* to talk to you, Angie. May I call you Angie?"

Angie was too shocked to rebuke her for trespassing, and Emilia took that as her cue to advance, placing a comforting hand on Angie's arm.

"How are you getting on, Angie? I hear you had a terrible shock."

One of the girls at work had obviously blabbed. Angie was irritated and pleased in equal measure. To be sought out by the local press was an unusual and gratifying experience. Effortlessly Emilia guided Angie back onto the sofa, seating herself beside her.

"I'm bearing up," Angie replied bravely.

"Of course you are. You're a strong woman—that's what everyone says about you."

Angie very much doubted it, but was pleased by the compliment.

"And our article will reflect that."

Angie nodded, excitement mingling with unease.

"The *Evening News* wants to do a double-page spread on you. Your life, your important work at Zenith Solutions and your bravery in dealing with such an unpleasant incident. We'd like to pay tribute to you. Is that okay?"

Angie nodded.

"So let's get a few details straight. We can do your career history in a moment, but let's focus on the day itself for now. You received a package for your boss . . ."

"Mr. McPhail."

"Mr. McPhail. You open all his mail, presumably?"

"Of course. I am his personal assistant. This was a couriered package and I always open those straightaway."

Emilia was scribbling keenly now.

"And inside . . ."

"Inside . . . was a heart. The smell was terrible."

"A heart?" replied Emilia, trying to keep the excitement out of her voice. She hadn't really expected it to be true, but it was.

"Yes. A heart, a human heart."

"And can you think of any reason why someone would send such a thing to Mr. McPhail?"

"No," replied Angie firmly. "He's a brilliant boss."

"Of course. And the police have been in touch?"

"I spoke to Inspector Grace."

"I know her well. She's a good copper. Was there anything in particular she wanted to know?"

Angie hesitated.

"I quite understand if you're uncomfortable disclosing details of your conversation," Emilia continued. "All I would say is that if I'm to convince my editor to give this story the center spread it deserves, then I am going to need *all* the details."

A long pause, then Angie spoke.

"She did seem particularly interested in getting a full list of Zenith's employees. Particularly those who were absent that day."

Emilia's writing hand paused for a second, then carried on scribbling. She didn't want to give away her excitement at this very interesting development. It was all fitting together nicely and would play well for her purposes.

Once again a major story had fallen into her lap.

37

Violet Robinson viewed her son-in-law with suspicion. She never doubted his love for Nicola, but she doubted his dedication. He was a man, and men were careless of the details and prone to take shortcuts. Nicola was certainly comfortable at home, and her basic needs were always catered to by Tony or by Anna if he was working, but Nicola was more than *basic*. She was a beautiful, intelligent and spirited young woman. Like her mother, Nicola had always taken great pride in her appearance, never leaving the house without makeup on, careful to ensure that not a hair was out of place. Too often Violet had had to take matters into her own hands, distressed by her daughter's pallor, by the stray hairs, by the lack of makeup. Tony didn't really know what to do in this area, and Anna—well, Anna was a plain girl who clearly felt it was what you were like on the inside that mattered.

"How long will you be gone for?" she asked Tony.

They were standing together in the living room, out of earshot of Nicola's bedroom.

"I won't be *gone*," Tony replied, choosing his words and tone carefully. "I will be here during the day—probably more than usual, in fact—it's just the nights. Anna has said she's happy to do the lion's share of the night work, but if there's any way you could—"

"I've already said I'll help, Tony. I'm happy to do it. Best to have family round her."

Tony nodded and smiled, but Violet could tell he didn't agree. He liked Anna better than her, and if Anna was up to doing seven nights straight, no doubt he would have paid her to do that, rather than corralling his mother-in-law to help.

"How long will this . . . night work go on for?"

"Not long, I hope."

Another evasive answer.

"Well, I'm happy to help for as long as is necessary, but you know how I feel about it. I hate the idea of Nicola waking up and finding a stranger at her bedside."

Violet's voice faltered, her underlying sense of loss suddenly ambushing her. Tony nodded sympathetically, but would never engage on this point. Had he given up on Nicola? Violet strongly suspected he had. Did he have other women? Violet suddenly wasn't sure, and it hurt her.

"Is it dangerous? What you're doing?"

A longer pause this time, and then an unnecessarily long reassurance. So it *was* dangerous. Was she being unfair, hating him for being so cavalier? He was a policeman and had a job to do—she understood that. But couldn't he have got moved off the front line to something safer? What if something happened to him? Violet's own husband—useless bastard that he was—had scarpered years ago. He was now living with his second wife and three children in Maidstone and never visited them. If anything happened to Tony, it would just be Nicola and Violet, locked together, waiting and hoping.

Suddenly Violet found herself crossing the room. She laid her hand on Tony's arm and, softening her tone, said:

"Well, take care, Tony. Take care of yourself."

And for once, he seemed to understand. This was a difficult moment for both of them—a shift in the status quo away from intensive care to a more expansive life for Tony—and for once they were in accord.

"You get on, Tony. Nicola and I will be fine here."

"Thank you, Violet."

Tony left the room to continue his preparations, leaving Violet alone with her daughter. Pulling her lipstick from her handbag, Violet applied it to Nicola's lips. It cheered her momentarily, but inside her nerves were still jangling. She had a nasty feeling that forces beyond her control were gathering and preparing to shake her world.

38

As the team congregated in the briefing room, Helen tried to gather her thoughts. She'd never felt so isolated on an investigation before. Charlie was keen to prove herself by nailing McEwan for the murders and Harwood seemed intent on backing her. Her superior did not want to credit Helen's growing conviction that they were dealing with a serial killer. Harwood was a politician, a protocol copper, and had never encountered this sort of individual before. Helen, because of her history and her training, had. Which is why she had to take the lead, to focus the team's investigation where it mattered.

"Let's assume for now," Helen began, "that our killer *is* a prostitute, murdering men who pay for sex. This is not something that's happened by accident—there's no evidence they tried to rape her or that there was a struggle—so she deliberately lured these men to out-of-the-way places and then killed them. This is something that's been brewing inside her, that she's been planning. There's nothing to suggest that she works in a team, so we are looking for a highly disturbed, highly dangerous individual who's probably been the victim of violence or rape, who may have a history of mental health problems and who clearly has a violent hatred of men. We should check out the hospitals, drop-in clinics, refuges, hostels, and see if anyone's presented there in the last twelve months who fits the bill. Also let's go through HOLMES 2 to see if there are any unsolved rapes or sexual assaults recently. Something must have set her off. However prone to violence she is, something must have triggered this terrible rage. Check also for crimes that *she* may have committed—assaults, stabbings—that may have been her flexing her muscles before she decided to kill. DC Sanderson, can you run this, please?"

"On it, boss."

"So who are we looking for?" Helen continued. "She obviously knows her way round the scene—Empress Road, Eling Great Marsh—so she's probably been an active prostitute recently. Her misspellings of both the word 'Evill' and the Matthewses' postal address suggest she may be ill-educated, even dyslexic, but she is clearly not stupid. She leaves virtually no trace wherever she goes—Forensics pulled a black hair from Reid's car, but it is synthetic, probably from a wig—and she possesses plenty of courage. She walked in and out of Zenith Solutions without anyone noticing anything about her. To risk capture in that way suggests that she is a woman on a mission. Someone with a point to prove."

Silence from the team as Helen's words sank in.

"So our prime focus is current or recent prostitutes. We should check out every rung on the ladder—high-class prostitutes, student escorts, illegals, the junkies giving it away at the docks—but with special focus on the lower end of the market. Matthews's and Reid's tastes seem to have been for the grubbier, nastier, cheaper girls. We need to cover the whole city, but I'm going to focus most of our manpower in the north. Bevois Valley, Portswood, Highfield, Hampton Park. Our killer picks up her clients in areas not covered by CCTV, but we have managed to track Matthews's and Reid's cars via traffic cameras. It looks like she picked up Matthews on the Empress Road and Reid somewhere near the Common. She's probably choosing these places because they are close to home, because she knows them, because they are 'safe.' So let's not rule anything out, but my guess is that she lives or works in the north of the city. DC McAndrew will lead our efforts in this area."

"I've got a team assembled, boss," DC McAndrew responded, "and we've broken down the area into sectors. We'll be onto it this afternoon."

"The next question is why did she choose Matthews and Reid? Were they picked at random or deliberately selected? The killer might have seen Matthews around and learned his habits and peccadilloes. But Reid was much younger and appears to have been relatively new to the scene. If he *was* selected deliberately, it would have to have been done by more subtle means. They were both family men, which could be an important link, but they moved in very different circles and were at very different stages of their family lives—Matthews had four kids of teen age and up. Reid had one baby daughter."

"They must have found her online. These days if you want a blow job, you just Google it, right?" chipped in DC Sanderson to muted chuckles.

"Probably, so let's check out Reid's and Matthews's digital footprints. DC Grounds, perhaps you could coordinate. Let's find out if these guys were deliberately targeted or just in the wrong place at the wrong time. Everybody clear?"

Helen was on her feet, marching back into the incident room. She was filled with energy and determination—a real sense of purpose. But as she crossed the office floor, she suddenly stopped dead, her newfound optimism dissipating in an instant. Somebody had left the TV on mute, the set playing silently to itself in the corner, but now Helen hurriedly grabbed the remote control and turned up the volume. It was the lunchtime news bulletin on BBC South. Graham Wilson, the regular anchor, was conducting an in-depth interview. And his studio guest today was Eileen Matthews.

Helen burned with anger and frustration as she raced to the Matthews residence. Eileen was desperate with grief—Helen understood that—but her direct intervention in the investigation risked sabotaging everything. Eileen had made up her mind that Alan was not involved with prostitutes and, convinced that the police were barking up the wrong tree, had decided to instigate her own hunt for her husband's killer. "Please help me find the man who did this to Alan" was a phrase she had repeated several times during the interview. *Man, man, man.* Five minutes of lunchtime TV had now set the public hunting for a killer that didn't exist.

Eileen had only just returned home from the TV studio when Helen arrived. She was visibly drained by the experience of talking publicly about her husband's death and wanted to shut the door on Helen, but Helen was too enraged to allow that. It didn't take long for hostilities to start.

"You should have consulted us first, Eileen. Something like this could really set our investigation back."

"I didn't consult you because I knew what you'd say."

Eileen was utterly unrepentant. Helen had to work hard to control her temper.

"I know you've had to deal with so much in the past few days that you feel overwhelmed with pain and grief, that you're desperate for some answers, but this isn't the way to go about it. If you want justice for yourself, for your children, you must let *us* take the lead."

"And let you blacken Alan's name? Drag this family through the gutter?"

"I can't hide the truth from you, Eileen, however painful it might be. Your husband used prostitutes, and I'm convinced that that was why he died. His killer was a woman—we're ninety-nine percent certain of that—and anything that directs the public's attention elsewhere risks allowing her to strike again. People need to be vigilant and we have to give them the right information in order for them to be so. Do you see?"

"Strike again?"

For once Eileen's tone was less strident. Helen paused, uncertain how much to share.

"A young man was murdered last night. We believe the same person is responsible for both murders."

Eileen stared at her.

"He was found in an area used by prostitutes . . ."

"No."

"I'm sorry . . ."

"I won't have you continue with this . . . this campaign of slander. Alan was a good man. A devout man. I know he wasn't always healthy . . . he had certain infections, but many of those can be contracted at the swimming baths. Alan was a keen swimmer—"

"For God's sake, Eileen, he had gonorrhea. You can't get that from swimming."

"NO! It's his bloody funeral tomorrow and you come here with these lies . . . *No! No! No!*"

Eileen shouted at the top of her voice, silencing Helen. Then the tears came. Helen felt a riot of emotions—sympathy, fury, disbelief. In the heavy silence that followed, she cast her eyes about the room, taking in the family photos that seemed to confirm Eileen's vision of Alan. He was the very image of the upstanding paterfamilias, playing football with his boys, standing proudly next to daughter Carrie at her graduation, leading the church choir, toasting his bride at their wedding all those years ago. But it was all propaganda.

"Eileen, you have to work with us on this. You need to understand the bigger picture. Otherwise innocent people will die. Do you understand?"

Eileen didn't look up but her sobbing subsided a little.

"I don't mean to cause you pain, but you have to face the truth. Alan's Internet history showed he had an active interest in both pornography and prostitutes. Unless someone else—you or the boys—used that computer, then it can only be Alan who was accessing those sites."

Eileen had previously told them that Alan didn't let anybody else into his study, let alone use his desktop, so Helen knew this one would land.

"These sites weren't accessed by accident. They were in his bookmarks . . . We have also done some investigation into his financial affairs."

Eileen was quiet now.

"There was an account he administered that contained money to pay for church repairs. Two years ago, it had a balance of several thousand pounds. Most of it's gone now, taken out in two-hundred-pound chunks over the last eighteen months. But no work has been carried out at your church. I sent one of my officers down there to speak to the minister. We know Alan wasn't a big earner and it looks very much like he was using church money to fund his activities."

Helen continued, softening her tone.

"I know you feel utterly lost right now, but the only way for you and your family to find your way through this . . . nightmare is to look the reality of it dead in the eye. You won't believe this, but I know what you're going through. I have experienced awful things, endured terrible pain, and burying your head in the sand is the worst thing you can do. For your girls, for your boys, for yourself, you need to take on board what I'm saying. See Alan for what he was—good and bad—and deal with it. Your church may well want to instigate financial investigations of its own and I'm sure we will have more questions for you. Fighting us is not the way to get through this. You need to help us and we will help you in return."

Eileen finally looked up.

"I want to catch Alan's killer," Helen continued. "More than anything else I want to catch Alan's killer and give you the answers you need. But I can't do that if you're fighting me, Eileen. So please work with me."

Helen's entreaty was sincere and heartfelt. There was a long pause, then finally Eileen looked up.

"I pity you, Inspector."

"Excuse me?"

"I pity you because you have no *faith*."

She hurried out of the room without looking back. Helen watched her go. Her anger had dissipated and now she just felt pity. Eileen had believed absolutely in Alan and would never truly come to terms with the fact that her mentor, her rock, was in fact a man of straw.

39

DC Rebecca McAndrew had been on the hunt for only a few hours, but already she felt tarnished and dispirited. She and her team had hit the high-end brothels first. They were far busier than she remembered. The recession had driven more and more women into the sex industry and the sudden influx of prostitutes from Poland and Bulgaria had further flooded the market. Competition was up, which meant that prices had come down. It was an increasingly cutthroat business.

Next they'd moved on to the student campuses, where they found a depressingly similar picture. Every girl they talked to knew of at least one fellow student who'd turned to prostitution to fund her studies. It was more and more a feature of everyday life as grants were cut and students struggled to pay their way through the many years of study. But the anecdotal tales of alcohol dependency and self-harming suggested that this new phenomenon was not without its costs.

Now Sanderson and her team were in the Claymore drop-in center, a free health-care service run by a combination of National Health Service workers and generous-hearted volunteers. Anyone could turn up here and receive free treatment, but it was in a grotty part of town, the queues were long and you always had to keep one eye on your possessions, so it generally attracted the drunk and the desperate. Many of the center's clients were young prostitutes—girls with infections, girls who'd been beaten up and needed stitches, girls who had young babies and simply couldn't cope. It was hard not to be moved by the awful situations they found themselves in.

Rebecca McAndrew often cursed the long hours that came with her job—she had been single for over two years now, partly because of the night work—but she realized the sacrifices she'd made were nothing compared to those made by the women who worked at Claymore. Despite being exhausted, despite being painfully short of resources, they worked tirelessly to help keep these girls together, without ever judging them or losing their tempers. They were modern saints—not that they were ever acknowledged as such.

As the team interviewed and questioned, a paradox struck Rebecca forcefully. In a world where it seemed harder and harder to find meaningful connections with other people—love, marriage, family—it had never been easier to find paid companionship. The world was in the doldrums, the country still in the grip of recession, but one thing was clear.

Southampton was awash in sex.

40

The streets were dark and so was Charlie's mood. After her bollocking by Helen, her first instinct had been to hand in her warrant card and run home. But something had stopped her and she was relieved now, ashamed of her thin skin. What had she been expecting? Helen didn't want her back and Charlie had played straight into her hands, allowing her enthusiasm to compromise her investigation into Sandra McEwan.

She burned with shame—what had happened to the talented cop she used to be?—and that shame drove her on now. Having failed in her first attempt to unmask Alexia's killer, Charlie had gone back to basics, hitting the streets in search of information. Perhaps by talking to the street girls who seemed to be at the heart of McEwan's war with the Campbells, she could dig up a lead. Schoolchildren were wandering home; it was only a little after four p.m., but already darkness was beginning to descend. That creeping, suffocating gloom that winter does so well. Charlie's spirits dropped a notch further.

The prostitutes who hung about the port were happy enough to take a look at Charlie's photo once they realized she wasn't going to bust them. Their memories were hazy, but one long-serving girl eventually pointed Charlie in the direction of the Liberty Hotel, a filthy and dilapidated place that rented rooms by the hour rather than by the day. Charlie had visited it before and her heart sank at having to return. It was a place full of loneliness and despair.

She pressed the buzzer. Once, twice, three times before eventually the door opened a crack. She shoved her warrant card in the face of the Polish thug who "greeted" her. Snarling, he let her inside, turning his back on her as he stalked up the stairs. Charlie knew he'd be little help—his job was to see all but say nothing—so she focused her attention on the working girls who appeared with impressive regularity from behind the many closed doors. The building was a tall terraced house, set over four floors. It was astonishing to consider exactly how much copulation took place here every night. Used condoms littered the floor.

Charlie was talking to a girl named Denise, who was seventeen at best. She and her boyfriend had a drug habit and clearly it was up to Denise to earn the money for both of them to indulge. Why do these girls value themselves so cheaply? This was the bottom end of the market—the more expensive girls plied their trade in the north of the city. Down by the docks you were expected to do anything for a few pounds, however painful or unpleasant.

A lot of coppers treated prostitutes like dirt, but Charlie always found herself wanting to help them. She was already maneuvering to get Denise away from her parasitic bloke, guiding her in the direction of a refuge she knew, when suddenly all hell broke loose.

A scream. Long, loud and desperate. Then the thundering of feet charging downstairs, doors being slammed, pandemonium. Charlie was on her feet and racing up the stairs. As she turned the corner, she collided head-on with a terrified prostitute. It knocked the wind out of her temporarily, but still the screaming went on, so Charlie dragged herself onward, past more worried faces, forcing the breath back into her lungs as she mounted the stairs. As she reached the top landing, she was surprised to find that she had blood on her shirt.

The screaming was coming from the last door on the right. Removing her baton from its holster, she extended it, ready to fight. But as soon as she entered the room, she knew that she wouldn't be needing it. The battle had already been fought and lost. In the corner of the room, a teenage prostitute was screaming incessantly, frozen by shock. Nearby on the blood-saturated bed was a man. His chest had been ripped open, revealing his pulsating heart to the open air.

Suddenly it all made sense. The reason Charlie had blood on her shirt was that she had collided with the killer as she fled the scene of her latest attack. Stunned, Charlie turned to run after her, then paused. The man was still alive.

Charlie had a split second to decide. She hurried over to the man, pulling her coat off and clamping it to his chest in an effort to stem the blood loss. Cradling his head, she urged him to keep his eyes open, to talk to her. Charlie knew that the killer had such a good lead that she had probably got away and her best chance of IDing her was to prize some information out of her victim before he died.

"Call an ambulance," she barked at the screaming girl, before returning her attention to the man. He coughed up a hunk of blood. The mist of it settled on Charlie's face.

"Can you tell me your name, love?"

The man gurgled but managed nothing.

"The ambulance is on its way now. You're going to be okay."

His eyes were beginning to close.

"Can you tell me who did this to you?"

The man opened his mouth. Charlie leaned forward, putting her ear to his mouth to hear what he had to say.

"Who attacked you? Can you give me her name?"

The man was struggling to breathe, but he was determined to say something.

"Her name? Please tell me her name."

But the man said nothing. All Charlie heard was the last breath escaping his body. The killer had got away and Charlie was left holding her latest victim.

41

Helen stalked the street outside the Liberty Hotel, her eyes raking the walls of the dilapidated terrace for CCTV cameras. They had had a lucky break—Charlie literally bumping into their killer—and as a result of her testimony and the crumbs gleaned from the Polish sex worker who'd disturbed the attack, they had their best description of the suspect so far. She was Caucasian, in her twenties probably and tall, taller than your average girl, with long, powerful legs. She wore dark clothes, probably leather, had a pale face and long black hair cut in a fringe. But no one had seen her face well enough to give more than generic descriptions. The guy who took the money from the girls clearly never dragged his attention away from the TV long enough to actually look at who went in and out of the building. The other working girls said she wasn't a regular—a couple of them had crossed her path as she took her client upstairs, but she had kept her head down, didn't meet their eyes and, besides, they had their own clients to attend to. It was infuriating to be so close and yet have so little. A grab from a CCTV camera could change everything, however, so Helen scoured the walls. It was an area where crime was rife, so people often employed extra security here, but her investigation revealed only one camera, poised above the entrance to a down-at-heel off-license. It hung limply, pointing at the wall, clearly the victim of vandalism. Was this the work of children or had their killer disabled it? It would be of little use either way.

Heading back to the hotel entrance, Helen spotted Charlie, who was now wearing a paper suit and a blanket. Her clothes had been taken away for forensic analysis and she was being looked after by a young woman police officer.

"Would you like me to call Steve?"

Charlie looked up to see Helen standing over her.

"Lloyd . . . DC Fortune's already done it."

"Good. Go home, Charlie. You've had a big shock and you've done all you can. We'll speak later."

Charlie nodded, still taciturn with shock. Helen placed a comforting hand on her shoulder, then moved on, impatient to see what the crime scene might offer them. Climbing the stairwell to the top floor, she paused to interrogate a group of Forensics officers crowded round a partial footprint. The outline of a heel and toe was printed on the wooden board in blood.

"Is it hers?" Helen asked.

"Well, it's not Charlie's, so . . ."

"Can you get a size off it?"

The Scene of Crime officer nodded, so Helen moved on. These small details could be surprisingly significant. She was momentarily cheered, but her good humor evaporated as soon as she took in the crime scene. It was drenched in blood. The victim lay on the bed, his hands and legs still tied to the bedstead, his chest opened up like a tin can. His heart, which only thirty minutes ago had been pumping fit to burst, now lay still. Helen leaned over the body, taking care not to touch it. Focusing on the wound, she could see that the tissue around the heart was untouched. Clearly the killer had been disturbed before she could take her prize. Helen looked at the victim's face—didn't recognize him—then quickly looked away. It was contorted in agony.

She retreated to watch the Forensics officers at work. In addition to the evidence garnered from the victim's body, they would also be analyzing a medium-sized Tupperware box that lay discarded on the floor. Was this what their killer put the hearts in? A Tupperware box. It was so common, so domestic, it was almost funny. It could have been bought in a hundred stores in Southampton, so they would have to hope that their killer had left some residue of her identity on it. Helen knew she couldn't bank on it, though—their killer had hardly put a foot wrong so far.

As Helen took in the crime scene, her mind was full of questions. Why this sudden change in MO? The killer had been so cautious thus far—why bring her latest victim to a place where she could be disturbed or, worse, identified? Was she getting careless? Or were the punters harder to isolate now? Had word got out about the danger? Were clients seeking safety in more public places? She had brought him here during the day, when she knew there would be others around. Was he special in some way? Could she get him only at this time of day? It was a strange turn of events.

One thing that Helen was sure of was that the killer would now be rattled. She had been disturbed during the act and had fled empty-handed. Worse, she had run straight into a cop waving a warrant card and had escaped only through sheer good fortune. She must fear now that the police would have a good description of her and possibly forensic evidence too. Experience had taught Helen that such a scare would make the killer react in one of two ways. Either she would vanish for good or she would step up her killing spree. Which option would she take?

Only time would tell.

42

It was time to say good-bye. Tony had been putting it off, but it was getting late now. He hesitated on the threshold of Nicola's bedroom, then stepped inside.

"Could you give us a moment, Anna?"

Anna stopped reading aloud and looked up from her book, momentarily doing a double take at Tony's appearance before recovering her poise.

"Of course."

She disappeared discreetly. Tony paused, looking down at his wife. Her right eyelid flickered—which was her way of greeting her husband.

"I've got to go now, love. Anna's going to be with you for the rest of the day and through the night. I'll come and see you in the morning, okay? We can read a bit of Dickens if you'd like. Anna says you've nearly finished it."

No response from Nicola. Had she understood what he was saying? Or was she upset and refusing to communicate? Once more Tony was swamped by guilt.

"I'll tell Anna she can read late tonight if you like. You can always sleep in tomorrow. I'll put the cot bed next to you and we can snuggle. Be like old times."

Tony's voice caught. Why was he stringing this out when he knew it was better just to go?

Leaning down, he kissed his wife's brow. He paused, then kissed her again, this time on her lips. They seemed dry, even a bit chapped, so he plucked the lip balm from the bedside table and gently applied it.

"Love you."

Tony turned and left and thirty seconds later the front door closed gently behind him.

Tony walked round the corner to where he'd parked his unmarked car. It was a dented Vauxhall saloon, the car of choice for traveling salesmen up and down the land. He bleeped it open with the fob. Stooping to open the driver's door, he caught sight of himself and paused. He was wearing a crumpled business suit, had painted flecks of gray in his hair and had added a pair of executive-type glasses. It was him, but not him. A vision of a man who was lonely, tired and bereft. There was more than a hint of truth in the image, but Tony refused to dwell on that. He had work to do.

Climbing into the car, he fired it up and moved off. It was time to dance with the devil.

43

A TART WITH *YOUR* HEART

Emilia Garanita surveyed the headline with undisguised pleasure. She was particularly pleased with her wordplay, as was her editor, who had splashed it across the front page. Would this be the best-selling edition of the *Evening News* ever? She sincerely hoped so. With a bit of luck, it might even be her passport out of regional journalism.

The papers had gone out a couple of hours ago. Clearly word was spreading—her mobile phone hadn't stopped ringing and her Twitter feed was going ballistic. Nothing sells papers like a serial killer, and Emilia intended to make the most of it. The pieces she'd written last year on Marianne's killing spree had gained her a reputation locally, but because of Grace's obstruction on that case, she had got to the story too late. She wouldn't make the same mistake again.

Emilia swallowed her guilty hope that the killer would not be caught too quickly. She knew it was wrong to think like that, but truth be told, she enjoyed the fact that Grace was being given the run-around, that the killer appeared to strike at will without leaving a trace. And besides, who honestly felt sympathy for the victims? They were typical men—deceitful, mendacious, driven by base desires. There were already signs in the messages posted on the paper's forum and on Twitter that the wider public felt that these men had got what was coming to them. For centuries prostitutes had been the unheralded victims of male violence; was it such a bad thing that the boot was now on the other foot? "Go, girl," Emilia said to herself, suppressing a smile.

There was only one blot on the landscape, and that was Emilia's failure to interview Christopher Reid's widow, Jessica. She had rung and visited often, but the Family Liaison officer knew Emilia's tactics well and had seen her off. She had subsequently returned, slipping a financial offer through the door's mail slot, with a note explaining how the money could be put to good use in the difficult months ahead and offering sympathetic coverage in the paper, but as yet there had been no response and Emilia doubted there would be. Grace would keep her away from public view while the killer was at large. Still, Emilia had overcome bigger challenges than this before. She would just have to be inventive. There was more than one way to skin a cat.

The office was thinning out now. There was little point in Emilia hanging about—the praise and adulation she'd received earlier had died down as her colleagues departed for home. Grabbing her bag and coat, she headed to the lifts. There was a new bar on the waterfront that she'd been meaning to check out for a while and now seemed the perfect time to do exactly that.

She had just left the office when her mobile rang. It was one of her tame PCs—he'd been a source of valuable intel for several months now. As she listened to his breathless report, a broad smile spread across Emilia's face. Another murder, and this time it involved a familiar face: DC Charlie Brooks. Turning on her heel, Emilia marched straight back into the office.

This story just kept getting better and better.

44

"She's asleep. You can't see her."

Steve was a bad liar, but Helen didn't contradict him. There was real fury in his eyes and Helen was careful not to provoke him.

"It's important I talk to her, so can you ask her to call me the minute she wakes up?"

"You don't let up, do you?" Steve replied, half laughing in his bitterness.

"I have a job to do, Steve. I'm not trying to rile you or disturb Charlie, but I have a job to do and I won't let personal friendships get in the way."

"Friendships? That's a fucking joke. I don't think you're capable of friendships."

"I didn't come here to argue with you . . ."

"You don't care about anyone but yourself, do you? As long as you get what you wa—"

"*Enough!*"

They both turned to see Charlie approaching. She hadn't been in bed; she'd merely been eavesdropping from the living room, as Helen had suspected all along. Anger flashed across Steve's face momentarily, in embarrassment at being revealed as a liar. Then he recovered himself and hurried over to Charlie. But she was staring past her husband at Helen.

"You'd better come in."

"Think, Charlie. Is there anything else you remember? Her face? Her smell? Her expression?"

"No, I've told you."

"Did she say anything when she bumped into you? Did you hear an accent of any kind?"

Charlie closed her eyes, unwillingly casting her mind back to that moment.

"No. She just kind of grunted."

"Grunted?"

"Yup, I'd winded her so . . ."

Charlie petered out, feeling Helen's irritation and disappointment. The Polish prostitute who'd got the wrong room and disturbed the attack spoke broken English and was deeply suspicious of the police. Her description of the killer was basic, hence the pressure Helen was now piling on Charlie to conjure a rabbit from the hat. Some half-remembered detail could give them the break they so desperately needed.

"Okay, let's leave it for now. You're obviously tired," Helen said, rising. "Perhaps things will be clearer tomorrow after you've had some sleep."

She was halfway to the door when Charlie said:

"Here."

Helen turned to see Charlie holding out her warrant card.

"You were right."

"What do you mean?"

"I can't do this. I thought I could, but I can't."

"Charlie, there's no need to rush into this—"

"Someone died in my arms today," Charlie shouted, her voice shaking even as she said it. "He died right in front of me. I had to wash his blood off my face, out of my hair. I had to wash his blood out of . . ."

She collapsed into sobs, huge breath-robbing sobs. Refusing to look at Helen, she planted her face in her hands. Her warrant card lay on the coffee table where she'd dropped it.

So this was it. All Helen had to do was pick it up. Charlie would be paid off, and that would be that. Helen had got what she wanted.

But Helen knew immediately that she wouldn't pick it up. She had wanted to be rid of Charlie, but now, on the cusp of victory, she felt ashamed of her selfishness and cowardice. What right did she have to drive Charlie out, to consign her to a wilderness of bitterness and regret? She was supposed to help people. To save them, not damn them.

"I'm sorry, Charlie."

Charlie's sobbing paused momentarily, before continuing in a lower key. Helen seated herself next to Charlie.

"I've been a bitch. And I'm sorry. It's . . . it's my weakness, not yours . . . I still have Marianne on my skin, in my blood. I can't shake her. Or Mark. Or you. Or that day. I've been screaming and shouting, running away, hoping that I could rub out the memories if I pushed everything and everyone away. I wanted to push you away. Which was cruel and selfish. I'm really sorry, Charlie."

Charlie looked up, her eyelashes wet with tears.

"I knew what you were feeling, but I didn't help you. I kicked you when you were down and that's unforgivable. But I'd like you to forgive me if you can. It was never about you."

Helen paused a moment before continuing:

"If you want to walk away, start a family, do normal things, then I won't stand in your way. I'll make sure you get whatever you need to start over. But if you change your mind, I want you back . . . I need you back."

Charlie's crying had ceased now, but she still refused to look up.

"We're hunting a serial killer, Charlie. I haven't said that out loud till now, because I didn't want it to be true. Didn't believe it could happen again. But it is true, and now I . . . I can't stop her."

Helen's voice wavered momentarily before she recovered her composure. When she next spoke, her voice was firm but quiet.

"I can't stop her."

Helen left shortly afterward, having said too much, yet still not enough. She had failed to be a good leader, copper or friend. Was it too late to pull something from the wreckage? She had lost Mark, she would be a fool to lose Charlie too. But maybe it was too little, too late. Perhaps it was now her destiny to face this killer alone. It wasn't a fight she thought she could win, but she would fight it nevertheless.

45

Why hadn't Alison hidden it from her? Surely it was Alison's job to suck up all the shit that the world threw at Jessica and keep her safe from the storm. Instead, because Alison had been busy playing with Sally, she hadn't heard the letterbox rattle, hadn't heard the paper hitting the mat. So it had fallen to Jessica to pick it up.

A TART WITH *YOUR* HEART. Jessica dropped the paper as if it were on fire and fled upstairs. She felt light-headed as she reached the landing, the sudden awfulness of it all ramming its way down her throat again. She started to retch, then choke. Stumbling to the bathroom, she could feel the vomit rising. Crashing through the door, she threw up in the bath, her stomach heaving again and again. Finally, it was over, but all her strength had leached out of her, and she curled up in a ball on the bath mat and put her head in her hands.

She wanted to die. It was just too awful. She had already given up hating Christopher for his betrayal and his stupidity and now she just missed him, wanting him back fiercely. That was the easy bit—it was the other stuff that she couldn't shake. The violence of his death, the fact that they couldn't bury him yet, the fact that his heart . . . his poor heart . . . was in an evidence bag somewhere . . .

Jessica heaved again, but there was nothing left to give, and she remained where she was, beached on the floor.

Why was the world so cruel? She had expected anger and incomprehension from her family—and boy, had she got that—but everybody else? The police had advised her not to look at e-mails or Twitter, but how can you live your life like that? She wished now that she'd heeded their advice. Within minutes of the story breaking, the trolls had started their work. E-mailing her directly, posting on forums, filling the world with their hate. Christopher deserved to be killed. Jessica was a frigid bitch who'd driven her man to his death. Christopher was an AIDS-ridden pervert who would burn in hell. Their daughter had syphilis and would go blind.

The police had told her that they were there for her, that they would protect her, but who were they kidding? There was no pity left in the world, no goodness. There were just vultures picking over the entrails, feeding on sadness and pain.

Jessica had always been an optimist, but now she saw how naive she'd been.

A loud noise from downstairs. Sally banging on her xylophone. Then the sound of childish laughter, before she resumed playing her tune. It was as if her daughter were in a parallel universe—a place where happiness and innocence still existed. Jessica was tempted to shut the door, cram her fingers in her ears, but she didn't. That parallel universe was all she had now and maybe it would save her. In the lonely hours of the night, Jessica wanted to die, but she knew now that she had to live. She had to swallow her pain and bring up Sally to trust and enjoy the world.

Her life was over, but Sally's was just beginning. And that would have to sustain Jessica for now.

46

Christopher Reid lay on the slab, his glassy eyes staring up at the stained ceiling panels. None of the killer's victims deserved their fate, but Helen couldn't help feeling that Christopher deserved it less than Matthews. Matthews was a nasty hypocrite who enjoyed dominating women. But Reid was a guy who missed sex. Why hadn't he talked to his wife? Found a way to rediscover their intimacy instead of resorting to paying for sex? Did he view his wife as prudish or innocent? In Helen's experience, women were just as sexually imaginative as men if they were given the chance to express themselves. Had a simple failure of communication condemned Christopher to a repellent death?

"So this guy is the same as but different from your first victim," Jim Grieves announced as he approached the trolley. "He was incapacitated with chloroform, administered with some sort of soaked rag. Forensics might be able to give you more. There's no evidence of restraints being used in this case, nor anything this time to suggest he was hooded."

"So he must have been comfortable in her presence."

"That's for you to decide," Grieves continued, shrugging. "All I would say is that the 'surgery' was more skilled this time, so perhaps your girl is getting better at this and doesn't need to use so much force in either the initial attack or the mutilation."

Helen nodded.

"Cause of death?"

"Well, he was incapacitated in the car, but killed in the ditch. Too much blood for him to have been killed elsewhere. He was killed by a single knife wound to the throat that severed his carotid artery."

"Just one wound?"

"Yup. She didn't spend any more time on this guy than she had to. Heart was removed relatively cleanly, even though she probably began the procedure as he was dying."

Helen closed her eyes—the awful image planted itself in her brain and refused to budge. She expected Jim to carry on, but he said nothing. She opened her eyes again and immediately saw why he had stopped.

Detective Superintendent Ceri Harwood had joined them.

Grieves made his excuses and left—he didn't really do stroppy women. Harwood was simmering and Helen braced herself for the onslaught.

"Have you seen the paper?" Harwood said, slapping the TART WITH *YOUR* HEART headline down on the table.

"Yes," Helen replied simply. "I picked it up on the way over."

"I've had to request more support from West Sussex Police—Media Liaison here can't cope with the level of press interest that bloody headline has generated. It's not just British press either—we've had France,

Holland, even bloody Brazil on the phone. Who was sitting on Angie? How did Garanita get to her?"

"Family Liaison had a chat with her, but she wasn't the victim of a crime, and I couldn't justify uniform babysitting her, not when there's so much going on—"

"What did you say to Garanita? She quotes you directly."

"Nothing unusual. I gave her the basic facts and promised our cooperation, as you requested."

"Did you say we were hunting a serial killer? Did you use those words?"

"No."

"Well, Garanita bloody did. That's all anyone wants to talk about now. A prostitute who kills her clients. Revenge on the Ripper. It goes on and bloody on."

"It's not ideal. But it is the truth, ma'am."

Harwood shot Helen a look.

"Have you ruled out Sandra McEwan as a suspect?"

"Yes."

"So what can we give them?"

"Give who?"

"Don't be obtuse, Helen. The press. What can we give the bloody press?"

"Well, we've got a partial description we can put out. And I think we need to appeal directly to possible punters to stay off the streets. I'm happy to—"

"And risk driving her underground?"

"It's about saving lives. We don't have a choice. Three men are already dead."

"So we've got nothing to give them?"

Harwood's anger was all too clear now.

"Well, we've got lots of lines of inquiry, but I don't think opening ourselves up to the press in that way is going to help, and with the very greatest of respect," Helen continued, talking over Harwood's attempted interruption, "I don't think our agenda should be dictated by what the press are saying."

"Grow up, Helen," was Harwood's withering response. "And don't you dare say 'with the greatest of respect' to me ever again. I can have you taken off this case in a second."

"Except that wouldn't play very well in the press, would it?" Helen retorted. "I'm a copper, ma'am, not a spin doctor. I chase up leads and hunt killers. I *catch* killers. You can't do that through protocols, or liaison or bloody politics. You do it through intelligence, risk taking and sheer bloody hard work."

"And this conversation is a waste of your valuable time?" Harwood replied, daring Helen to agree.

"I'd like to get back to my duties now," was all Helen said in response.

Helen left shortly after, biking fast back to Southampton Central. She cursed herself for opening up another front in this war, but she'd had little choice. What would happen next was hard to say. All that was clear was that Harwood was no longer her friend, but her enemy.

47

Finally he had a bite. Tony had been driving the streets for hours, slowly climbing inside his new identity as a lonely businessman looking for sex. He'd been up and down Bevois, but the streets were strangely quiet. It was a Tuesday night—a long way from payday— but still he'd expected to see more business than this.

He'd tried Empress Road, only to find it deserted. Too much police activity round there recently to encourage a vibrant night trade. So he'd diverted a little farther north to Portswood. This was more promising, but the girls who hung their heads through his car window didn't fit his spec. They were mixed race, Polish, too short, too fat, too old, too transgender. The description of the killer hadn't been that detailed, but it ruled out most of these girls. As he terminated negotiations and drove off quickly, he received a healthy dose of abuse.

In frustration, he'd driven south to the docks. He was both

angered and relieved by his lack of progress. He wanted to find this girl, wanted to bring this thing to a close, but still his heart thumped, beating out his fear and anxiety. He assumed he'd be able to handle himself against her, but how could he know that for sure? She was organized, ruthless and violent. What if she got the upper hand?

Tony shook the thought from his mind. He must remain focused on the job in hand. Driving the side streets near the Western Docks, his eyes slid back and forth, searching for signs of business. The girls that worked down here were the busiest, servicing a never-ending stream of punters from the cruise ships and dockyards. Prostitutes loomed into view intermittently, but he could tell even from a distance that none of them fitted the bill.

But then there she was. She was pacing up and down on the deserted street and when Tony pulled up alongside her, he could see she was agitated, distressed. Instinct made him stroke the accelerator, something telling him to get away from this girl, but then his brain kicked in and he put the car into neutral.

"You up for business?" he called out, keeping his voice steady.

The girl jumped as if startled, as if somehow she hadn't heard the car approaching. She was dressed in black leggings, which emphasized her long, muscular legs. Her upper half was swathed in a military coat that seemed too big for her and was incongruous in comparison with the rest of her outfit—had she stolen it? Her face was striking, though—dark brown eyes, strong nose and full lips. Recovering her poise, she regarded him—making some mental calculation—then slowly, carefully she approached him.

"What are you after?" she said.

"Company."

"What sort of company?"

"Nothing out of the ordinary."

"Hour or the night?"

"Just an hour, please."

Tony cursed himself internally. What kind of punter says "please"?

The girl narrowed her eyes, perhaps trying to work out if he was as green as he looked.

"Fifty pounds."

Tony nodded, and then without being asked, the girl pulled open the passenger-side door and climbed inside. Tony put the car in first and pulled away.

"I'm Samantha," she said suddenly.

"Peter," Tony replied.

"That your real name, Peter?" she countered.

"No."

The girl chuckled.

"Married, are you?" she said.

"Yup."

"Thought so."

The conversation was over. She told him where to go and the car drove off into the night.

48

The incident room was full to bursting when Helen arrived. It was only six thirty a.m., but she'd demanded an early start and the team hadn't let her down. As they crowded into the briefing room, Helen was surprised to see Charlie among their number. The two women looked at each other—a swift, silent exchange. Charlie had made her decision. What had it cost her? Helen wondered.

"So one thing is clear," Helen began. "This is about exposure. The killer wants to *shame* her victims, wants to hold them up to public ridicule, to express her disgust for them. Cutting out their hearts and sending them to his home, in Alan Matthews's case, and to his workplace, in Christopher Reid's, was guaranteed to create *noise*. With the headlines in the latest *Evening News,* we can assume the killer has got what she wanted. The private lives of her victims will now be picked over in massive detail. They've already gone to town on Alan Matthews—he's an elder of his local Baptist church with a predilection for unpleasant sex—and they are doing the same with Christopher Reid—the hidden secrets of the clean-cut family man and so on. So this is all about exposure. This is *personal*."

"Do we think she knew them, then?" DC Fortune interjected.

"Possibly, although there is no evidence that they'd actually used her services before. That said, DC Grounds and his team have come up with something interesting. Andrew?"

"We have found a concrete link between the two victims," DC Grounds announced. "They had both browsed a Web forum called Bitchfest."

He winced slightly as he said it, then carried on briskly.

"It's basically a forum in which local men who've used prostitutes share their experiences. They talk about where to find particular girls, what their names are, what they charge. They rate breast size, sexual prowess, the tightness of their . . . vaginas—the list goes on."

DC Grounds looked relieved to have got through this first bit. He was a married father of three and not entirely comfortable relaying these details to younger, female colleagues.

"Matthews contributed using the alias 'BigMan.' Reid hadn't contributed but had had conversations with other men in the forum, using the name 'BadBoy.' The forum has a long history and we're still wading through it, but it appears that other men in the forum had recently reviewed a new girl who would let you do 'anything' to her."

Grounds looked around at the sea of dispirited faces. It was a good lead, but a sad indictment of humanity. Sensing a dip in morale, Helen stepped in.

"We've also had some feedback from SOC. The blood we extracted from Charlie's clothes"—heads turned in Charlie's direction—"was that of the third victim. ID in his wallet suggests his name is Gareth

Hill. We're triple-checking that before contacting his family and I'll confirm as soon as I can. So the blood was no help, but they did recover samples of what we think is the killer's DNA from the scene. Forensics lifted it late last night."

A buzz went round the room.

"It doesn't match any of our records, but it's the first concrete evidence we have and could be crucial in securing a conviction. Just as important, it tells us something about our girl. The DNA was found in saliva on the victim's face. It had settled in a series of thin layers spread one on top of each other. So this wasn't her spitting on him deliberately or an occasional excretion of saliva as she worked on the body. The patterns suggest that this was her talking to him or more likely shouting at him, given the amount of saliva and the pattern of its spread. Was she denigrating him as she killed him? Letting him know exactly what she felt about him? Possibly. No saliva was found on the first two victims, suggesting what?"

"That the other killings were more rushed? That she had less time to enjoy herself?" Charlie interjected.

"Yes. Or that she cleaned the other victims up. There is some evidence of an alcohol-based cleanser on their faces—we're not sure yet whether this was something they used as part of their daily routine or something she used to destroy evidence. If it's the latter, it suggests our killer possesses a degree of cunning as well as a deep, real anger against her victims."

A sense of determination seemed to be growing within the team—finally they looked to be getting somewhere. Helen seized on this energy.

"We will follow up on all those lines of inquiry, but I also want us to think laterally. If she hates these men and wants to expose them, then she will presumably want to enjoy her triumph. I've asked for extra manpower so we can watch the families of the victims in case she shows up. I want surveillance at the funerals, at their homes, places of work—I've asked DC Fortune to run this for now. Also, you will no doubt have noted the absence of DS Bridges. He is doing some undercover work for us on this case, which I am coordinating, and for now this is on a need-to-know basis. If it becomes relevant to your inquiries, you will be informed. But for now assume he doesn't exist—DC Brooks will be temporarily filling his shoes."

Once more all eyes swung to Charlie, whom Helen had suddenly promoted, albeit on a temporary basis. Would people support this decision or resent it? Charlie kept her eyes straight ahead.

"Last thing—we're going to shake our killer's cage a little. She's probably already rattled following her near miss, so I want to turn up the heat. I'm going to let the press know that we have her DNA and that it's only a matter of time before we ID her. I want to make her angry. I want to make her careless."

Helen paused a moment before concluding:

"It's time to take the fight to the enemy."

49

Caffè Nero was packed to bursting, which is why Helen had chosen it. It was on the high street in the smart suburb of Shirley. A million miles away from the grubby brothels and ill-lit streets patrolled by Southampton's sex workers.

Helen was pleased to see that Tony had arrived and was waiting for her, tucked away in a booth at the back as agreed.

"How are you doing, Tony?"

He looked drawn, but oddly cheerful.

"I'm okay. I'm actually . . . okay."

"Good. So this will be our regular spot to debrief. We'll arrange our meets by text and meet here only. I should say up front that if at any time you feel it's not working or that pursuing this avenue of investigation is putting your life at risk, then you call me and walk away immediately. Your safety is my number one priority."

"I know the drill, boss, and there's no need to look so serious. It really is okay. I was shitting myself last night, but it turned out fine. In fact, I think I might have something."

"Tell me."

"Well, I didn't have much luck to start with. I trawled Bevois, Portswood, Merry Oak without any joy, so I headed south to the docks and picked up a girl there. Samantha. Early twenties but an old hand on the street."

He had Helen's full attention now.

"We went to a hotel she knows. I told her I liked to watch, so I let her do her thing and then afterward I chatted to her as I drove her home. She was cagey at first, but she had obviously heard rumors about a girl killing punters. She doesn't know anything useful, but there's another girl who occasionally works the docks who's been talking. Saying she's seen the girl. Apparently there's a warrant out on her for a couple of things, so she's not going to be coming forward, but if I can get to her, then . . ."

Helen's heart was beating faster, but she reined in her excitement.

"Okay, follow it up. Be careful, though, Tony. It could be a setup—we've got no way of knowing how people will exploit this situation. But . . . it sounds promising."

Helen couldn't suppress a small smile, which was reciprocated by Tony.

"Anyway, go home and get some sleep. You've earned it."

"Thanks, boss."

"How is Nicola, by the way?"

"She's all right. We take it one day at a time."

Helen nodded. She respected and liked Tony for his conscientious, patient care of his wife. It must be hard to live a life that you never wanted, after the life you'd planned for had been so brutally snatched away from you. He was a good man and she hoped they would be okay.

Walking away from the café, she had a spring in her step. The course they were pursuing was fraught with danger, but she sensed that finally they were getting closer to their killer.

50

Picking up an unmarked pool car, Charlie sped out of the back entrance, anxious to get this over with. Jennifer Lees, the Family Liaison officer assigned to accompany her, would take the lead, but it would be Charlie who would have to ask the awkward questions. Normally Helen would interview the victim's family in the first instance, but she had disappeared on undisclosed business, leaving Charlie to carry the can.

They pulled up outside a run-down terraced house in Swaythling. This was the home Gareth Hill shared with his mother—"shared" in the past tense, as his mutilated body was currently lying on a slab in Jim Grieves's mortuary. They couldn't formally identify him as the third victim until his next of kin had done so, but they knew they had the right man. He had minor convictions for shoplifting, drunkenness and even one pathetic attempt at indecent exposure, so they already had his picture on file. Once the formalities were done, that file would be marked *Deceased* and sent upstairs to the incident room for evaluation.

An enormous woman of seventy-plus opened the door. Her blotched ankles were swollen, her stomach jutted out generously and her jowls hung deep from her plump face. But hidden amid all that flesh were two incongruous, ratlike eyes that stared fiercely at Charlie now.

"If you're selling something, you can piss—"

Charlie held up her warrant card.

"It's about Gareth. May we come in?"

The whole house stank of cats. They seemed to be everywhere, and as if scenting danger they clamored round their owner now, demanding her attention. She stroked the largest one—a ginger tom called Harvey—as Charlie and Jennifer broke the news to her.

"Dirty little boy."

Jennifer turned to Charlie, this unexpected response rendering her temporarily speechless.

"Did you understand what we said, Mrs. Hill?" Charlie asked.

"Miss Hill. I've never been a Mrs."

Charlie nodded sympathetically.

"Gareth has been murdered and I—"

"So you keep saying. What did he do—try and run off without paying?"

Her tone was hard to read. She sounded angry, but was that distress punching through too? This woman's armor was hard, toughened by years of disappointments, and she was hard to read.

"We're still investigating the circumstances, but we suspect this was an unprovoked attack."

"Hardly unprovoked. If you wallow in the gutter . . ."

"Where did Gareth say he was going last night?" Charlie interrupted.

"He said he was going to the pictures. He'd just got his benefits so . . . I thought he must have come in after I was asleep. I thought the lazy oaf was still in bed . . ."

At last her voice wavered, as the reality of her son's death struck home. When her defenses finally collapsed, they would collapse *big*, so Charlie carried on the conversation a bit longer, then excused herself to head upstairs. She had learned as much as she could, and she wanted to be away from this woman's sharp grief. Charlie knew she was weak to let another's distress spike so sharply with her own sense of loss, but she couldn't help it.

Pushing into Gareth's bedroom, she tried to gather her thoughts. It was truly a sight to behold. Empty fast-food wrappers littered the floor, lying in company with used tissues, old magazines and discarded clothes. The whole place looked and smelled dirty, as if someone had existed rather than lived here. It was stale. Stale and empty.

Gareth wasn't an attractive man, and he could hardly have brought girls back here anyway. The mess was bad enough, but would he have had the balls to parade another female in front of his mother, presuming he could have persuaded one to return home with him in the first place? Charlie thought not. His probation reports suggested he had learning difficulties and cripplingly low self-esteem. The evidence of his home life seemed to confirm that. This was a house that trapped people rather than protected them.

Looking around the detritus, Charlie saw that the only item of value in evidence was the computer. Perched in glorious isolation on the cheap desk, it stood proud. Its aluminum casing and familiar logo looked fresh, as if this totemic item had been kept clean and safe while all else had been allowed to go to seed. No doubt this treasured possession was Gareth's passport to life, and Charlie felt sure that the key to his death lay within it.

51

The Bull and Last did the best steak sandwich in Southampton. It was also off the radar of most coppers, a middle-class hangout favored by yummy mummies and businessmen, so it was one of Helen's favorite haunts when she needed a bit of time to herself. After she'd left Tony, she suddenly realized how incredibly hungry she was. She'd hardly eaten for days, surviving on coffee and cigarettes, and now she desperately needed some fuel. Sinking her teeth into the thick sandwich, she immediately felt better—the protein and carb fix hit the spot.

She had to get her head out of the case for a few minutes. When you are deep in an investigation of this magnitude, you become utterly obsessed. It haunts your thoughts, day and night. The longer it goes on, the easier it is to become snow-blind, to lose your sense of perspective and your clarity of vision. It was healthy to come here and people-watch for a little while, speculating on the emotional lives of the wealthy women who enjoyed flirting with the handsome waiters.

A local freesheet lay discarded on the table. She'd avoided picking it up and even as she did so now, curiosity finally getting the better of her, she flicked quickly through the first few pages. They were full of news on the recent murders, trumpeting the fact that police now had the killer's DNA, but Helen didn't linger on these. She liked to get deeper inside the local rags, to the small adverts, the petty crimes reported in the court circulars, the horoscopes— and all the other nonsense that was used to fill up these papers.

Flick, flick, flick, then suddenly she froze. She looked away, then looked back, hoping she had imagined it. But there it was. A photo of a house. The same house Helen had seen Robert and his mate Davey breaking into two days ago.

And above it the damning headline: PENSIONER FIGHTS FOR LIFE AFTER SURPRISING BURGLARS.

She made it to Aldershot in record time, driven there by instinct and anxiety. The details of the newspaper report had made for grim reading—a seventy-nine-year-old former teacher had surprised intruders and been savagely beaten. His skull fractured, he was now in an induced coma in Southampton General. It was touch-and-go whether he would survive.

She risked a direct approach to his house, a cover story about an attack on one of Robert's colleagues at the supermarket up her sleeve, but no one was at home. So she visited the Red Lion, the Railway Tavern and a clutch of other Aldershot drinking holes. Striking out, she visited their preferred off-licenses before finally getting lucky at the arcade. They were playing the slots—no doubt spending the proceeds of their recent crime.

After a while they lost interest and left, heading their separate ways after an excess of fist bumping. Helen followed Robert cautiously, waiting for the right moment to approach him. The streets were busy with shoppers, but when Robert diverted into the park, Helen seized her chance.

"Robert Stonehill?"

He spun round, suspicion writ large on his face.

"I'm a police officer," she continued, flashing her warrant card. "Can I have a word?"

But he'd already turned to go.

"It's about Peter Thomas. The man you and Davey beat half to death."

Now he paused.

"And don't even think about running. I've caught faster guys than you, believe me."

"I'm not here to arrest you, but I want you to tell me the truth."

They were seated on a park bench.

"I want you to tell me what happened."

A long pause as Robert debated what to say, then:

"It was Davey's idea. It's always bloody Davey's idea."

He sounded bitter and depressed.

"The old boy was a teacher of his. S'posed to be rich."

"And Davey thought it would be easy pickings?"

Robert shrugged.

"Davey said he'd be out. He's always out on Thursday nights. Plays cards at the Green Man. He said we'd be in and out in twenty minutes."

"But . . ."

"But the old boy walked in. Had a bloody great poker in his hand."

"And?"

Robert hesitated.

"And we ran. Legged it back to the window, but the old boy came after us. Gave me a bloody great whack on the leg."

Robert peeled down the top of his trousers to reveal a huge purple bruise on his hip.

"After that, Davey just went for him. Kicking, punching, whatever."

"And you just stood by?" Helen replied, incredulous.

"I gave him a kick and that, but it was Davey who . . . He stamped on his head, for fuck's sake. I bloody pulled him off. He would've killed him."

"He might have already killed him. He's in a coma, Robert."

"I know. I can read, all right?"

His retort was full of defiance, but Helen could see the boy was scared and upset.

"Have the police spoken to you? Or Davey?"

"No," he said, turning to her, confused. "You going to arrest me?"

The million-dollar question. Of course she had to arrest him and Davey.

"I don't know, Robert. I'm considering it, but . . . let's see what happens with Mr. Thomas. It's possible he will make a full recovery . . ."

It sounded weak and Helen knew it.

"And I know that there are mitigating circumstances in your case, so . . . so I'm going to give you a second chance."

Robert looked stunned, which only made Helen feel more pathetic and wrongheaded.

"You're a decent guy, Robert. You're smart, and if you committed yourself to something worthwhile, you could have a good life. But you're on the wrong path now, hanging out with the wrong guys, and you *will* end up in jail if you carry on like this. So here's the deal. You will stop seeing Davey and his mates. You will work hard and look for opportunities to better yourself. You will try to live a decent life. If you do that, then I will let this go. If you fuck up, though, I will throw you in jail, right?"

Robert nodded, relieved but confused.

"I'm going to take an interest in you. And I want you to repay my faith. If you feel you're struggling or that you are going to get into trouble, I want you to call me."

She scribbled her mobile number down on the back of one of her official business cards.

"This is a big chance for you. Don't fuck it up, Robert."

He took the card, looked at it. When he looked up again, Helen saw gratitude and relief on his face.

"Why? Why are you doing this for me?"

Helen hesitated, then eventually replied:

"Because everyone needs someone to watch over them."

Helen walked quickly away from the park. Now that she had done the deed, she just wanted to be away. She had taken a big risk coming here, and in making contact with Robert had done something she'd vowed she wouldn't do. She had crossed the line. Yet despite this, despite all the dangers that lay ahead, she didn't regret it. While there was still a chance of saving Robert, it was worth it.

52

Jessica Reid marched up the street, tears stinging her eyes. She swallowed hard to stop the sobs escaping—she wouldn't give those women the satisfaction of breaking down in front of them.

She had debated whether to keep Sally in nursery. Her first instinct had been not to return, to hide away from the world, but Sally liked it there, so Jessica had nailed her courage to the mast and taken her down. Sally needed some stability—best to keep to the familiar routine.

As soon as she'd got there she'd realized that she'd made a mistake. Sally trotted off to play, but no one was paying any attention to her. All eyes were glued to Jessica. There were a few sheepish smiles of support, but nobody approached her. Clearly no one knew what to say to the stupid, duped wife.

As she walked away, she could hear hushed conversations strike up. She could only imagine what they were saying. The prurience, the speculation. Did she know? Did she allow it? Did he bring diseases home with him?

It was all so unfair. She had done *nothing* wrong. Sally had done *nothing* wrong. But it was they who had been branded, as accessories to his behavior. How could she have been so bloody stupid? She had given Christopher her heart and trusted him with it, even after their first bust-up over his use of pornography. She'd thought he turned over a new leaf, but he hadn't. Instead he'd lied and lied and lied. Why hadn't he talked to her? Why had he been so selfish?

She was back in the house now, though how she'd got there she couldn't really say. Without hesitating, she charged upstairs. Flinging open the chest of drawers, she grabbed an armful of Christopher's things and threw them out of the window down onto the drive below. Again and again and again. Cleansing the house of his presence.

Grabbing some lighter fluid and matches from under the kitchen sink, she marched out through the still-open front door. Dousing the messy pile generously, she threw a match onto it, then watched the clothes—clothes she'd bought for him—burn.

Snap, snap, snap. From their vantage point in a van across the road, the plainclothes police officers recorded every second of her despair before calling it in.

DC Fortune took in their report, then rang off. The show was about to start and he didn't want to miss a minute of it. He had given his fellow officers the dull gig—no one really expected their surveillance of Jessica Reid to throw up anything. The plum job was the Matthews funeral, which was about to get under way.

Lloyd Fortune stretched, yawned, then settled himself down into position. Watching and waiting. That was the drill on these sorts of operations. Looking across the road, Lloyd saw the Matthews family leave the house. There were plenty of people on hand to support them— extended family, friends from the church—so many that four funeral cars had been hired. Lloyd scanned the heads to pick out the family members from among the well-wishers. He caught a glimpse of the elder daughter shepherding a grandmother into the first car. Like the others, she looked blank with shock, even after three days had passed.

Lloyd surveyed the street. Was their killer out there? Watching? Enjoying her success? *Snap, snap, snap* went the camera, taking in every passerby, every parked car. Lloyd, exhilarated by the prospect of seeing the killer in the flesh, felt his pulse quicken.

The first car was on the move now. And the second. Lloyd nodded to Jack to start the engine. It hummed quietly. They waited patiently—Eileen and the twins slipping into the final car—then it was their turn. Pulling away from the curb, they followed the flotilla of grief toward its final destination—St. Stephen's Baptist Church.

53

He hesitated before typing. How did one begin these things?

Hello Melissa. A mutual friend . . .

No, that wasn't right.

Hello Melissa. My name is Paul and I would like to meet you.

That was better. Tony leaned back in his chair, amused by how much effort that had taken. And how nervous he'd been. Satisfied that the thing was now in train, he went to shut his computer down. But as he did so, a response pinged up.

Hello Paul. When would you like to meet?

Tony hesitated, then typed.

Tonight?

What time?

Tony hadn't expected to be making arrangements so quickly. Still, needs must.

Ten?

Pick me up on the corner of Drayton St. and Fenner Lane. I'll be wearing a green coat. What car you drive?

Vauxhall.

Color?

Silver.

Looking for company? Or something special?

Company.

How long?

Couple of hours?

£150 for two hours.

Okay.

Cash.

Sure.

See you later, Paul.

See you later, Melissa.

XXX.

End of conversation. Tony caught himself smiling. He was in his own bloody kitchen. Instant messaging prostitutes. Still, it wasn't the kind of thing you could do in a café, so . . .

Tony switched off the computer. Nicola's mum would be here soon and she didn't need any more ammunition. Best go and get some rest.

He had a big night ahead of him.

54

Charlie was in full flow when Helen entered the incident room. The team had broken from their tasks to hear the latest developments.

"We've had a trawl through Gareth Hill's hard drive. His computer seems to have been his one and only window on the world—he used it *a lot*. And one of his favorite sites was the Bitchfest Web forum."

She had everyone's attention now.

"This prostitute rating site was also visited by Alan Matthews and Christopher Reid—they used the pseudonyms 'BigMan' and 'BadBoy.' Gareth Hill's moniker was 'Blade.' They entered into extremely graphic conversations with other men about the girls in Southampton. They were particularly interested in girls up for denigration and rough sex and received various pointers from other users, specifically from 'Dangerman,' 'HappyGoLucky,' 'Hammer,' 'PussyKing,' 'fillyerboots' and 'BlackArrow.' Several girls were discussed, but the one who came up time and again was a prostitute who calls herself 'Angel.'"

Helen felt a shiver inside. Could this be their killer?

"Interestingly," Charlie continued, "Angel doesn't advertise, doesn't have a Web site. She's totally offline. She gets her punters by word of mouth alone, current clients tipping off other men about where to find her. She's elusive and, it should be said, expensive, but she's clearly willing to do anything if the money is right."

"So she's hard to find and a closely guarded secret?" Helen interjected.

"Exactly."

"Good work, Charlie. So top priority is to find these other forum users. Let's focus on those who've used Angel's services and who might have chatted with Matthews, Reid and Hill. These men can lead us to Angel, so let's find them fast. I'm going down to the surveillance points, but want to be kept up to speed with developments. DS Brooks will run things in my absence."

As Helen departed, Charlie set about organizing the team. It had cost her a lot to come back to work, but perhaps it had been the right choice after all. "DS Brooks"—she liked the way that sounded, and knew there and then that she wanted back in.

55

Helen stopped in her tracks the moment she saw her. Anger flared inside her at the sight of Emilia Garanita leaning casually against her Kawasaki in the bike park outside the station.

"You're in a restricted area and currently obstructing police business, Emilia, so if you wouldn't mind?"

It was said politely, but without warmth. Emilia smiled—always that same Cheshire cat smile—and slowly peeled herself off the bike.

"I've tried calling you, Helen, but you won't answer. I've talked to a number of my uniform friends, I even had a quick heart-to-heart with your boss, but nobody seems to know what's going on. Are you clamming up on me again?"

"I don't know what you mean. I gave you the tip-off about the DNA and much more besides."

"But that's not the whole story, is it, Helen? Harwood feels it too. Something's going on in that team of yours and I want to know what it is."

"You want to know what it is?" Helen replied slowly and with maximum sarcasm.

"Don't tell me you've forgotten our little deal already? I said I wanted exclusive access on this story and I meant it."

"You're getting paranoid, Emilia. As soon as there are any new developments, I'll let you know, okay?"

She moved to get on her bike, but Emilia grabbed her arm.

"No, not okay."

Helen looked at her as if she were mad—did she really want to be charged with assaulting a police officer?

"I don't like being lied to. I don't like being looked down on. Especially by a degenerate like you."

Helen shrugged her off angrily, but was unnerved. There was real venom and a newfound confidence in Emilia's tone.

"I want to know, Helen. I want to know everything. And you're going to tell me."

"Or?"

"Or I tell the world your little secret."

"I think the world knows everything about me already. I don't think you'll shift any papers rehashing that old stuff again."

"But they don't know about Jake, do they?"

Helen froze.

"I see you don't deny knowing him. Well, I've had a long chat with him and—after a little gentle persuasion—he told me everything. How he beats you up for money. What is it with some women that they just have to give men the upper hand?"

Helen said nothing. How the hell did she know all this? Had Jake really spoken to her?

"So here's the deal, Helen. You will tell me everything and you will give me exclusive access. I want to be ahead of the nationals every step of the way on this, and if I'm not . . . then the whole world will know that heroic Helen Grace is actually a dirty little pervert. How do you think Harwood would like that?"

Emilia's words hung in the air as she walked off. Helen knew instinctively that she wasn't bluffing and that for the first time she was in the woman's thrall. Emilia had dangled the sword of Damocles over Helen's head and would take great pleasure in dropping it.

56

St. Stephen's Baptist Church reared up above her, gray and austere in the spitting rain. Churches were supposed to be places of refuge, warm and welcoming, but Helen found them cold and dispiriting. She had always felt she was somehow being judged by them and found wanting.

Her mind was still reeling from her discussion with Emilia, but she wrenched it back to the task at hand. She had stewed on their conversation for too long and was nearly late as a result—she had had barely five minutes with DC Fortune before haring up the path—and she could hear the organ music swelling inside. Slipping quietly into the building, she seated herself in a pew at the back. From here she would have a good view of everyone who attended. It was surprisingly common for murderers to attend the funerals of their victims—serial killers in particular seemed to relish the feeling of power as they watched the body being buried, the vicar intoning, the black-clad mourners clinging to one another. Helen scanned the female faces—was their killer sitting somewhere in this church?

The service ground on, but Helen barely took in the words. She had always quite enjoyed the high style of the Bible and she liked to let its ornate phraseology wash over her, but in terms of their content the words might as well have been in the original Greek and Hebrew. The lessons seemed to conjure up a world that was totally alien to her—an ordered, divine cosmos in which everything happened for a reason and in which good would prevail. There was a level of reassurance in it that Helen could never swallow—the random madness and violence of her world seemed at odds with the cozy catchalls of religion.

Still, she couldn't deny that for many the church and its teachings were a comfort. That was very much in evidence now. At the front of the church, Eileen Matthews was surrounded by fellow worshippers, literally being held up by family and friends. The laying on of hands is meant to create a religious rapture in the receiver but also has the very practical purpose of keeping the weak and the vulnerable upright— and so it was proving now. As the chanting increased and the fervor grew, Eileen started to babble. Quietly at first, then louder, strange non-words flying out, her accent changing from south coast to something foreign. She sounded Middle Eastern, a touch Jewish perhaps and distinctly medieval—a torrent of guttural nonsense phrases flew from her mouth as the divine spirit entered her. Helen had seen speaking in tongues before on TV, but never in the flesh. It was odd to witness—it looked more like possession to her than rapture.

Eventually the frenzy subsided and the male members of the congregation guided Eileen back to her seat, allowing Helen a chance to examine the female faces front on as they returned to their seats. She realized with a jolt that she was the only single woman there. Every other female present had a husband and every one of them seemed to be very much in his thrall. As the service came to an end, the congregation rose, dividing along gender lines. The men chatted confidently together as the women listened. Alan Matthews, in addition to being an elder of the church, was a member of Christian Domestic Order, a group that promoted the patriarchy of the Bible, upholding the husband as leader in all things and condemning wives to the role of helpmeet. Women were subservient in every way, and spanking was advised if they failed to live up to their duties. Eileen Matthews had probably suffered chastisement at the hands of her husband, who clearly loved to dominate women, and Helen suspected the other women in this congregation had too. The fact that many of them probably submitted willingly didn't help in Helen's eyes. Looking around the church now, Helen saw passive, inert women who lacked the confidence or bravery to do anything for themselves. Unless one among their number was a phenomenal actress, there was no one here who would have the gumption, determination and balls to perpetrate this terrible string of murders. Was the killer elsewhere, then, watching from the shadows? Slipping out of her seat, Helen walked quickly round the perimeter, eyes scanning this way and that for possible concealed vantage points, but she found nothing.

DC Fortune had scarcely fared better. He had snapped everyone in and out of the church and had been assiduous in photographing every member of the public who passed by. Junior officers dressed as gardeners covered the back of the church, but had seen nothing apart from a man and his dog.

"Keep an eye out as people leave the church and make sure you get a picture of the chauffeurs too. Go with the cortege back to the family home, but tell one of your boys to remain behind. I want that grave watched night and day. Chances are, if our killer comes, she'll come in the dead of night."

"Yes, ma'am."

"Good. File what you've snapped so far and keep on it, Lloyd. You never know when she might turn up."

Did Helen really believe that? As she walked back to her bike, she felt the killer once more slipping away from them. Surveillance was a good move, but had yielded nothing so far. Would she have suspected this move? Did she know what they were thinking?

Helen felt once more on the back foot, ineptly dancing to a tune played by their killer, and now by Emilia Garanita too. Had Jake really spilled the beans? It seemed unlikely—no, actually it seemed impossible—but how else had Emilia found out about them?

She was due to see him this evening, but pulling her phone from her pocket, she texted him to cancel. She wasn't ready to speak to him yet. A small part of her wondered if she would ever speak to him again.

57

There is a fantasy that sustains you when you're on active service. It's the dream that sustains every soldier when he's stuck in some godforsaken dust bowl being shot at and shouted at. It's the fantasy that there's something better waiting for you at home. In this fantasy, your girl is keeping the home fires burning, hankering for your return. She will welcome you back with open arms, fill you with good food, take you to bed and be the doting, angelic wife. This is the very least you deserve for the months of fear, loneliness and anger. But it seldom works out that way.

Simon Booker was an ordinary citizen now. His best mate had been blown up two days before they were due to ship out. On the plane home, Simon had told his superior officer he was quitting. He used to love the army, but he wanted out now. It had brought him nothing but disillusionment and despair.

He was convinced that Ellie had been seeing other men while he was away. He didn't have any evidence; it was just a feeling. Still, it gnawed away at him and he wondered which of his so-called mates were laughing behind their hands now, exchanging stories of what his Mrs. was like in the sack. He avoided them, just like he now avoided Ellie. He couldn't talk to her about what life had been like over there, about what it felt like to see Andy split in fifty pieces, and he certainly didn't want to talk about what she got up to while he was away. So he went to the Doncaster and the White Hart. And when he came home, struggling to fit the key into the lock as his hand shook and his brain swam in cheap lager, he would trudge up to the box room where the computer was, walking past the open bedroom door.

He always locked the door. Despite his anger toward Ellie, he still didn't want her to catch him at it. Was that out of shame or from some buried desire not to hurt her? He wasn't sure, but he locked the door nevertheless.

The porn had been good to start with, but recently he'd grown tired of it. Now his site of choice was Bitchfest. It was a whole new world for him. This was the new frontier of sex and he found in the forum a camaraderie he'd thought he'd lost forever. Here men could talk frankly about what they wanted. And advise one another on how to go about getting it.

For a long time he'd held off acting on his impulses, but "Happy-GoLucky" had given "Angel" such rave reviews that he'd decided he couldn't resist. A lot of men had cried off prostitutes in the wake of stuff in the newspapers and in other forums. Stories of blokes getting killed while on the job. And he wasn't stupid—he knew you had to watch your back. The world was full of killers, liars and thieves. So he was taking precautions. He'd told Ellie he was seeing old army pals, but the contents of his holdall suggested otherwise. Inside was a pack of condoms and a change of clothes. And nestling underneath, unseen, was an iron bar.

58

"So what do we know about him?"

Helen and Charlie were in a pool car heading for Woolston.

"Real name—Jason Robins." Charlie replied, flicking through her notes. "But his alias in the Bitchfest forum was 'Hammer.' He wasn't the most regular contributor—I think that prize goes to 'PussyKing'—but he posted every couple of days and when he did he went to town. A lot of bragging about what 'Angel' had done to him, how he'd actually made her come, the usual crap."

"How did you find him?"

"Most of the users are pretty discreet—they obviously use aliases and post on work computers or at Internet cafés. They are hard to track down even if you have the IP address. Jason's not so bright. He uses the 'Hammer' alias on other sites as well, one of which was a pay-per-view porn site. He used his credit card to pay for some material—"

"And you got his home address from that."

"Exactly."

Right on cue they pulled up outside a block of flats on Critchard Street. It was a bit shabby, a bit unloved, the small flats rented by people who were making do until something better came along. Helen and Charlie climbed out of the car, looking up and down the street. Night was falling and apart from the odd worker hurrying home, everything was quiet. A light burned in the living room window of the house in front of them—"Hammer" was at home.

They sat at the IKEA table—a stilted threesome with untouched cups of tea sitting in front of them. Jason Robins had assumed the worst when he'd opened the door to two police officers, asking stutteringly if Samantha and Emily had been involved in some kind of accident. When Helen had assured him that this was nothing to do with his family, he'd calmed down, suspicion slowly replacing his fear.

"You may have read about a series of murders in Southampton recently," Helen began. "Murders linked to the sex trade."

Jason nodded but said nothing.

"A couple of the victims used an online prostitute rating forum."

Helen let her words hang in the air, pretending to consult her notebook before continuing:

"It's called Bitchfest."

She looked up as she said it, keen to see how Jason would react. He didn't react at all—not a nod, not a smile, nothing. In Helen's eyes this was as damning as an admission. Jason was sitting stock-still, clearly worried that the slightest reaction might give him away. Helen eyed him.

"Are you aware of that forum, Jason?"

"No."

"Have you ever visited it?"

"Not my kind of thing."

Helen nodded and feigned writing something in her notebook.

"Do you ever use the alias 'Hammer' while online?" Charlie asked.

"'Hammer'?"

"Yes, 'Hammer'—have you ever used that alias while visiting other Web forums or sites offering adult material?"

Jason seemed to mull over the question, keen to be seen to be taking it seriously.

"No. No, I haven't."

"I ask because someone using that alias has a credit card registered to this address in the name of Jason Robins."

"Must be fraud."

"Have you reported any fraudulent activity on your card?"

"No, I wasn't aware of it, but now that you've told me I'll ring them straightaway. Get it canceled."

Silence descended briefly. Jason was wound tight as a drum, a sheen of sweat sticking to his brow.

"Are you separated from your wife?"

Jason seemed to relax as the questioning took a new turn.

"Yes, I am. Not that it's any of your business."

"But you're not divorced?"

"Not yet. But we will be."

"So presumably you're currently involved in negotiations about custody of your daughter, Emily?"

"That's one way of putting it."

"How would you put it?"

Jason shrugged and took a sip of his tea.

"I can understand why you're being cagey, Jason. You're in a tricky place, and the last thing you need is the police outing you as a guy who visits adult Web sites and uses the services of sex workers. It wouldn't play well in court—I get that. But listen to me carefully. People are dying out there, and unless men like you have the courage to step up to the plate, more people will die. I could charge you with wasting police time, obstructing an investigation and more, but I know that you're a decent guy, Jason. So I'm asking you to help us.

"We need to know about Angel," Charlie continued. "Where you meet her, what she looks like, who else might know her. If you can give us everything you know, then we will protect you. We'll keep your name out of the papers and minimize the disruption to your life. We've no interest in making your life any harder—we just want to catch this killer. You can help us do that."

A long silence ensued, broken only by the *ticktock* of the kitchen clock. Jason finished his tea.

"Like I said before, I've never heard of this 'Hammer.' So if you'll excuse me, I'd like to go and call my credit card company."

Helen and Charlie said nothing as they walked away from the house, both too angry to risk speaking. It wasn't until they were safely inside the car that Helen finally spoke.

"Lying little shit."

Charlie nodded.

"Stay on him, Charlie. Ring him, e-mail him every day or so with a couple of extra questions, a couple of extra details. He may just be embarrassed or he may know something—keep squeezing him until you find out which."

"It'll be my pleasure."

"In the meantime, we have to work harder to find the others. 'HappyGoLucky,' 'Dangerman,' 'fillyerboots,' 'BlackArrow'—I want them hunted down. Someone out there knows where we can find Angel."

"Sure. Do you want me to take the lead—"

"Yup. Run them to ground and I'll rendezvous with you back at the nick. But drop me in the city center first."

Charlie looked up, intrigued.

"I've got a date that I'm keen to keep."

59

They walked down the lonely corridor, her plastic, high-heeled boots squeaking with every step she took. Trailing just behind, Tony took her in. "Melissa" was far more attractive than he'd expected her to be. Long, sleek legs encased in shiny black boots, a tight backside, a sensual, full-lipped face framed by a short black bob. Tony knew not all prostitutes were yellow-toothed junkies, but he was still surprised at how well presented she was.

He had picked her up at Hoglands Park, a skateboarders' hangout in the north of the city that was virtually deserted at night. He'd radioed in as he approached the venue and later had spotted the tail car in his rearview mirror as they'd headed south toward the docks, but still he felt a spike of fear now that he was alone with her. They had driven in silence to the Belview Hotel, a down-at-the-heels B&B that wasn't fussy about its clientele. Tony had paid for the night up front, then they'd headed to the first floor. En route, they'd passed a middle-aged man descending in the company of a half-dressed Polish girl. He had looked straight at Tony, who'd dropped his eyes to the floor, unwilling to be drawn into this unpleasant camaraderie.

Soon they were inside room 12. Melissa slung her bag and coat down on the only chair in the room, then sat down on the bed.

"So what can I do for you, *Paul*?"

She stressed the last word, as if she knew it was a lie.

"I'm all yours."

She smiled a broad, sexy smile, full of mischief. Tony was surprised to feel a twinge of desire for this acquiescent plaything and sat down on the chair to hide the beginnings of an erection.

"I like to watch," he replied as calmly as he could. "Why don't you do your thing for a while and we'll take it from there?"

She looked at him curiously. Then:

"It's your money, honey," she replied, shrugging.

Taking the hint, Tony reached into his wallet and pulled out £150. Pocketing it, Melissa lay down on the bed.

"Do you want me to keep my boots on, while I . . ."

"Yes."

"Good. I like it better that way."

Melissa let her hands wander over her body. She had a muscular, toned physique that was certainly fit for purpose and the more she got into it, the more Tony desperately wanted to look out of the window. It was absurd, really. He knew he had to play the part and keep his eyes glued to her. He knew, in spite of his now full erection, that this was just part of the job, a setup designed to yield valuable information. And yet he still felt extremely uncomfortable, the level of his arousal surprising and alarming him.

As Melissa feigned her way to climax, she urged him to get involved, to treat her how she deserved to be treated. Tony had to think on his feet to avoid physical contact, instead firing off a volley of obscenities to bring her to "orgasm." She was a good actress—anyone listening in would have assumed she'd just had the greatest sexual experience of her life. Afterward, she reclothed herself, shooting a look at the cracked clock on the wall.

"You've still got ten minutes left, baby—do you want me to suck you off?"

"I'm fine. Can we talk?"

"Sure. What you want to talk about?"

"I wanted to ask if we could do this again."

"Of course. I'm always up for fun."

"You been doing this long?"

"Long enough."

"You like it?"

"Of course," she replied. Tony knew she was giving him the lie she thought he wanted to hear.

"Ever have any trouble?"

"Now and again," she replied, not looking him in the eye.

"How do you deal with it?"

"I've got ways. But usually there are other girls around."

"To keep an eye out for you?"

"Right. Do you mind if I use the loo, honey? I've got to be out again soon."

She walked off to the bathroom. Moments later the toilet flushed and she emerged, making straight for her coat and bag.

"Could I pay you for some more of your time?"

She paused.

"You want me to do it again?"

"No, no, I just want to talk. I . . . I'm alone in the city. I won't see my family until the weekend and I . . . well, I just like to talk."

"Okay," she replied, sitting down on the bed.

Tony fished another fifty pounds from his wallet and handed it over.

"So, where are you from?"

"Lots of places. But I was born in Manchester, if that's what you mean."

"Still got family there?"

"None that are worth bothering with."

"Right."

"How about you, Paul? You from round here?"

"Born and bred."

"That's nice. Good to have a home."

"You live near here?"

"Just stopping with a friend. As long as I'm getting work, I'll stay put."

"Are you making decent money?"

"Pretty good. I'm more open-minded than some."

"Do you ever work with other girls?"

"Sometimes."

"Do you do threesomes?"

"Sure."

"There's a girl I'm interested in hooking up with. Angel. Perhaps you know her?"

Melissa paused, then looked up.

"I'm not sure you want to get to know her, honey."

"Why not?"

"Just trust me—you don't. Besides, there's nothing she can do for you that I can't."

"But if I wanted a threeso—"

"I can find you another girl."

"But I want Angel."

Another long pause.

"Why?"

"Because I've heard good things about her."

"Who from?"

"Other guys."

"Like hell you have."

"Sorry?"

"This is your first time, isn't it? You're as green as they come."

"So?"

"You don't look the type to be jawing with other fellas about what toms like me get up to."

Tony was surprised to feel affronted, but gathered himself.

"Okay, maybe I am new, but I know what I want. I'm happy to give you cash if you can set it up."

"What have you heard about her, then?"

"Just that she likes to be hit, denigra— Abused, you know. She'll let you do things that other girls don't."

"And who's told you about her?"

"Guys."

"Guys?"

"You know, other g—"

"Who?"

"People I've chatted to—"

"Give me their names."

"I don't really—"

"Give me their names."

"Er . . . I think one was called Jeremy. And—"

"Where did you meet them?"

"Online."

"How?"

"On a forum."

"What was the name of the forum?"

"I can't remember the name—"

"And you want to meet Angel?"

"Yes!"

"Because you want to question her? Like you're questioning me?"

"No, no," Tony replied, but he had hesitated a nanosecond too long and he knew it.

Melissa was already on her feet.

"A bloody cop. I knew it."

"Melissa, wait."

"Thanks for the chat and the cash, but I've got to go."

Tony put a hand on her arm to stop her.

"I just want to talk to you."

"You lay one more finger on me and I will scream the bloody house down. Then every hooker for miles around will know you're a pig, right?"

"I just need to find Angel. It's really important that I find . . ."

"Go fuck yourself."

She walked out, leaving the door open behind her. Tony's first instinct was to go after her, but what was the point? Defeated, he sat down heavily on the bed. Melissa was their best lead and he'd blown it completely. It had cost him quite a lot to inhabit this role—had raised questions he didn't want to ask himself—and he'd ended up with nothing.

Next door the sound of frantic copulation cranked up, beating out the rhythm of his failure. Picking up his coat, he hurried out. He wanted to be away from this place. Away from the sex. And away from this crushing defeat.

60

The caravan stood alone on the open wasteland. Framed by the gypsy fires that burned nearby, it looked almost beautiful. Inside, it was less pleasant, mildewed and rotting, the detritus of drug use littering the floor. Still, it would do for tonight—a mattress was slung down on the floor, ready for action.

"You a soldier, then?" she asked.

"Was. Afghanistan."

"I love soldiers—you killed any ragheads?"

"A few."

"My hero. I should give you one on the house."

Simon Booker shrugged off the suggestion. He didn't want her pity. Or her charity. That wasn't why he was here. He pulled some notes from his wallet, laying them on the stained Formica breakfast bar. As he did so, he noticed his wedding ring and began to tug at it.

"Don't worry about that, love. I won't tell if you don't. It's thirty for oral, fifty for straight, hundred for anything else. And I'm going to need you to use a condom, love. Don't want any of the diseases you picked up from those foreign whores, do I?"

Simon Booker nodded and turned, bending down to retrieve his condoms from his bag. He couldn't find them at first and had to root around a bit before eventually locating them. As he stood up, he was surprised to see Angel standing by the door.

"You stay the fuck away from me!" she spat at him.

"What? I was just getting the—"

"What's the iron bar for?"

Shit. She'd obviously spotted it as he'd rooted through his holdall.

"It's nothing. Just for protection. But I'll put it outside if you like."

He moved toward it.

"Don't you dare touch it. If you do, I'll shout. I've got mates over there. People who look out for me. Do you know what gypsies do to the likes of you?"

"All right. Keep your hair on."

Simon was irritated now. He wanted to have sex, not a full-blown slanging match.

"You put it outside, then. I don't want any trouble," he said.

She looked scared but slowly edged her way to the bag, keeping an eye on him the whole time. Picking up the bag, she lobbed it outside—it landed with a dull thud. She breathed out, composing herself.

"Right, then, shall we start again?" she said, her smile wide but forced.

"Sure."

"Come and give me a kiss, then. And once I've got to know you better I'll put your big dick in my mouth."

That was more like it. Simon crossed the floor. Hesitantly at first, he put his hands on her waist. She responded by lacing her arms round his neck and pulling his mouth toward hers.

"Let's get this started, shall we?"

As Simon Booker closed his eyes, Angel brought her knee sharply up into his groin. As he froze, stunned, she did it again and again. Crumpling to the floor, he gasped for breath. He wanted to puke. Oh, God, the pain was horrible.

He looked up to find Angel standing over him. The smile was gone now and in her hand she held the iron bar from his bag. Without warning, she brought it crashing down on his head. Once, twice, three times just to make sure. Then she crossed the floor to shut the caravan door. She locked it from the inside and paused to catch her breath. Staring down at her victim, she could feel her excitement rising.

It was time for the fun to begin.

61

Heads turned as she marched through the newsroom toward Emilia Garanita's office. In the wake of her eye-catching work on Marianne, Emilia had been awarded a corner office from which to plot her next exclusive. It was airless and cramped, but it was one in the eye for the other hacks, which was why Emilia liked it so much. And it afforded her a good view of the newsroom and of Helen Grace, who was now striding toward her.

Helen Grace had never before set foot in the offices of the *Evening News*, so whatever it was, it was going to be good. Was this the first countermove in their battle or was it a very public capitulation? Emilia sincerely hoped it was the latter. She would *try* to be gracious.

"Helen, how nice to see you," she said, as Helen entered her office.

"It's nice to see you too, Emilia," her guest replied, closing the door behind her.

"Coffee?"

"No, thanks."

"Quite right," Emilia replied, ostentatiously opening her laptop. "We've got a lot to get through. We're too late for tonight's edition, but if you give me everything you've got now, we can sort out a killer spread for tomorrow. If you'll pardon the pun."

Helen regarded her quizzically, then leaned forward and pushed the laptop back down, closing it.

"We won't be needing that."

"Sorry?"

"I haven't come here to give you any news. Just a warning."

"Excuse me?"

"I don't know how you know what you think you know about me, and to be honest I don't really care. What I do care about is a journalist at a respectable paper attempting to blackmail a serving police officer."

Emilia eyeballed her—the temperature in the small room had just dropped considerably.

"So I'm here to give you a clear and simple message. Print what the hell you like about me, but if you *ever* attempt to bribe, blackmail or intimidate me again, I will see you in prison for it. Understand?"

Emilia stared at Helen, then responded:

"Well, that's your choice, Helen, but don't say I didn't give you fair warning."

"Do what you need to," Helen replied tersely. "But be ready for the consequences."

She turned to leave, but as she got to the doorway, she paused.

"We sink or swim together on this one, Emilia. So ask yourself how much you hate me. And how much you value your liberty."

Emilia watched her go—anger and adrenaline pulsing through her. Should she break her or back down? Either way, Emilia was about to make the biggest call of her life.

62

Tony slammed the car door shut behind him and slumped down in the driver's seat. How could he have messed up so badly? And what was he going to say to Helen?

This was his big chance to be back on the front line again, to prove that he'd still got it—and he had completely ballsed it up. He could try to contact Melissa again, but what was the point? Now that she knew he was a cop, it was game over. The only thing he could do was confess all to Helen as soon as possible and start formulating a new plan. Some of the other girls must have seen Angel. It was inconceivable that she could ghost in and out of these fleshpots undetected. What he had to do—

He jumped as the passenger door opened. He had been so caught up in his own little world that he hadn't heard anyone coming. He turned to confront the intruder . . . and was surprised to see

Melissa climbing into the passenger seat. She didn't look at him, simply saying:

"Drive."

They drove in silence for a full ten minutes before Melissa indicated an alleyway adjacent to a derelict restaurant. It was quiet down here, not a soul around to disturb them. As he turned to look at her, Tony was surprised to see that she was shaking.

"If I tell you what you want to know, I'll need money. Lots of money."

"Not a problem," Tony replied. He'd figured out on the way over that it could only have been the prospect of financial gain that induced her to get into his car.

"Five grand up front. More to follow."

"Agreed."

"And I'll need somewhere to stay. Somewhere she can't find me."

"We can offer you a safe house and round-the-clock protection," Tony replied without hesitation.

"Round-the-clock—you promise?"

"I promise."

"Shake on it," Melissa demanded, and Tony obliged.

Melissa let out a deep sigh—she looked exhausted by the evening's events. Then, without looking up at Tony, she whispered:

"The girl you're looking for is Lyra. Angel's name is Lyra Campbell."

63

Cold. Freezing, freezing cold.

Simon Booker's eyes crept open, briefly flicking, then closed once more as the harsh light of the naked bulb assaulted them. His head was so foggy; he was so confused. What the hell had happened to hi—

There she was, watching him. Angel. With the iron bar. Now it slowly came back to him, jagging sharply as the memories flashed through his mind.

He was weak. His face was sticky with blood, his mouth horribly parched. But still he tried to get up. Only to find he was held firm. Looking around, he saw his arms were tied together with thick green wire and secured to the wall behind him. He was naked and kneeling on the mattress, his clothes nowhere in sight. He tried to shout at her, only to become aware of the tape stuck firmly over his mouth.

"You pathetic little shit."

Simon Booker jumped as her venom broke the silence.

"You sad little lowlife."

She was walking toward him, the iron bar still in her hand. She tossed it from hand to hand.

"Did you think you could *trick* me?"

Simon shook his head vigorously.

"You did, didn't you?"

He shook his head even harder.

"Trick me, then attack me?"

She swung the bar down as hard as she could on his kneecap. He screamed, the duct tape enveloping his agony, making it hard to breathe. Now she brought it down on his other kneecap, the bone crunching on impact. Simon howled once more, trying to turn his body away from the blows that rained down on his legs, his thighs, his chest. Again and again and again. She paused briefly, shouted something unintelligible, then swung the bar between his splayed legs to connect with his groin.

He screamed fit to burst, as tears flooded his eyes.

"What the fuck did you think you were doing?" she bellowed at him before laughing. "Oh boy, you are going to pay for that. I'm going to send you back to your frigid wife in pieces, right?"

The tears were pouring down his face now, but they seemed to have no impact on her. She raised the bar to strike his face, then suddenly paused, reining in the tempest of violence that threatened to overwhelm her. Breathing heavily, she turned and put the iron bar in her rucksack.

The respite was brief, however, as she now drew a long knife from her bag. Feeling its blade with her gloved finger, she turned to her victim. Marching over, she held the blade to his throat. He prayed for her to do it, to end his suffering right now. A little more pressure would sever his carotid artery and that would be that.

But Angel had other ideas. She raised the blade and crouched down, rocking back and forth on her haunches. A smile danced around the corners of her mouth.

"You've paid for a whole hour, so we might as well have a little fun, mightn't we?"

And with that the butchery began.

64

Helen had only just returned to Southampton Central when she got the call from Tony Bridges. She and Charlie had been running over the latest leads on the other forum users—"BlackArrow" had scaled down his posting, but the obsessive "PussyKing" was still giving them plenty to work with—but Helen abandoned the search now without a second thought. Half an hour later, she was alongside Tony in the interview room. Melissa sat opposite them, cradling a mug of tea.

"Tell me about Lyra Campbell."

"Money first."

Helen slid the fat envelope across the table. Melissa counted the notes quickly, then stuffed the cash into her bag.

"She's from London, I think. Not sure where exactly, but she talks like a Londoner. Like you."

Despite Helen's many years in Southampton, her South London accent had never entirely deserted her.

"Did a bit of streetwalking up there, then came down to Portsmouth with a boyfriend. When that didn't work out, she moved to Southampton."

"When?"

"'Bout a year ago. Ended up working in the same gang as me."

Melissa sniffed and took a swig of her tea. She hadn't once looked up. It was as if mumbling at the floor might prevent Lyra from hearing her betrayal.

"Which gang?" Tony queried.

"Anton Gardiner."

Tony looked at Helen. The name was familiar to both of them. Anton Gardiner was a violent drug dealer and pimp who ran girls in the south of the city. He worked alone and lived in the shadows, occasionally attracting the attention of the police by acts of incredible violence against his girls or his rivals. He was rumored to be wealthy, but as he didn't believe in banks, this was hard to confirm. What was undoubtedly true was that he was sadistic, unpredictable and unbalanced. He often picked up girls from care homes and shelters—which meant that Helen had a particular hatred of him.

"Why did she choose Anton?"

"She wanted drugs; he could get them."

"And how did they get on?" Tony continued. Melissa just smiled and shook her head—no one "got on" with Anton.

"Where is Lyra now?" Helen asked.

"Don't know. Haven't seen her in over a month."

"Why?"

"She took off. Had a row with Anton and then . . ."

"What about?"

"About why he was such a sadistic fuck."

For the first time, Melissa looked up. Her eyes flashed with anger.

"Go on," Helen continued.

"Do you know what he does to his new girls?"

Helen shook her head. She had to ask, but didn't really want to know.

"He gets them to strip, then bend over and hold their ankles. He tells them they have to stay like that *the whole day*. He leaves you alone for the first few hours. Leaves you until your legs are cramping, your back is in agony, and just when you can't take it any longer, he does you. An hour later, he does you again. Over and over. That's how he breaks you."

It was clear that Melissa was talking from personal experience, her voice trembling as she spoke.

"And if you ever step out of line or don't bring in enough cash, he does the same again. He doesn't care about anything or anyone. He just wants the money."

"So what did he do when Lyra left?"

"No idea. Ain't seen him."

"You've not seen him since?" Helen said, suddenly alert.

"No."

"I need you to be clear on this one, Melissa. Did you see Anton during or after his confrontation with Lyra?"

"No. *She* told me about it, not him."

"Did you look for him?"

"Not at first. You don't go looking for someone like that. But after a few days, I asked a few questions. I needed a fix. But he wasn't at any of his usual places."

"Do you know where Lyra might be hiding out?"

"Probably somewhere near Portswood. She always lived round there. Never told me where she was sleeping."

"And when she was working, did she call herself Lyra?"

"No, that was just between us. When she was on the job, she was always Angel. An angel sent from heaven, she used to tell the punters. They loved that."

Helen called time on the interview shortly afterward. It was very late and Melissa was completely drained. There would be time for more later, and besides, the priority now was to get a sketch that they could release to the public. She sent Tony and Melissa to a custody suite with a police artist, then returned to her office. She wouldn't sleep tonight, so there was no point going home.

Had they just made the breakthrough that would bring this awful killing spree to an end? All this time they had been trying to get a handle on what had triggered this explosion of violence. Had Anton been the unwitting trigger? Had he precipitated this savage rage? If so, chances were he was lying dead in a fleapit somewhere. Helen wouldn't mourn him, but she needed to find him if the pieces of this jigsaw were to fit together.

Her phone rang, making her jump. Jake again. He'd left a number of messages, wondering why she hadn't been to see him, checking if she was okay. Were his inquiries genuine or the product of a guilty conscience? Helen surprised herself by not wanting to know. Normally she would tackle everything head-on, but not this time. This time she didn't want to, in case the answer upset her. Her mind shifted to thoughts of Emilia. What was she up to right now? Was she contemplating pardoning Helen or busy planning her execution? If she printed her story, Helen would be off the case. She couldn't allow that to happen, not now that they were finally making progress, but nevertheless she hadn't backed down. She'd seen other officers make a deal with the devil, and within months they'd become irredeemably compromised, often corrupt. There was nothing to do in these circumstances but tough it out and see who was still standing at the end.

Helen grabbed a coffee and headed back to the incident room. This was no time for fear or introspection—there was work to be done. Somewhere out there was an avenging Angel with a taste for blood.

65

The house was quiet when Charlie returned home. Steve had eaten and gone to bed—the kitchen was scrupulously clean, as it always was when he was in charge. Charlie picked at a few leftovers, then headed upstairs to shower. The hot water pummeled her, briefly reviving her, but she was utterly spent and soon hurried to bed.

Steve didn't stir as she entered, so she crept into bed as quietly as she could. They weren't sleeping in separate beds, which was one small mercy, but communication between them was almost nonexistent. Ever since she'd decided to answer Helen's plea to return to the investigation, Steve had made little attempt to hide his anger and disappointment. It was unbearably sad that just as Charlie was finally finding her feet at work, her domestic life was falling apart. Why couldn't things just work out for once? What did she have to do to be happy?

She lay awake staring at the ceiling. Steve stirred, as he often did, and Charlie flicked a glance at him. She was surprised—and unnerved—to find him staring at her.

"Sorry, love, I didn't mean to wake you," she said softly.

"I wasn't asleep."

"Oh." Charlie couldn't read him in the half-light. He didn't seem angry, but he didn't seem friendly either.

"I've been lying awake thinking."

"Right. What about?"

"About us."

Charlie said nothing in response, unsure where this was going.

"I want us to be happy, Charlie."

Tears suddenly filled Charlie's eyes. They were tears of happiness and tears of relief.

"So do I."

"I want to forget all the stuff that's happened and be like we were before. To live the life we always wanted to lead."

"Me too," Charlie said, just about managing to get the words out. She clung to Steve now and he to her.

"And I want us to try for a baby."

Charlie's sobbing subsided slightly, but she said nothing.

"We always wanted kids. We can't be ruled by bad things that happened before. We have a life to lead. I want to have a baby with you, Charlie. I want us to start trying again."

Charlie buried her head in Steve's chest. The truth was that she desperately wanted a baby too, desperately wanted them to be a happy, normal family. But she was also aware that this wasn't compatible with her career and that Steve had just thrown down the gauntlet.

He would never put it so crudely, but he had just told her that it was time to choose.

66

The eyes. It was all there in the eyes. Set in a slender face and framed by long black tresses, they demanded your attention, fixing you with an intense piercing gaze. There were other features that should have drawn your attention—the full lips, the strong nose, the slightly pointed chin—but it was those big, beautiful eyes and the intensity of her stare that gripped you.

"How accurate a likeness is this?" said Ceri Harwood, looking up from the sketch she'd been studying.

"Very," Helen replied. "Melissa was up all night with our best artist. I only let her go once we were one hundred percent sure we'd got it right."

"And what do we know about Lyra Campbell?"

"Not a lot, but we're working on it. We've got uniform out looking for Anton Gardiner, and this morning we're going to sweep his area of operation, talk to every girl that we know has worked for him, see if anyone can tell us any more about her."

"And what's your working theory?"

"In some ways it's not that extraordinary. She falls into prostitution, then makes another bad choice in taking Anton as her pimp. He brutalizes her. This in combination with the job takes its toll on her psychologically. The drug and alcohol abuse, the stress, the sexual assaults, the diseases—and then one day Anton crosses the line. Does something to her that makes her snap. She attacks him, probably kills him. Either way, she takes out the years of misery on him and this sets her off. We know from Forensics that she talks or shouts at her victims—perhaps she denigrates them, avenges herself upon them . . ."

"The floodgates have opened and now she can't stop?" Harwood interrupted.

"Something like that."

"You sound almost . . . sympathetic toward her."

"I am. She wouldn't be doing this unless she'd been to hell and back, but my real sympathies lie with Eileen Matthews and Jessica Reid and the others. Lyra is a vicious killer who won't stop until we bring her in."

"My thoughts exactly. To that end I'm going to suggest that I take today's press conference, while you get out there and lead the team. Time is of the essence and I want the press and the public to know that our very best people are on the case."

There was a brief, pregnant pause before Helen replied:

"It is customary for the senior investigating officer to handle the press and it's probably best if I do it. I know all the hacks round here—"

"I think I can handle a few journalists. I've had more experience with this sort of thing than you and it is imperative that it runs smoothly this time. I'll ask DS Brooks to sit in to answer any specifics if that becomes necessary. I really think you'll be better used out there."

Helen nodded but could feel the ground shifting beneath her feet once more.

"It's your call."

"Indeed. Keep me up to speed with any developments."

"Ma'am."

Helen turned and left. As she walked down the corridor back to the investigation room, her blood boiled. Now that they were finally making progress, she was being nudged out of the picture. She had seen it before—senior officers who climb high by riding on the coat-tails of others—and she'd always abhorred it. She had to put her irritation to one side, though. They had a killer to catch. But even as she locked her anger away, it fizzled and burned.

Helen had hoped she would be able to work with Harwood. That she would be a pleasant change from Whittaker. But the truth was, Helen deeply disliked her.

And they both knew it.

67

"Thanks for staying with me, Tony. I'd have gone crazy on my own."

It was nearly ten a.m., but neither Tony nor Melissa had slept. Once they had completed the sketch, they had been whisked across town in an unmarked car to a safe house in the center of Southampton. A plainclothes officer sat in a car out front to ward off any casual callers, while Tony and Melissa holed up inside. She had insisted that Tony stay and he'd been happy to do so—now that they were making progress, he didn't want to take any chances.

Despite the exhaustion that gripped them both, they were too wired to relax. Tony knew where the "emergency" bottle of whisky was kept, so he'd dug it out and they'd both had a couple to try to take the edge off the day. Slowly the relaxing effect of the alcohol had done its work, reducing the anxiety and adrenaline a little.

Melissa hated silence—hated her own thoughts—so they had

talked and talked. She had asked him questions about the case, about Angel, and he'd answered as best he could and in return he'd asked her questions about herself. She told him she'd fled an alcoholic mother in Manchester but had left her younger brother behind. She often wondered what had become of him and clearly felt guilty for deserting him. She had got herself into endless trouble as she'd free-wheeled south, but in spite of everything she had survived. The booze and drugs hadn't killed her and neither had the job.

The darkness of the night had cocooned them, making Melissa feel anonymous and out of harm's way. But as the sun rose and another day dawned, her anxiety began to grow. She paced the house, peering through the curtains, as if expecting trouble.

"Shouldn't there be someone out back as well?" she asked.

"It's all right, Melissa. You're safe."

"If Anton finds out what I've done. Or Lyra—"

"They'll only find out once they're in the dock and facing a stretch. Nobody knows you're here. Nobody can touch you."

Melissa shrugged as if she only half believed him.

"All you've got to think about is what you do next. Once it's all done with."

"What d'you mean?"

"I mean . . . you don't have to go back to the streets. There are programs that can help you get out. Addiction treatment, counseling, training . . ."

"You trying to save me, Tony?" she replied, teasing.

Tony felt himself blushing.

"No . . . well, kind of. I know you've been through a lot, but this could be the break you need. You've done something strong, something good. You shouldn't waste this opportunity."

"You sound just like my dad used to."

"Well, he was right. You're better than this."

"You really don't know anything, do you, Tony?" she replied, though her tone was not unkind. "You ever worked vice?"

Tony shook his head.

"Thought not," Melissa continued. "If you had, then you wouldn't be bothering."

"I hope I would."

"You'd be one in a million," Melissa replied, laughing bitterly. "Do you know what girls like us do? What we've been through to end up like this?"

"No, but I can im—"

"We've lied and cheated and stolen. We've been beaten up, spat on, raped. We've had knives held to our throats, been choked half to death. We've done heroin, crack, uppers, downers, booze. We've not changed for a week, puked in our sleep. And then we've got up and done it all again."

She let her words hang in the air, then carried on:

"So I appreciate you trying, but it's too late."

Tony looked at Melissa. He knew she was telling the truth, but it seemed such a horrible waste. She was still young and attractive—she clearly had a good brain and a big heart. Was it fair to consign her to a lifetime of brutality?

"It's never too late. Take this chance. I can help you—"

"For God's sake, Tony. Have you listened to a word I've said?" she spat back. "I'm broken. There's no way back for me—Anton saw to that."

"Anton's gone."

"Not in here he isn't," she said, rapping the side of her head viciously. "Do you know what he did to me? What he did to us?"

Tony shook his head, wanting to know and not wanting to know.

"Normally he'd just use his lighter or a cigarette. Burn us on the arms, the back of the neck, the soles of our feet. Somewhere that'd hurt like fuck but wouldn't put the punters off. That was for small things. But if we'd done something really bad, he'd take us on a little trip."

Tony said nothing, watching Melissa intently. It was as if she were no longer talking to him, instead inhabiting some dark memory elsewhere.

"He'd drive you out to the old cinema on Upton Street. Belonged to a mate of his—it was a dirty great hole full of rats. All the way we'd be begging him to forgive us, let us go, but that'd only make him more angry. Once we got there, he'd . . ."

She hesitated before continuing.

". . . he had this bicycle chain, big chunky thing with a padlock on the end, and he'd hit you with it. Over and over again until you couldn't get up and run even if you wanted to. He'd be shouting and hollering as he beat you, calling you every name under the sun, until he'd run out of steam. And when you were lying there . . . like a rag doll in the dirt and the blood and the filth wishing you were dead . . . he'd piss on you."

Her voice was shaking now.

"Then he'd bugger off and leave you there for the night. People said some girls froze to death there, but if you didn't . . . then the next day you'd clean yourself up and go back to work. Praying that you'd never make him angry again."

Tony looked at her. Her whole body was shaking.

"That's the kind of people we are, Tony. He did that to us and now that's all we're good for. That's all I am now. That's all I can be. Do you understand?"

Tony nodded, though he wanted to tell her she was wrong, that she could be saved.

"The best that I can hope for is that it won't kill me. That just for a little bit I can be safe."

"You're safe now. I'll make sure of it."

"My hero," she replied, smiling through her tears.

She allowed herself to be held. He was supposed to carry on questioning her, but suddenly he didn't want to ask her about the darkness and the filth and the violence. He wanted to take her away from that, take her to a better place. He wanted to save her.

And he knew he would risk everything to do it.

68

"Lyra Campbell is now our number one suspect in this investigation. She is a highly dangerous individual, and we would urge members of the public *not* to approach her. If they see her, or have any information on her whereabouts, they should call the police immediately."

Detective Superintendent Ceri Harwood was holding court with the assembled members of the press. Charlie had never seen the media suite so busy—there were journalists from more than twenty countries, some of them reduced to standing in the corridor outside. They were scribbling furiously as Harwood brought them up to speed, but their eyes never left the enlarged sketch that dominated the screen behind her. Magnified, that face, those eyes, were even more beguiling and hypnotic. Who was this woman? What was her special power over people?

Charlie handled the operational questions. Inevitably Emilia Garanita asked why DI Grace wasn't at the press conference—she seemed particularly disappointed that her sparring partner wasn't present—and Charlie was happy to bat that back, underlining the many and enduring virtues of her boss. At that point Harwood cut in, leading the Q&A in another direction, and twenty minutes later the whole thing wrapped up.

When the final journalist had left, Harwood turned to Charlie. "How did we do?"

"Good. The message will be out there in a couple of hours and . . . well, you can't hide forever. Normally once the e-fit's out we pick them up within forty-eight hours. Along with a few unfortunates who look a bit like them."

Harwood smiled.

"Good. I must remember to call Tony Bridges. It's thanks to him that we are where we are."

Charlie nodded, swallowing her instinct to remind the station chief that it had been Helen's idea to put someone undercover.

"How do you feel the investigation has gone so far, Charlie? You've been away for a while and have probably come back with fresh eyes . . ."

"It's gone as well as it could have in the circumstances."

"Have the different parts of the operation pulled their weight? Have we got anything from the surveillance yet?"

"No, not yet, but—"

"Do you think we should persist with it? It's cripplingly expensive, and now that we have a concrete lead . . ."

"That's DI Grace's call. And yours, of course."

It was a coward's answer, but Charlie felt deeply uncomfortable discussing the running of the investigation behind Helen's back. Harwood nodded, as if Charlie had actually said something quite profound, and then she sat down on a table edge.

"And how are you getting on with Helen?"

"Fine now. We've had a good talk and things are . . . fine."

"I'm glad, because—strictly between me and you—I was worried. Helen had some very robust opinions about your return to Southampton Central. Opinions that I felt were unfair. I'm pleased that you've proved her wrong and that the old team is back together again."

Charlie nodded, unsure what the appropriate response was.

"And I hear you've been made temporary DS, while Tony is busy. How are you finding that?"

"I'm enjoying it, of course."

"Would you be interested in making it a permanent promotion?"

The question took Charlie by surprise. Immediately memories of her conversation with Steve reared up. In truth, they had been plaguing her all morning.

"I'm taking it one step at a time. I have a husband and maybe one day . . ."

"Children?"

Charlie nodded.

"It doesn't have to be a choice, you know, Charlie. You can do both—take it from me. You just need to be clear with everyone and then . . . well, for a talented female officer like you, the sky is the limit."

"Thank you, ma'am."

"Come and talk to me whenever you need to. I like you, Charlie, and I want you to make the right decisions. I see great things for you."

Shortly afterward, Harwood departed. She had a lunch date with the police commissioner and it didn't do to be late. Charlie watched her go, deeply unnerved. What game was Harwood playing? What was her role in it?

And what did it mean for Helen?

69

The team spread over Southampton, searching for Lyra. North, south, east and west, leaving no stone unturned. Extra uniform and community support officers had been drafted in, and led by CID detectives, they visited brothels, mother-and-baby drop-ins, health clinics, social security offices, Accident and Emergency departments—clutching their e-fits and appealing for information. If Lyra was hiding in Southampton, they would surely find her now.

Helen led the hunt in the northern reaches of the city, firmly believing that the killer would operate from somewhere familiar and safe. She kept her radio volume turned up high, hoping that at any moment it would squawk into life with news of a breakthrough. She didn't care who got Lyra, didn't care who brought her in—she just wanted this to be over.

But still Lyra proved elusive. Some claimed to have seen her, some thought they might have known her under a different name, but so far no one had confirmed speaking to her. Who was this woman who could exist in such a bubble, so devoid of human contact? They had been at it for hours, spoken to scores of people, but still they had nothing concrete. Lyra was a phantom who refused to be found.

Then, just after lunchtime, Helen finally got the break she'd been craving. As the hours had ticked by, as each working girl had claimed ignorance of Lyra's existence, she had started to wonder if Melissa had made it all up to get some attention and a bit of cash, but then suddenly and unexpectedly they got a positive ID.

Helen picked her way through the litter-strewn tenement building on Spire Street, utterly depressed by what she saw. Working girls and junkies lived cheek by jowl in the leaky, derelict flats that were due for gutting and redevelopment next year. Many of the squatters had kids, who ran round Helen's legs as she stalked the building, running from the policewoman in mock horror, hiding from her in dirty and dangerous corners of this ruined building, squealing all the while. If she could have, Helen would have scooped them all up and taken them somewhere decent. She made a mental note to contact Social Services as soon as she had a spare second. It couldn't be right for kids to be living like this in the twenty-first century, she thought.

A group of women sat round a small heater, breast-feeding, gossiping, recovering from last night's work. They were hostile at first, then sullen. Helen had the distinct impression that they were holding out on her, but she persisted nevertheless. These girls might be far gone, but they all had families of some sort or other and were not immune to emotional blackmail. Helen played on this now, painting a grim picture of the bereaved families burying their defiled fathers, husbands and sons. Still the women offered nothing—whether this was from fear of Anton or fear of the police, Helen couldn't tell. But then, finally, the quietest one of the group spoke up. She wasn't much to look at—a shaven-headed junkie with a mewling baby in her arms—but she told Helen that she'd known Lyra briefly. They'd worked for Anton together, before Lyra disappeared.

"Where did she live?" Helen demanded.

"I don't know."

"Why not?"

"She never told me," the girl protested.

"Then where did you see her?"

"We worked the same places. Empress Road, Portswood, St. Mary's. But her favorite was by the old cinema in Upton Street. You could usually find her there."

Helen carried on quizzing her for a few moments longer, but already she had what she needed. All the places the girl had mentioned were in the north of the city, which fit her theory. But more than that, it was the mention of the old cinema that had set Helen's heart beating. Tony had filled her in on his latest debrief with Melissa, which had also pinpointed the cinema as one of Anton's haunts. It seemed too much of a coincidence to be ignored. Was this where Anton and Lyra had come to blows? Had he been killed there? Would she still be haunting this lonely and desolate spot?

Helen called it in immediately, ordering a plainclothes CID officer to secure the old cinema swiftly and quietly, so that an SOC team could slip in and do their work. Simultaneously a surveillance team would set up camp on the street. Already Helen was impatient for results. Something in her gut told her that the old cinema would prove crucial in cracking this case. Maybe they were finally getting close to Lyra. Maybe their phantom was about to become flesh.

70

The car slipped quietly along the street, shadowing her. Charlie had been so wrapped up in her own thoughts that she hadn't noticed it at first. But there was no doubt that she was being followed. The car was keeping its distance but also keeping pace—did they want to know where she was going or were they just waiting for the right moment to pounce?

Suddenly the car sped up, roaring past her before mounting the pavement and coming to an abrupt halt. Now the door swung open. Charlie's hand immediately reached for her baton.

"Have you missed me?"

Sandra McEwan, aka Lady Macbeth. An unwelcome reminder of past mistakes.

"I'll take that as a 'yes.' Sometimes it's so hard to put your feelings into words, isn't it? Oh, excuse the amateur dramatics," McEwan continued, nodding to the car slewed across the pavement. "Some-times the boy gets overexcited."

"Get it off the pavement now and be on your way."

"By all means," McEwan replied, nodding at her lover to move the car. "Though I was rather hoping you'd come with us."

"Dogging's not really my thing, Sandra. We'll have to take a rain check."

"Very funny, Constable. Or is it Sergeant these days?"

Charlie said nothing, refusing to give her the satisfaction.

"Either way, I would have thought you'd be interested in meet-ing the lowlife who killed Alexia Louszko."

As she spoke, she opened the back door of the car and gestured to the empty interior.

"I'll happily give you a ride, if you can spare the time."

Charlie acquiesced, and before long they were speeding out of the city. Charlie had no fears for her own safety—Sandra McEwan was too smart to target coppers and she certainly wouldn't abduct them on a busy street full of witnesses—but nevertheless Charlie wondered what game they were playing. She questioned Sandra en route, but her inquiries were met with stony silence. Clearly they were going to have to play it Sandra's way today.

The car rattle-bumped to a stop on a desolate patch of wasteland overlooking Southampton Water. It had been bought by a foreign property company, but they had run into planning trouble and two years later the ground remained unbroken. It had since become a mecca for illegal dumping and was now liberally decorated with build-ing waste, burned-out cars and chemical drums.

Sandra opened the door and gestured Charlie out. Irritated, Char-lie acquiesced.

"Where is he, then?"

"Over there."

Sandra pointed to a burned-out Vauxhall not fifty yards away. "Shall we?"

Charlie hurried toward the vehicle. She now knew exactly what she would find and wanted to get it over with. Sure enough, nestled in the boot of the car was the brutalized body of a young man—one of the Campbells' thugs, no doubt.

"Terrible, isn't it?" Sandra said, without an ounce of pity in her voice. "Some kids found him like this and told me. My first thought was to call the police."

"I'm sure."

The man was lying in exactly the same position as Alexia had been when she was found. His face had been caved in and his hands and feet removed in identical fashion too. This was tit-for-tat killing, a message to the Campbells that their aggression would be met head-on. An eye for an eye.

"Your SOC team will find a hammer in his inside coat pocket. Word on the street is that it's the hammer that killed Alexia. I'm sure your forensics will confirm that for you. Sad to see a man like that, but then perhaps there's a natural justice in it, eh?"

Charlie snorted and shook her head in disbelief. She had no doubt that McEwan would have been present when the man was tortured and killed, conducting operations with gleeful malice.

"I'd say that was case closed, wouldn't you?"

Smiling, she headed back to her car, leaving Charlie alone with a faceless corpse for company and a very bitter taste in her mouth.

71

Helen was on her way back to Southampton Central when she got the call. She could feel her phone buzzing and swerved her bike into a bus lane in order to answer it. She had expected it to be Charlie with an update. For a moment she even thought it might be news of a positive sighting of Lyra. But it was Robert.

She had been summoned back to Southampton Central by Harwood, but she didn't hesitate now, speeding round the ring road, then north toward Aldershot. Harwood could wait. In less than an hour, she was walking through the atrium of the Wellington Avenue police station. She had met a good handful of the CID officers based here at various Hampshire Police conferences, and one of them—DI Amanda Hopkins—greeted her now.

"He's holed up in interview room one. We offered him a lawyer, or to call his mum, but . . . well, he won't speak to anyone but you."

It was said in a friendly manner but was an appeal for information.

"I'm a friend of the family."

"The Stonehills?"

"Yup," Helen lied. "What sort of state is he in?"

"Shaken up. A few superficial injuries, but he's basically okay. I've got the other two in cells. We've already interviewed them— they are all blaming each other, so . . ."

"I'll see what I can get out of him. Thanks, Amanda."

Robert was slumped on a plastic chair. He looked in a bad way—as if he had slightly imploded—with numerous scratches on his face. His right arm was in a sling. He stirred on seeing Helen, sitting up straight.

"I got this for you," Helen said, placing a can of Pepsi on the table. "Shall I open it?"

He nodded, so Helen obliged. Grabbing it with his good hand, he drank it down in one go. His hand shook as he did so.

"So, are you going to tell me what happened?"

He nodded, but said nothing.

"I can try to help you," Helen continued, "but I need to know—"

"They jumped me."

"Who?"

"Davey. And Mark."

"Why?"

"Because I wouldn't run with them anymore."

"You told them you weren't interested."

"They said I was yellow. They thought I was going to grass on them."

"Were you?"

"No. I just wanted out."

"So what happened?"

"I told them to do without me. That I wanted to be left alone.

245

They weren't happy. They left, but then they came back. Threatening me. Telling me they'd cut me."

"So what did you do?"

"I fought back. I wasn't going to be pushed around."

"What with?"

There was a long pause, then:

"Knife."

"Sorry?"

"A knife. I keep one on me—"

"For God's sake, Robert. That's how you get killed."

"Saved my life tonight, though, didn't it?" he spat back, unrepentant.

"Maybe."

He lapsed into silence.

"So let me get this straight. They attacked you first."

"For sure."

"And you fought back?"

He nodded again.

"Did you injure them?"

"Got Davey a bit on the arm. Nothing bad."

"Okay. Well, we can probably make that one play, but you're going to have to cough to carrying the knife. Nothing to be done about that. I can probably get you out of here and back home, if I promise to stand for you."

Robert looked up, surprised.

"But I'm going to need you to promise me that you won't carry again. You get caught with a knife a second time and I won't be able to help you."

"'Course."

"Do we have a deal?"

He nodded.

"Right, let me talk to them. We'll leave Davey to stew for a bit, shall we?" Helen replied, a smile creeping through. To her surprise, Robert smiled back, the first time she'd ever seen him do so.

She was nearly at the door when he spoke.

"Why are you doing this?"

Helen paused. She considered her answer.

"Because I want to help you."

"Why?"

"Because you deserve better than this."

"Why? You're a copper. I'm a thief. You should bang me up."

Helen hesitated. Her hand was on the door handle. Would it be safer to turn it and go? Say nothing?

"Are you my mother?"

The question hit her like a sledgehammer. It was unexpected, painful, and rendered her speechless.

"My real mother, I mean?"

Helen took a breath.

"No, no, I'm not. But I knew her."

He was looking at her intently.

"I've never met anyone who knew her before."

Helen was glad she wasn't looking at him. Tears had suddenly sprung to her eyes. How much of his life had he spent wondering about his birth mother?

"How did you know her? Were you a friend or . . . ?"

Helen hesitated. Then:

"I'm her sister."

Robert said nothing for a second, stunned by Helen's confession.

"You're . . . you're my aunt?"

"Yes, I am."

Another long silence as Robert took this in.

"Why didn't you come and see me sooner?"

His question cut like a knife.

"I couldn't. And I wouldn't have been welcome. Your parents had carved out a good life for you—they wouldn't have wanted me butting in, raking up old ground."

"I don't have anything of my mother. I know she died when I was just a baby, but . . ."

He shrugged. He knew virtually nothing of Marianne and what he did know was a lie. Maybe it was better to keep it that way.

"Well, maybe if we meet again, I can tell you more about her. I'd like to. Her life wasn't always happy, but you were the best thing in it."

Suddenly the boy was crying. Years of questions, years of feeling incomplete, catching up with him. Helen was fighting tears too, but fortunately Robert had dropped his head, so her distress went unnoticed.

"I'd like that," he said through his tears.

"Good," Helen replied, recovering her composure. "Let's keep it between us for now. Until we know each other a little better, eh?"

Robert nodded, rubbing his eyes with his hands.

"This isn't the end, Robert. It's the beginning."

Thirty minutes later, Robert was in a cab heading home. Helen watched the cab go, then climbed on her bike. Despite the many problems that lay ahead, despite the many dark forces swirling around her, Helen felt exhilarated. Finally, she was beginning to atone.

In the aftermath of Marianne's death, Helen had devoured every aspect of her sister's life. Many would have buried the experience away, but Helen had wanted to climb inside Marianne's mind, heart and soul. She wanted to fill in the gaps, find out exactly what had happened to her sister in prison and beyond. Find out if there was any truth in Marianne's accusation that *she* was to blame for all those deaths.

So she had dredged up every document that had ever been written for or about her sister and on page three of Marianne's custody file she stumbled upon the bombshell that had shaken her world—a sign that her sister still had the power to hurt her from beyond the grave. Helen was only thirteen at the time of Marianne's arrest, and she had been spirited away to a care home straight after her parents' murders. She hadn't attended her sister's trial in person—her testimony had been prerecorded—and she was told only the verdict, nothing more. She hadn't seen her sister's swollen belly and Hampshire Social Services had kept mum about it, so it was only when skimming the medical assessment on her arrest sheet, expecting nothing more than the familiar bruises and scars, that Helen had discovered her sister was pregnant when arrested. Five months pregnant. Later DNA tests would prove that Marianne's dad—the man she had murdered in cold blood—was the child's father.

The baby had been taken away from Marianne minutes after delivery. Even now, after everything that had happened, that image still brought tears to Helen's eyes. Her sister cuffed to a hospital bed, her baby forcibly taken from her after eighteen hours of labor. Did she fight them? Did she have the strength to resist? Helen knew instinctively that she would have. Despite the brutality of its conception, Marianne would have cared for that baby. She would have loved it fiercely, feeding off its innocence, but, of course, she was never given the chance. She was a killer, who received no sympathy from her captors. There was no humanity in the process, just judgment and retribution.

The baby had vanished into the care system and then to fostering, but Helen had diligently pursued Baby K through the reams of paper and bureaucracy until she'd traced him. He'd been adopted by a child-less Jewish couple in Aldershot—who'd named him Robert Stonehill—and he was doing fine. He was rebellious, lippy, frustrating—with scant qualifications to show for his years of schooling—but he was okay. He had a job, a solid home and two loving parents. In spite of the loveless nature of his birth, he had grown up nurtured and loved.

Robert had dodged his inheritance. And Helen knew that because of that, she should have left him well alone. But her curiosity wouldn't let her. She had attended Marianne's funeral by herself, her killer and sole mourner, only to discover that she was not alone after all. Someone else had escaped the wreckage. So for Marianne's sake, as much as her own, she would keep an eye on Robert. If she could help him in any way, she would.

Helen turned the ignition of her bike, revved the engine and roared off down the street. She was so caught up in the moment, so relieved, that for once she didn't check her mirrors. Had she done so, she would have realized that the same car that had followed her all the way from Southampton was now following her back.

72

Since his daddy's return, life had got better for Alfie Booker. They
had been living in a flat while his dad was in the army. But when he
came back, they moved to a caretaker's house that bordered school
playing fields. His dad cut the grass and swept up the leaves. Painted
the lines on the football pitches. It was a good job, Alfie thought,
and he liked to go with his dad as he did his work.

His dad argued with his mum a lot and was happier when he was
working, so that was the best time for Alfie to be with him. He never
said much, but he seemed happy to have his son by his side. They
made a funny pair, but Alfie wouldn't have changed it for the world.

His dad hadn't come home last night. His mum said he had, but
Alfie knew that wasn't true. His work boots were where he'd left them
yesterday afternoon and he was nowhere on the grounds. Alfie had
covered every blade of grass, listening all the while for the telltale

drone of the riding mower. He didn't know what was going on, but he didn't like it.

He turned the corner and saw a tall figure walking toward the sports pavilion. It was Sports Day later that day and his first thought was that it was one of the games masters, but he didn't recognize him. The figure wasn't broad enough to be his dad, so who was it? He was walking with real purpose toward the pavilion, so he obviously had something of importance to do. Instinct drew Alfie toward the figure, his curiosity getting the better of him.

As he got closer, he slowed. It was a woman. And she was placing a box by the pavilion entrance. What was in the box—a trophy? A prize?

He called out as he ran over. The woman spun round, stopping Alfie in his tracks. She wasn't smiling and had a nasty face. To his surprise, she turned and walked off without saying a word.

Alfie watched her go, confused. Then he turned his attention to the box. There was a word he couldn't understand written on it. He tried to spell it out: *F. I. L. T. H.* But it made no sense to him. Why was it written in red ink?

He looked around, wondering what to do. There was no one to tell him he couldn't open it.

Double-checking that the coast was clear, Alfie stepped forward and opened the box.

73

It was hours after the event, but Tony's mind was still reeling. His heart was beating nineteen to the dozen, fired by a mixture of fear, adrenaline and anxiety.

He tried to gather his thoughts but they spun round and round, eluding him. He hadn't felt like this in ages, yet a little voice was shouting inside him, abusing him, shaming him. It was all he deserved, yet oddly he didn't care. He didn't care at all. Which Tony was thinking these thoughts? He didn't recognize him.

He had always been a by-the-book copper. Some said he was stolid. Others more charitably said he was professional, exemplary. Helen certainly respected him. The thought suddenly made his head hurt. What would she think if she could see him now? It wasn't uncommon, but that didn't make it any better.

Melissa stirred next to him, turning over in her sleep. He took in her naked body. It was marked with tattoos and ancient scarring in places, but was still muscular and alluring. His eyes flicked to the bedroom curtains again, checking for the umpteenth time that they were pulled together. On the street outside, a colleague of his was sitting in an unmarked car. Would he have noticed anything? The light going on and off in the bedroom? Surely he would have assumed it was Melissa going to bed finally. But what if he'd done a perimeter check of the house and noticed that Tony wasn't downstairs?

When it happened he hadn't thought of the risk at all. He had held her close, enjoying the warmth of her body against his, then she'd looked up at him and drawn him toward her. They had kissed. Then kissed some more. Despite the fact that she was both a prostitute and their key witness, Tony had not hesitated, his desire driving him on. They were in bed minutes later—Tony was stunned to think of his utter recklessness—he had never once paused to draw breath.

He was like a boy again, full of foolish, hopeless thoughts. He wanted to laugh, shout and cry. But all the while that same little voice kept calling to him. Banging out its questions with deafening power. Where was this leading? And where would it end?

74

She pushed the bell down hard and didn't let go. She had already rung it twice, done a perimeter of the house, but it remained resolutely closed to her, despite the fact that it was obviously occupied. The curtains were closed and she could hear the TV playing inside.

Eventually she heard footsteps, accompanied by a volley of cursing. Emilia Garanita smiled to herself and kept her finger on the bell. Only when the door swung open did she finally take her finger off, restoring peace once more.

"We don't buy at the door," the man said, already shutting the door.

"Do I look like I'm selling fucking dusters?" Emilia replied.

The man hesitated, taken aback by her forceful and unrepentant response.

"I know you," he said eventually. "You're what's-her-name . . ."

"Emilia Garanita."

"Right. What do you want?"

He was clearly anxious to get back to his viewing. Emilia smiled before continuing.

"I want a file."

"Excuse me?"

"You do work at the probation service, Mr. Fielding?"

"Yes, and as such you should know that there is no possible way I could ever give a journalist any information. It is all confidential."

He said the word "journalist" with real distaste, as if he were somehow operating on a superior plane. Emilia loved these moments.

"Even if she was going to save your life?"

"I beg your pardon?"

"Your professional life, I mean."

Now Fielding was quiet. Could he tell what was coming?

"Got a few friends in uniform. They told me an interesting story about a middle-aged guy getting caught on the Common engaging in lewd acts in the back of a Ford Focus."

She let her eye drift to the Ford Focus parked in Fielding's drive.

"Story goes he'd picked up the girl at a bar . . . but she was only fifteen. Whoops! Apparently the guy begged and pleaded and eventually the officers let him off, each with a hundred pounds in their pocket. Still, they kept a record of the license plate and a description of the dirty bastard. I've got their police notepad right here."

She pretended to rummage in her bag. Now Fielding stepped outside the house, pulling the door shut behind him.

"That's blackmail," he said indignantly.

"Yes, it is, isn't it?" Emilia replied, smiling. "Now, are you going to give me what I want or shall I start writing my story?"

It was a rhetorical question. Emilia could tell from the look on his face that he was going to do exactly what she wanted.

75

"Hello, Alfie, my name is Helen and I'm a police officer."

The boy looked up from his drawing.

"Is it okay if I sit down with you?"

The boy nodded, so Helen crouched down next to him.

"What are you drawing?"

"Dinosaur pirates."

"Cool. Is that the *T. rex*?"

Alfie nodded, then said matter-of-factly:

"He's the biggest."

"I can see that. He looks scary."

Alfie shrugged as if it was no big deal. Helen found herself smiling. The six-year-old was a cute kid who had handled the strange events of the day remarkably well. He seemed more confused than upset. Which was more than could be said for his mother. She hadn't been told the worst yet—and she wouldn't be until they had a body—but she was already a wreck. Family Liaison were doing their best, but she was very vocally distressed, which was starting to affect Alfie. Helen knew she needed his undivided attention.

"Can I show you something special?"

Alfie looked up. Helen slipped her warrant card onto the table.

"This is my police badge. Do you know what a police officer is?"

"You catch burglarers."

"That's right," Helen said, suppressing a smile. "And do you know what this is?"

She slid her police radio onto the table.

"Cool," he said, immediately picking it up.

"Press that button there," Helen suggested. Alfie did so and got a good blast of static for his trouble. He seemed pleased. As he toyed with it, Helen continued:

"Would you mind if I ask you a few questions?"

The boy nodded without looking up.

"I want you to know that you are not in trouble at all. It's just that the lady with the box—the lady you saw—well, she might have taken something that didn't belong to her. So I need to find out who she is. Did she talk to you?"

Alfie shook his head.

"Did she say anything at all?"

Another shake.

"Did you see her face?"

A nod this time. Helen hesitated, then pulled a photocopy of the e-fit from her bag.

"Was this the lady you saw?"

She showed him the picture.

He looked up from the radio, took in the picture, then shrugged and returned his attention to the radio. Helen put a hand on his, gently stopping him. He looked up.

"It's really important, Alfie. Could you take another look at the picture for me, please?"

Alfie obliged with good grace, as if he were getting another go in a game. This time he looked at it more carefully. There was a long pause and then he half nodded.

"Maybe."

"Maybe?"

"She was wearing a hat. It covered her face a bit."

"Like a baseball cap?"

Alfie nodded. Helen sat back on her haunches. They could ask him some more questions—about her height and build—but it would be hard to get a positive ID off him. He was only six, after all.

"What did she do?"

"I'm sorry?"

"What did she take?"

Helen shot a look at Alfie's mum, then lowered her voice.

"Something very special."

Helen looked at his face, so full of curiosity. She didn't have the heart to tell him that he would never see his daddy again.

76

Helen was so engrossed in her chat with Charlie that she didn't hear Harwood coming. An increasingly frustrated Charlie had spent days trying to run PussyKing's true identity to ground—he was Bitchfest's principal contributor and should have been easy to find. But because he never used a home or office computer and was adept at creating fake addresses via encrypted IPs, PussyKing remained forever just out of reach. Helen and Charlie were debating their next move, when:

"Could I have a word, Helen?"

It was said with a smile, but without warmth. This was a public summons in front of the team and was designed to send out a message. What that message was Helen wasn't yet clear about.

. . .

"I've been trying to get hold of you all day," Harwood continued once they were in her office. "I know events are moving fast, but I will not tolerate this breakdown in communication. Is that clear?"

"Yes, ma'am."

"This only works if every link in the chain is connected, right?"

Helen nodded but privately wanted to tell her to blow it out her arse.

"So what's been going on?" Harwood continued.

Helen brought her up to speed with the developments in the hunt for Lyra Campbell, the work being done at the old cinema and the latest killing.

"No body yet, but we believe the victim is Simon Booker, former paratrooper and veteran of Afghanistan."

"A war hero. Bloody hell."

Helen sensed it was the possible headlines that were upsetting Harwood, not the man's fate. She concluded her briefing, then moved to excuse herself, but Harwood stopped her in her tracks.

"I had lunch with the police commissioner today."

Helen said nothing. Was this another front opening up?

"He's very worried. The investigation is already massively over budget. The cost of surveillance alone is huge and has yielded nothing. Then there's the extra uniforms, the overtime, the auxiliary SOC team and the dogs, and to what end? What concrete progress have we made?"

"It's a tough investigation, ma'am. She's a clever and a resourceful kill—"

"All we've had for our money is a slew of negative headlines, which is why the commissioner has asked for an internal review of the investigation."

So this *was* a new front. Had he asked or had Harwood led him to it? Helen's blood boiled, but she said nothing.

"I know you have experience in this area and that the team are—by and large—loyal to you, but your methods are irregular and costly—"

"With the greatest of respect, four people are dead—"

"Three."

"That's fucking semantics. We all know Booker's dead."

"It may be semantics, Inspector, but it says so much about you. You rush to judgment. Right from the start you've wanted this to be about Helen Grace chasing another serial killer. That's the only narrative you know, isn't it? Well, I think it's misguided, unprofessional and dangerous. We have budgets, protocols and targets that cannot be ridden over roughshod."

"And what's your target, Ceri? Chief Super? Chief Constable? Police Commissioner?"

"Watch your tongue, Inspector."

"I've met people like you before. Never do the work, but always on hand to take the glory."

Harwood leaned back in her chair. She was clearly livid but refused to show it.

"Tread very carefully, DI Grace. And consider this an official warning. You're a gnat's breath away from getting taken off this investigation. Bring her in or step aside. Is that clear?"

Helen left soon after. One thing was crystal clear. As long as Harwood was around, she was on borrowed time.

77

It was getting dark now, but that would only add atmosphere to the composition. The low light and the grainy image would help capture the feel Emilia was going for. By rights she should have asked for one of their regular snappers to come with her, but she knew how to operate a digital SLR as well as the next man and there was no way she was letting anybody else in on this story until she had the whole package.

Adrian Fielding had been remarkably helpful, once he'd realized Emilia would happily destroy his career if she didn't get what she wanted. The file on Robert Stonehill began in undramatic fashion, a pitiful list of his recent minor misdemeanors, but got much more interesting once Emilia discovered he'd been adopted. There were scant details of his biological mother in the main file, but it was obvious enough that he'd been born in a prison hospital. As soon as Emilia had discovered this, she knew who he was—Helen Grace had truly cared for only one person—but being a good journalist she'd cross-referenced Robert's age with the date of Marianne's arrest. After that it was a short step to Marianne's arrest sheet and the jigsaw was complete.

Emilia could barely keep her hand still as she raised the camera. The boy had been sent out to buy milk and was waiting impatiently in the queue. *Snap, snap, snap.* The detail wasn't brilliant, but the shots would look snatched and dangerous. Emilia waited some more, watching as Robert paid. Now he was leaving the shop. Emilia raised the camera again. As if choreographed, he paused as he exited, casting his eyes up to the heavens as rain began to spit. The sodium glare from the streetlamp caught his face, rendering him ghostly and unnatural. *Snap, snap, snap.* Then he pulled his hoodie up and looked almost straight at her. He couldn't see her hidden in the gloom, but she could see him. *Snap, snap, snap.* The young man born of violence caught on the darkened streets wearing a hoodie—the uniform of violent and disillusioned thugs the country over. Perfect.

Now that she had what she needed, Emilia was going to act. She should of course ring the editor of the *Evening News*, but there was no way she was going to do that. There was a contact she'd been cultivating at the *Mail* for just such an occasion. If she was quick, she could get it on the front page of tomorrow's edition.

This was her ticket out. She had the price. She had the package. And she had her headline:

SON OF A MONSTER.

78

Helen was still chewing on her confrontation with Harwood when she arrived at the old cinema on Upton Street. Hugging the shadows, she slipped inside via the fire exit. The building was supposed to be up for sale soon, though who would want to buy it was beyond Helen. As soon as she stepped inside, she was assaulted by a rich aroma—the smell of years of rotting wood and decaying vermin. It made her gag and she quickly put her mask on. Gathering herself, she held on to the shaky rail and made her way downstairs.

The Crown Cinema had been popular with families in the 1970s. It was a traditional picture palace, right down to the galleried theater seating and heavy velvet curtains that concealed the screen. At least, it had been in its heyday. Its owners had gone bust during the recession in the 1980s, and subsequent attempts to resurrect it had fallen afoul of the out-of-town multiplexes and the arthouse cinema down by the waterfront. Now the main auditorium was a travesty of its former glory, a fractured mess of torn-up seats and building rubble.

The SOC team was grouped in a corner near the screen. The levels of activity and excitement meant progress. Helen hurried over. The phone call she'd received just after her confrontation with Harwood had been the one small piece of good news she'd had all day. She wanted to see it with her own eyes before she got carried away.

The SOC team parted as she approached. There he was. He was still mostly buried in the rubble, but enough had been lifted off to reveal the top of his head and a raised arm. The fingers on the exposed arm pointed upward in accusing fashion. The skin, though covered in dust, was dark and suggested the victim was mixed race. But that wasn't what really interested Helen. More important still was the fact that the hand had only four fingers, the one having been removed some years earlier, by the look of the historic wound.

They didn't know much about Anton Gardiner—his parentage, his early life—but they did know that he had had his ring finger cut off in a tit-for-tat gang punishment ten years earlier. Was he the trigger for Lyra's killing spree? Was he the cause of all this? Helen shivered as she looked at his mutilated corpse, a pulse of excitement flowing through her. Was Anton's ravaged hand finally pointing them in the right direction?

79

It was cold and dark and she was losing patience. It was getting harder and harder to find room to breathe. The police presence was huge all over the city now and she'd had to be exceedingly cautious, walking the streets in tracksuit bottoms and a hoodie, as if out for a late-night jog. Once she'd found a secluded patch down by the Western Docks, she'd stripped off to reveal a short skirt and stockings. A tight top exposed her generous frame, with a short fur jacket as the icing on the cake. Despite the frustration and stress of the evening, she felt good as she unveiled herself. Now all she had to do was stand and wait for the dirty dogs to come to her.

Twenty minutes later, a lone figure came into view. He was slightly unsteady on his feet and was muttering a song in a foreign tongue. *A sailor, probably a Polish one,* she thought. Angel's heart started to beat faster. Sailors were dirty, unhygienic and coarse, but they always had money when on shore leave and they usually came pretty quickly, having been starved of sex for so long.

The man paused when he spotted her. Casting around to check that he was alone, he sauntered over. He was surprisingly pretty—twenty-five at the most, with a slender face and female lips. He was drunk, to be sure, but not unattractive. Angel was surprised he had to pay for it.

"How much?" His accent was thick.

"What do you want?"

"Everything," he replied.

"Hundred pounds."

He nodded.

"Let's go."

And with that he sealed his fate.

Angel walked ahead, leading him through a maze of cargo containers to a small supervisors' yard. It was here that cargo was supposed to be checked and logged, but in truth it was where a fair portion of the imported goods mysteriously disappeared, only to reappear on the black market. It would be deserted tonight—they hadn't had a delivery all week.

As she led him to his death, Angel fought to suppress a laugh. Her whole body was shaking with adrenaline and excitement. Would she ever kick this habit? Surely not when it felt so good. This was the best bit. The calm before the storm. She loved the pregnant deception of it all.

They were now alone in the darkened yard. Taking a deep breath, she turned.

"So shall we get started, honey?"

His right fist collided with her jaw, sending her crashing into the container behind her. Stunned, she raised her hands to defend herself, but the blows kept coming. She pushed him away, but the next blow nearly took her head off and she fell heavily to the ground.

What was happening? She tried to scramble to her feet, but he was already on top of her. Instinctively she lashed out. She had dealt with violent punters before, but always with the help of Mace—she had never engaged in hand-to-hand combat like this.

Now he was pinning her down, his strong hands encircling her throat. Squeezing harder, harder, harder. She rammed her fingers into his left eyeball, but he jerked his head away, out of her reach. She could see the blood pumping through a vein in his neck and she slashed at it with her fractured nails. Surely he would release his grip if he started to bleed out? It wasn't meant to be like this. She wasn't meant to die in this miserable place.

She fought for all she was worth. She fought for her life. But it was too little too late, and after only a few seconds the lights went out.

80

Tony was relieved to see that Nicola was asleep. It was late, but she often struggled to get to sleep. Tony knew that had she been awake, had those deep blue eyes looked up at him as he entered, he would have confessed everything to her. He wouldn't have been able to hold back, such were his feelings of confusion, exhilaration and shame. As it was, he just had to exchange a few stilted sentences with Violet— staring at the floor and claiming tiredness—before she went on her way and he was left alone with his wife.

Tony had never been unfaithful before and he still loved Nicola. Loved her even more, if that was possible, now that he had the shame of his infidelity weighing on his conscience. He didn't want to hurt her—he'd never wanted to hurt her—and they had always told each other everything. But what was he going to say to her now?

The truth was that he was still buzzing. He and Melissa had

made love twice more before he eventually left. The policeman at the door looked at the thick file under his arm and seemed to buy that he had been diligently taking Melissa's testimony all the while. Tony felt another pulse of shame; not only had he betrayed Nicola, he had betrayed his colleagues too. He had always been a good copper—where had this sudden fall from grace come from?

He knew where. Of course he did. He'd tried for so long to tell himself that his life with Nicola was the norm. That it was okay. He often told inquiring friends that he had married for life and that if these were the cards that they'd been dealt, then that was fine by him. But it wasn't and never had been. Not because he wanted more, but because *Nicola* had been so much more.

She had opened up everything for him. Whereas he came from a family of nomadic low achievers, she came from a family that was successful, cultured and driven. Whatever she did—whether in work or play—she did with utter determination, a will to succeed and a real sense of fun. And he missed her. He really, really missed her. Romantically she was impulsive and surprising, sexually she had been imaginative and mischievous, and emotionally she was always so giving. She could give him nothing of that now, and though he berated himself for thinking she was turning into his friend, that was the bitter truth of it. She would never be a burden, but she might be something less than his wife.

This, he had always thought, was the real betrayal. But what about Melissa, then? This was something new, something dangerous. It was crazy, but he already had feelings for her. It couldn't be love—because he'd only just met her—but it felt like something similar. Having been starved of love and affection for so long, he was now overdosing on it.

And he didn't want to stop.

81

Helen stood stock-still, barely able to breathe.

The first signs of trouble had come with repeated calls to her mobile from Southampton Central's Media Liaison unit, flagging repeated attempts by the *Mail* to get access to her. Then the same again from Hampshire Police HQ, and this time it was the editor of the *Mail* who had called. There was confusion all round—Media Liaison had assumed it was to do with their current investigation into the killings in Southampton, but actually they wanted to talk to Helen about someone called Robert Stonehill.

At the first mention of his name, Helen had switched off her phone and raced back to the nick. Once there, she had demanded sight of tomorrow's front pages. Most led on the ongoing hostage crisis in Algeria, but the *Mail* had gone for something different. SON OF A MONSTER was splashed across the front page and beneath it a grainy, sinister-looking picture of Robert, shot from a distance on a long lens. Marianne's police mug shot leered out underneath, with the details of her crimes rehashed with relish.

Dropping the paper, Helen sprinted from the media suite, down the stairs and out to her bike. As she raced to the outskirts of the city, one question kept swirling round and round her head. *How? How had they found out?* Emilia must be involved somehow, but Helen hadn't told anyone about Robert, so unless he had . . . No, it didn't make any sense. When had Emilia suddenly become omniscient, able to penetrate the most secret chambers of Helen's life?

All she wanted to do was find Robert and comfort him. Protect him. But as she approached Cole Avenue, she could already see the press pack assembling. A TV crew had just pulled up, and there was a growing crowd of hacks ringing the doorbell, demanding an interview. Helen's first instinct was to barrel through them to find Robert, but wisdom prevailed and she stayed where she was. Her presence would only inflame the story, and the Stonehill family had enough to deal with already.

How could she help him? How could she stop the shitstorm that *she* had brought crashing down on this innocent young man? This was her fault and she cursed herself bitterly for her weakness in ever contacting Robert. He had been happy. He had been ignorant. And now this.

In trying to save him, she had damned him.

82

She was splayed out on the ground, lifeless and pliable, her arms snaking out in capitulation. She was his now and he took his fill. He didn't bother to wear a condom. In a few hours he would be on his way to Angola aboard the PZR *Slazak*. By the time they found her, he would be long gone. He always made good use of his shore leave, and this time had been no exception.

It had taken him a while to gather himself after he'd strangled her. It always did. The adrenaline raged through him—his heart beating as if it were going to burst—and stars danced in front of his eyes. He was breathless and exhausted even in his triumph. The cuts on his face stung sharply and his senses were supercharged—every drip of water sounded like an approaching footstep, every blast of wind like a shrieking woman. But there was no one else here. It was just him and his prey.

She was just like all the others. Sinful, dirty and cheap. How many

had he killed now? Seven? Eight? And how many had fought back—
really fought back? None. This one had been tougher than most, but
like all the others, she *knew*. She knew that she was fallen—that she
had given away any chance of salvation thanks to her own depravity—
and that was why they were happy when he relieved them of their suffering. Did they know or care that they were going straight to hell?

He shuddered to a finish. Closing his eyes, he savored the moment. The tension that had been building up within him week upon
week was already starting to dissipate. Soon he would feel that all-
pervading calm that was so rare but so precious to him.

He opened his eyes, hoping to indulge himself with one last
look at her bloodless face. But as soon as he did so, he froze.

Her eyes were open. And she was looking straight at him.

Next to her was her bag. And in her right hand was a very large
knife.

"Bitch!"

The knife punctured his face with a sickening crunch. He blacked
out and within less than a minute Wojciech Adamik was dead.

83

She was on him in a flash. As she put her key in the lock, she felt him coming up fast behind her. Spinning, she grabbed the outstretched arm, swinging her attacker hard into the wall, while raising the key in her hand to eye level. She could blind her assailant in a second if she had to.

It was Jake. Breathless, panting, Helen dropped her arm to her side.

"What the fuck are you doing?"

Jake could hardly speak, winded by his collision with the hard brick wall, but eventually he said:

"Waiting for you."

"Why couldn't you ring like any normal person? Or wait downstairs?"

"I've tried ringing you, Helen. You know I have—I've left . . . what . . . five, six messages? You've not responded to any of them."

His raised voice echoed round the stairwell of the building. Downstairs, James had just crashed through the front door, with another young nurse in tow, so Helen quickly slipped the key in the lock and pushed Jake inside her flat.

"I was worried. I thought something might have happened to you. Then I thought I must have done something wrong. What's going on?"

Jake was now in her front room, surrounded by her books and journals. It felt profoundly odd to have him in her space, the context somehow all wrong.

"Emilia Garanita knows about us. She knows what I come to you for and she is threatening to expose me in the press."

Jake looked stunned, but Helen had to ask the question anyway.

"Did you tell her?"

"No, of course not. A hundred times, no."

"Have you told anyone else? Anyone who might know her, who might have a big mouth?"

"No, why on earth would I do that? What happens is between us and no one else—you know that."

Helen stared at the floor. Suddenly the weight of the day's events caught up with her and she started to cry. Furious with herself, she kept her head bowed, refusing to show her weakness, but her shoulders started to shake. Things had gone so horribly, horribly wrong and most of it was down to her own weakness and stupidity. Was she destined always to be on the losing side?

Jake crossed the room and enveloped her in a warm hug. It felt good. Some people despised her, others questioned her, still others thought she was odd. But Jake had never judged her, had always cared for her, despite the unusual nature of their relationship. Helen had been starved of unconditional love all her life, but she realized in that moment that this was what Jake wanted to give her.

She had always kept him at a distance, even when he'd signaled his desire to get closer to her. Which is why it surprised him as much as Helen when she finally looked up and said:

"Stay."

84

Sunlight flooded through the thin curtains. Charlie felt the warmth of the new day on her face and slowly opened her eyes. Memories, thoughts and feelings swirled round her fuzzy head, then suddenly she turned over, anxious to see if she'd dreamed it or not. But Steve wasn't there—he hadn't come home last night. It was no dream.

Charlie had tried ringing him repeatedly, but the calls had all gone straight to voice mail. Was he okay? Had something happened to him? She was sure Steve wouldn't have left her. His stuff was all here, and besides, he was a bigger man than that. He would never walk out without an explanation.

So where was he? And why hadn't he come home? After he had issued his ultimatum, Charlie had asked for time to think. She desperately wanted them to be together, to be a happy family, but to give up her career, give up everything she'd fought to achieve, was a huge sacrifice. But would any of it be worth it without Steve by her side? This was a circle Charlie couldn't square.

Perhaps she'd never understood the depth of his grief over the baby they'd lost. Steve had had a name in mind for it if it was a boy. He had teased her with that when she was first pregnant, refusing to let her in on the secret. He had never mentioned it subsequently, despite Charlie's attempts to get him to talk about it. After a while she'd stopped asking and because he was so solid, so self-contained, perhaps she had underestimated the effect it had had on him.

He was so insistent. So determined that she should do something else. Something safe that would allow them to start a family together. He had swallowed enough anger, enough anxiety, enough fear. Now it was up to Charlie to decide what life she wanted.

Except Charlie didn't know. Couldn't decide. The only thing she did know for sure was that she hated being alone in this big house.

85

He was under siege. They had had to disconnect the doorbell and pull out the phones in the end, but still the barrage of inquiries didn't stop. Journalists shouted through the letterbox, banged on the doors and the windows, asking for comments, for a photo opportunity. They were remorseless, merciless.

Robert had taken refuge with his parents, Monica and Adam, in their bedroom upstairs. They'd sat on the bed together, trying to block out the sound of the commotion outside by cranking up the radio. No one had really known what to say at first, too shocked to process the day's events, but finally Robert found his voice.

"Did you know?"

His first question had been tinged with bitterness and anger. Monica nodded, but was crying too much to speak, so Adam falteringly told Robert what he needed to know. His parents had known who his mother was when they'd adopted him, but they'd never wanted to know the details of her crimes, fearing that their horror would seep into their relationship with their cherished child. As far as they were concerned, the child was innocent. The slate was wiped clean, and by good fortune and the grace of God both he and they had been given an amazing opportunity. They had always referred to him as "their little blessing."

Robert didn't feel like a blessing now. After a couple of hours of fraught, painful discussion, he had retired to his bedroom, needing to be alone. He had lain on his bed, his iPod turned up to the max, trying to block out the hysteria of his life. But he couldn't, and he couldn't sleep either, so he'd just spent the time staring at the clock as it made its slow progress through the night.

Had Helen done this to him? He'd worked out who Helen really was even before Emilia Garanita told him. He'd shrugged Emilia off when she'd collared him at the convenience store, but not before she'd laid out the basics. Helen was his aunt, and his mother was a serial killer. As far as he could see, Helen had tried to protect him . . . but still she was the only person who knew his real identity. The only one who had a personal interest in him. Had she brought the walls crashing down on him?

His iPod lay discarded on the floor now and he could hear his parents arguing. They didn't deserve this either. What did it mean for their family now? They had loved him unconditionally for all of their time together, but they hadn't signed up for this. They were an ordinary, nice couple who'd never done a thing wrong in their lives.

He stole a glimpse out of the window and his heart sank. There were even more journalists out there than there had been before. They were under siege now. And there would be no escape.

86

Helen left the flat promptly, but the roads were already clogged with traffic and her ride to the police mortuary took twice as long as usual. She cursed herself for not leaving earlier, but she had been thrown by waking up next to Jake. It had been so long since that had happened that she'd been unsure of the etiquette. As it was, she allowed him a shower and breakfast, then asked him to leave. Oddly, that didn't feel awkward and their parting was friendly, even fond. They had talked into the small hours and then Helen had fallen asleep; she woke several hours later, fully clothed but refreshed. She wasn't quite sure what to make of it, but she knew that she didn't regret it.

On her ride to the police mortuary, Helen's thoughts turned once more to Robert. Should she attempt to contact him? Parking up, she pulled out her phone and swiftly typed a message. Her finger hovered over the button—would he want to hear from her? What could she possibly say? What if her message fell into the wrong hands or was hacked? Emilia would certainly stoop to those levels if she felt she could get away with it.

But she couldn't just say nothing. Couldn't leave Robert to face this alone. So she'd written a short text saying how sorry she was, how he should sit tight while she got local uniform to move the press on, and asking him to text her to let her know how he was. It was inadequate, grossly so in the circumstances, but what else could she say? Blasted by the cold wind ripping through the deserted mortuary car park, Helen hesitated once more, then pressed the Send button. She hoped with all her heart that it would make a difference, however small.

Jim Grieves was unusually quiet this morning, the first sign that he was aware of the chaos in Helen's life. More surprising still, he'd patted her arm as they'd walked to the slab. Helen had never known Jim to display any physical affection to anyone before, and she was touched that he felt the need to let her know he was rooting for her. She smiled her thanks; then they got on with the task at hand. Slipping on their masks, they approached the desiccated remains of Anton Gardiner.

"He's been dead about six months," Jim Grieves began. "It's hard to be precise. The vermin in that place have had a fine time. They've picked off his skin and most of his internal organs, but by dating the dried blood in his mouth cavity and nasal passage . . . six months is a reasonable guess."

"Was he murdered?"

"Absolutely. Your man *suffered* before he died. Both ankles were broken, kneecaps and elbows too. And his windpipe was cut deep— the blade edge severing his vertebrae. Whoever did this virtually cut his head off."

"Was he killed on-site?"

"Doesn't look like it. The lack of blood at the scene, the absence of any clothes, and the small hole that the body was forced into suggest that he was killed elsewhere, then hidden there. Before rigor mortis set in, your killer or killers scrunched him up and buried him—his bones were already broken, so he would have been more easy to manipulate."

"What about his heart?"

Jim paused, aware of the importance of the question.

"Still there. Or fragments of it. And what's left is still attached. It's been eaten by the rats—you can see the teeth marks if you look close."

Helen peered down at the interior of the dead man's chest.

"Like I say, we've found blood under the fingernails, in his nasal passage and in his mouth. Two blood types so far, so if you're lucky your killer's blood might be in there. Should have DNA for you in a few hours."

Helen nodded, but her attention remained fixed on what had once been Anton's beating heart. So much seemed to fit with the killer's MO, but the heart hadn't been removed. Was Anton a nursery slope for Lyra? Did she graduate from torture to mutilation with her later victims? Was Anton Gardiner the spark that set the blaze burning in her mind?

It was time to find out more about the life and times of the murdered pimp. Helen thanked Jim and headed for the exit, leaving the unusually taciturn pathologist alone with the man who had been eaten by rats.

"So what do we know about this guy?"

Helen was addressing the team, who were now crowded round her in the incident room.

"Anton Gardiner, small-time pimp and drug dealer," DC Grounds began. "Born 1988 to Shallene Gardiner, a single mum with numerous convictions for shoplifting. No father on his birth certificate and we're unlikely to make any headway on that score. We don't know much about Shallene, but we do know she was generous with her favors."

Despite the subject matter, a few female members of the team suppressed smiles. There was something endearingly old-fashioned about DC Grounds.

"Anton went to school at St. Michael's, Bevois, but left without any qualifications. His charge sheet starts when he's about fifteen. Possession, theft, battery. And then it just gets longer and longer. We never pinned anything major on him, though, and his times in prison were brief and to the point."

"So what about his girls?" Helen responded. "What have we got on that?"

"He ran girls from the mid-aughties onward," Charlie replied. "Had a fairly big stable. Picked up a lot of girls from care homes, got them onto drugs, then made them work for him. I've spoken to a few girls who had 'dealings' with him, and by all accounts he was a nasty piece of work. Controlling. Violent. Sexually sadistic. And very paranoid. He was always convinced that people were watching him, that his girls were plotting to leave him, and he would often inflict terrible beatings on them for no good reason. He never used a bank—didn't trust them—never carried ID and always had a knife close at hand, even when he slept. He was a guy forever looking over his shoulder."

Helen let that thought settle, then added:

"Was he successful?"

"He made good money," DC Sanderson replied.

"Any known enemies?"

"The usual suspects. No specific incidents around the time of his death."

"I'm guessing he wasn't married."

Sanderson smiled and shook her head.

"So why was he targeted?" Helen replied, wiping the smile off Sanderson's face. "And why was he hidden away? He's an unmarried, low-life pimp, so there's nothing to expose. He wasn't a hypocrite with a loving family waiting for him at home. He was what he was and made no attempt to hide it."

"And the heart was left intact," DC McAndrew added.

"Exactly—the heart wasn't removed. So what was the point? Why did she kill him?"

"Because he attacked her?" DC Grounds offered. "We know he used the old cinema to imprison and torture his girls."

"But he wasn't killed there," Helen interrupted. "He was murdered elsewhere, then buried at the cinema. It doesn't fit."

"Perhaps she bided her time—after he attacked her," DC Fortune said, picking up the thread. "Waited for the right time, then attacked him somewhere they wouldn't be disturbed. Maybe she dumped the body at the cinema as a message to other pimps—and the other girls."

"Then why bury it?" Helen countered. "Why hide him away if you want to make a point?"

Silence descended on the team. Helen thought for a moment, then:

"We need to find out where he died. Do we have any addresses?"

"We've got scores," DC Grounds replied, raising his eyebrows. "He liked to keep on the move. He was like a snail, moving round Southampton with his possessions on his back. Always trying to keep one step ahead of his enemies, real or imagined."

"Run them down, every last one. If we can find the crime scene, maybe we can link him to Lyra more clearly. We need to know the circumstances of his death. DC Grounds will take the lead."

Helen wrapped up the meeting and pulled Charlie aside. She wanted to quiz her on her progress in tracking down the other forum users, but she never got the chance. The front desk buzzed through with a development that stopped them all in their tracks—Angel had killed again.

87

"Looks like it was quite a struggle."

Charlie and Helen stood together in the freezing cargo yard, looking at the carnage in front of them. A young man—mid-twenties and heavily tattooed—lay on the tarmac, a large pool of blood encircling his head. A deep cut in the center of his face was being photographed by the SOC team, but what interested Helen was his torso. It had been slashed to ribbons in what looked like a frenzied knife attack, but his internal organs remained untouched.

Helen drew her eyes away from the grizzly sight in response to Charlie's comment. She was right. There was blood all over the place, splattered against the crates where someone had landed heavily, smeared over the ground where the struggle had taken place and spread in short bursts along the connecting pathway as the surviving party had fled. The footprints were small and looked to have been made by high-heeled boots—Angel.

"I guess she met the wrong guy this time," Charlie continued.

Helen nodded but said nothing. What had happened here? Why hadn't she drugged him like the others? It looked like a desperate fight to the death. Perhaps Charlie was right. Perhaps Angel's luck had finally run out.

"A sailor. Probably foreign. Probably unmarried. An odd choice for her." Helen spoke out loud, as she surveyed the strange tattoos on the body of the corpse.

"Perhaps victims are getting harder to find."

"But still she can't stop," Helen replied. It was a sobering thought.

Charlie nodded but said nothing. The body was partially clothed and Helen examined it more closely now. Presumably Angel had been disturbed by the encounter and had been unable to go to town on her victim in the usual way. His chest looked like it had been hacked at—there was none of her usual precision here. Just a frenzy of brutality.

"What have you got for me?" Helen asked the chief SOC officer.

"Deep laceration to the face. Virtually stabbed him through the eye. Death would have been instantaneous."

"Anything else?"

"Looks like he was involved in some kind of sexual activity tonight. He's got traces of semen on his penis and his hips are heavily bruised. Which suggests the sex was violent, possibly even rape."

Unbidden, Helen felt a flash of sympathy for Angel. Even after all these years, nothing affected Helen like sex crimes, and she only ever felt pity for the victims, however degraded they were. The aftermath of rape is like a slow death, a cancer eating away at you from the inside, unwilling to let you go, unwilling to let you live. Angel was unhinged, mad even, but an attack such as this would have plunged her further into the abyss.

She would be heavily bruised, perhaps badly injured too. Would she retreat from the world now and be lost from them for good? Or would she go out in one last blaze of glory?

88

The rain fell steadily and hard. It was attacking the city, not cleansing it, bouncing up off the pavement in angry bursts. Deep puddles were forming, blocking her path, but she didn't hesitate, marching straight through them. Water seeped into her trainers, soaking her aching feet, but she didn't stop. If she hesitated, she would lose her nerve and turn back.

She was frozen to the bone, her head pounding, her body screaming as the shock began to wear off. Sure that she stood out like a sore thumb, she quickened her pace. The faster she walked, the less she limped. She had a hoodie on and a baseball cap too, but still an observant passerby would clock the heavy bruising around her eyes and nose. She had a cover story ready, but she didn't really trust herself to speak. So she marched on.

Eventually the building came into view. Instinctively she hesitated—

through fear? shame? love?—then hurried toward it. She had no idea what to expect, but she knew that this was the right thing to do.

The place looked drab but friendly. She hammered on the door and waited, casting around to see if anyone was watching. But there was no one. She was alone.

No answer. She hammered again. For God's sake, every second made this worse.

This time she heard footsteps. She stepped away from the door, bracing herself for what was to come.

The door slowly opened and a stout, matronly figure emerged. She looked at the hooded figure and paused.

"May I help you?" Her tone was polite but cautious. "I'm Wendy Jennings. Have you come to visit someone?"

In response, the woman pulled back her hood and removed her cap. Wendy Jennings gasped.

"Dear God. Come inside, you poor girl. You need to have that looked at."

"I'm fine."

"Come on now. Don't be afraid."

"I don't want anything for me."

"Then what do you want?"

"This."

She unzipped her coat and brought out the soft bundle that had been hidden inside. Wendy looked down at the slumbering baby, swaddled in a warm blanket, and realized what was being offered to her.

"Take it, for God's sake," the woman hissed.

But now Wendy Jennings was drawing back.

"Listen, dear, I can see you're in trouble, but we can't take your baby just like that."

"Why not? This is a children's home, isn't it?"

"Yes, of course, but—"

"Please don't make me beg."

Wendy Jennings flinched at the tone. There was real distress there, but anger too.

"I can't care for her anymore," the woman continued.

"I see that and I understand, I really do, but there are ways of doing these things. Procedures we have to follow. The first thing we have to do is call Social Services."

"No social services."

"Let me call an ambulance, then. Get you seen to and then we can talk about your baby."

It was a trap. Had to be. She had hoped she would find someone good here, someone she could trust, but there was nothing for her here. She turned on her heel.

"Where are you going?" Wendy shouted. "Stay, please, and let's talk about it."

But she didn't respond.

"I mean you no harm."

"Like fuck you don't."

She hesitated, then turning, took a big step forward and spat in Wendy Jennings's face.

"You should be ashamed of yourself."

She marched off down the street without looking back, her baby clutched to her chest. Tears streamed down her face—fat, hopeless tears of impotence and rage.

Her last chance had gone. Her last shot at redemption.

Now there was only death.

89

It was hopeless. The police had moved the press pack back, reminded them of their responsibilities, but as soon as they departed, it started up again. The hammering on the door, the questions through the letterbox. A few had tried their hand round the back, clambering over the garden fence and rattling the back door. Peering in through the conservatory window like ghouls.

Robert and his parents now lived in perpetual darkness on the second floor. At first they thought they would be out of sight up there, but then they saw a photographer hanging out of a second-floor window across the road and they'd pulled the curtains firmly shut. Now they behaved like creatures of the night, huddling in the dark, eating food from tins and packets—existing rather than living.

At first, Robert had steered clear of the Internet, didn't want to go there. But when it's your only window on the world, it's hard to hold out. And once on it, he couldn't resist. The national papers had gone to town, bringing Marianne the bogeywoman back to life in all her glory. He didn't want his parents to see, knew it would hurt them, so locked away in his bedroom he read and read. Climbing inside his mother. He was surprised to feel a modicum of sympathy for her—she had clearly suffered terrible abuse and neglect—but her crimes made for grim reading. She had obviously been intelligent—more intelligent than he?—but not intelligent enough to pull herself back from the brink. Her life had ended in disgusting and depressing fashion. According to the *National Enquirer* Web site, the bullet had penetrated her heart and she had bled to death in her sister's arms. In the aftermath, Helen's life had been exposed and now it was his turn. Every failed exam, every minor indiscretion, every brush with the law had been seized on by the press. They wanted to portray him as a loser, a drifter, violent, a chip off the old block. A bad seed. He had been so enraged by the character assassination visited on him and his parents that when Helen Grace texted him with a message of support, he'd replied tersely and unpleasantly. Maybe the journalists could intercept their messages or maybe not. He didn't care.

Something had to be done. That much was clear. His parents were suffering terribly, unable to talk to or see their friends, tainted by association with him. Robert knew he had to draw the pack off, give them something else to think about. He owed that to the couple who had raised him since birth.

He toyed with the bandage that had recently swathed his injured arm, wrapping it over and over in his hands. A plan was forming in his mind. It was desperate and it meant the end of everything, but what else could he do? He was backed into a corner and now there was nowhere to run.

90

Tony was amazed at the transformation. He knew Melissa had asked for some fresh clothes and makeup, but even so he hadn't expected her to look so different. Up until now, he had seen her only in battle dress, the sex worker's uniform of boots, short skirt and low-cut top. Dressed in jeans and a jumper, with her hair tied back in a loose ponytail, she looked happy and relaxed.

She greeted him tentatively, as if not quite sure what to expect now that they had been apart for a little while. Truth be told, he hadn't been quite sure how to play it either, but now that he was here it seemed the most natural thing in the world to take her in his arms. Fearing detection, they had hurried upstairs, but this time passion wasn't on their minds. They simply lay side by side on the bed, holding hands and staring at the ceiling.

"I'm sorry if I've caused you trouble," Melissa said quietly.

She had obviously guessed that he was married, despite the fact that his ring was on his bedside table back at home.

"I didn't mean to."

"It's not your fault. So don't feel guilty . . . That's my job."

He managed a half smile and she responded.

"I don't want to make you unhappy, Tony. Not after you've been so good to me."

"You don't."

"Good. Because I've been thinking about what you said to me. And you're right. I do want to make a change."

Tony said nothing, unsure where this was going.

"If you can get me on to the right programs, to get off the drugs, then I'll do them. I don't want to go back on the streets. Ever."

"Of course. We'll do everything we can to help."

"You're a good man, Tony."

Tony laughed.

"I'm very far from that."

"People get hurt, Tony. That's the way life is. Doesn't make you bad. So don't go beating yourself up. You and I . . . we'll have what we'll have and then you can go back to your wife, no problem. I won't hold on to you, I promise."

Tony nodded, but not with any sense of satisfaction or relief. Was that what he wanted? A return to normality?

"Unless you want me to, of course," she continued with a smile. "But it's up to you. I've got nothing; you've got everything. If I were you, I'd do the smart thing and go back to your wife."

They lapsed into silence, staring once more at the odd cracks in the ceiling. A new future was being offered to him. It was completely insane, of course, and yet strangely made sense. But would he have the courage to seize it?

91

DC Grounds stood and stared. He had never seen anything quite like it. It was utter carnage.

Anton Gardiner had proved an elusive figure in death, as he had been in life—he had liked to move base constantly to keep the police and his competitors guessing. He hadn't owned any property, preferring short-term rentals, so that if he'd had to vanish suddenly, he would not have been left out of pocket. And in the end this had provided DS Bridges and his team with the breakthrough they needed. Anton Gardiner had dealt only in cash, hadn't liked the trail that checks and credit cards left, so a few hours hammering the phones, pressuring landlords into giving up the details of anyone who'd paid in cash for a short rental in the past twelve months—who might match Anton's description—had eventually yielded a result.

The landlord had been only too happy to help, opening up the basement flat on Castle Road for their inspection. But he was as shocked by what greeted them as Bridges was. Chairs were smashed, tables turned over, the only bed lay upside down on the floor, a shredded mattress lying on top of it—it was as if someone had declared war on the flat and shown it no mercy.

In the bedroom, beneath the ravaged bed, was a dirty brown stain that spread out in a jagged circle of at least a meter's diameter. DC Grounds instructed one of his officers to call for an SOC team, but he didn't need anyone else to tell him it was dried blood. Someone had bled out in this dingy room.

The stained patch of carpet was one of the few areas that hadn't been turned over. Even here, in this tiny room, the wardrobe had been smashed up, the corners of the carpet lifted. Scanning the other rooms in the flat, DS Bridges digested these developments. Two things were abundantly clear. First, someone—probably Gardiner—had been attacked and killed here. And second, someone had been looking for something.

But what was it? And why were they prepared to kill to get it?

92

"Are you absolutely sure?"

Helen was aware that she had raised her voice—several heads had popped up in the incident room—so she continued the conversation more quietly, pushing shut her office door.

"One hundred percent," said the voice on the other end of the phone. It belonged to Meredith Walker, chief forensics officer at Southampton Central. "We compared the DNA from the saliva on Gareth Hill's face with the DNA harvested from the two sources of blood on Anton Gardiner's body. There's no match. If the blood under Gardiner's fingernails is that of his killer, then he was killed by somebody else."

"Not by Angel?"

"Doesn't look that way. We're running it through the database to see if we can get a match. I'll let you know as soon as I have anything."

Helen ended the call. Once again this case had taken a lurch sideways. Whenever they seemed to get close to Angel, she drifted away again. Marching out of her office, Helen called Charlie over. Her news was hardly better—they were still no nearer to unmasking the other Bitchfest forum users. Which meant there was only one avenue to explore.

"Ask Sanderson to take over the search for now and come with me," Helen said to Charlie. "You and I have got a date with a liar."

93

"Hello, Hammer."

Jason Robins spun round to see Helen and Charlie entering his office. Rising from his desk, he hurried toward, then past them, shutting his office door quietly but firmly.

"Who let you in?" he demanded. "Don't you need a warrant or something?"

"We've just come for a chat. We told the girls at reception that we needed to speak to you urgently on a police matter, and once they saw our warrant cards they were more than happy to let us in."

Jason shot a look at the secretaries, who were now gossiping at their desks.

"I could do you lot for harassment. I've already had this one," he said, gesturing at Charlie, "e-mailing me day and night, phone calls . . . it's not on."

"Well, I'm sorry, but 'this one' has some more questions for you," Charlie countered. "Questions about Angel."

"Not this again."

"I have a picture that I would like you to look at."

"I've told you I don't know this 'Angel'—"

"Here," Charlie continued, ignoring his protests and holding out the sketch of Lyra. Reluctantly, Jason took it.

"Do you recognize this woman? Is she Angel?"

Jason looked up at Helen. Sweat was starting to form on his brow.

"For the last time, I never used Angel. I never met her. I was the victim of identity theft. Someone cloned my credit card and used it to—"

"So why haven't you reported it?" Helen barked, her irritation puncturing her professional poise.

"Sorry?"

"We spoke to your bank. Turns out you never reported any fraudulent activity on your card. In fact you've continued using it since our last interview. At Morrisons, at Boots—shall I go on?"

For once Jason had nothing to say.

"I'm going to give you one last chance, Jason. And if you don't cut the crap and tell me about Angel *right now*, I am going to arrest you for obstruction of justice," Helen continued, her volume rising. "I'm going to march you out in front of all your colleagues, but I'll make sure to leave DS Brooks behind. A few well-chosen questions from her will leave them in absolutely no doubt that their boss likes to sleep with prostitutes and then brag about it to other sad men online. We may even accidentally direct them to some of your posts. I'm sure they'd love to know more about Hammer and his big co—"

"All right, all right, keep your bloody voice down," Jason begged, shooting another look at his colleagues on the other side of the glass. Many of them were blatantly staring.

"Can we go somewhere else?" he entreated.

"No. Start talking."

Jason looked like he was about to protest, then slumped back into his chair.

"I never used her."

"What?"

"I never slept with Angel. In fact I only met her once."

"But your posts said you slept with her many times," Charlie interjected. "That you'd had her 'every which way.'"

There was a long silence. Jason's sweaty face was now pink with shame.

"I lied. I never slept with her. I've never slept with a prostitute."

"You made all that stuff up?" Helen replied, incredulous.

Jason nodded, his head hanging.

"I told the other guys what they wanted to hear."

"The other guys on the forum? 'PussyKing,' 'fillyerboots'—"

"Yes. I wanted to fit in. I wanted them to like me."

Helen shot a look at Charlie. His loneliness was tragic and for the first time Helen felt an ounce of pity for him.

"When did you meet Angel?"

"Four days ago. One of the other boys told me where I'd find her, so I went out looking. And there she was."

"What happened?"

"I picked her up. We drove toward the Common."

"And?"

"She wanted to talk. Was asking me questions. Small talk, you know. Then . . . then she asked me if I was married. And I don't know why, but it just hit me like a brick."

"How do you mean?"

"It set me off. It was just a simple question, but . . ."

Jason paused, emotion at the memory ambushing him now.

"But I started crying."

Finally he looked up. Helen was struck by the desperation in his expression.

"I told her everything. How I missed my wife. How I missed Emily."

"What did she do?"

"Not a lot. She didn't like me talking like that. She said a couple of things—'you'll get over it,' stuff like that—then asked me to stop the car."

"Then what?"

"She got out. She got out and walked away. And that's the last time I saw her—I swear to God."

Helen nodded.

"I believe you, Jason, and I know it's hard to talk about. But the truth is you had a very lucky escape. Believe me, things could have been a lot worse."

"And she's been . . . all these guys in the paper?"

"Yes, which is why it's so important we find her. So please take a good look at the picture and tell me—is that Angel?"

Jason picked up the sketch once more. He took a good look at it and then said:

"No."

Charlie shot a look at Helen, a look pregnant with alarm, but Helen ignored it. She could feel the case once more unraveling in front of her.

"Look again. Lyra Campbell is our number one suspect. This is a very good likeness. Are you sure that's not Angel?"

"Absolutely. It looks nothing like her."

And in that moment Helen knew they were back to square one.

94

Helen cursed herself bitterly. It was so obvious to her now how she and the rest of the team had been *played*. Sending Charlie back to base to gather the necessary evidence, Helen headed straight to the safe house, flanked by a pair of uniformed officers. Up until now Melissa had been treated like royalty—Helen wondered how she'd react to being bundled into the back of a squad car with a pair of cuffs on.

At first it seemed as if there was no one at home. Helen knocked on the door furiously—had Melissa somehow found out and done a runner? The officers outside insisted she hadn't left the building, but you could never be sure. Eventually, however, an eye appeared at the spyhole and then Melissa's throaty voice could be heard, asking accusingly who it was and what they wanted. She was surprised to find it was Helen. She was even more surprised—and aggrieved—to find herself in the interrogation room of Southampton Central half an hour later with the questions raining down on her.

"Why did you do it, Melissa?"

"Do what? What am I s'posed to have done?"

She spat the question back at Helen as if offended by the very implication of any wrongdoing. She really was in a vile mood.

"Why did you kill Anton Gardiner?"

"Are you kidding me?"

"Did he hurt you? Did you need money?"

"I never touched him."

Helen stared at her. Reaching to her right, she pulled a sheet of paper from her file.

"We've just received the full analysis of the blood found on Anton Gardiner's body. As you'd expect, he had a lot of his own blood on him—not surprising, given the level of violence visited on him. But there was another source of blood. There were traces of it beneath Anton's fingernails and even on two of his teeth—it appears he scratched and bit his attacker as he tried to defend himself."

Helen let that land, then continued:

"It's your blood, Melissa."

"Like fuck it is."

"I should say at this point that it would be advisable for you to have a lawyer present—"

"I don't need a lawyer. Who's been spreading lies about me?"

"We've got a match, Melissa. We ran the blood DNA analysis through the Police National Computer and your name came up."

Melissa glared, admitting nothing. Helen continued, pulling more sheets from her file:

"Three years ago you were involved in an altercation with another sex worker—Abigail Stevens. An argument over a client. She accused you of actual bodily harm, you did the same and, as is normal in these cases, both of you were asked for a DNA sample, which was taken via a mouth swab. It's standard practice to keep those on the national database for ten years."

Helen let this sink in before continuing:

"Now, maybe you thought we'd got rid of it, or perhaps you'd forgotten you'd ever even given it, but the fact remains it's your blood."

Melissa was about to interrupt, but Helen steamrollered over her.

"You killed Anton Gardiner and buried him at the old cinema. Then you heard the derelict building was coming up for sale. This gave you a bit of a problem, so when the chance came to palm your murder off on someone else, you took it. Anton was never one of Angel's victims; he was yours."

"You better have proof or you'll regret this."

"One of my officers carried out a search this morning of an address in Bitterne Park. Last known sighting of Anton put him near a basement flat he rented on Castle Road. The place had been torn apart, turned upside down, and there were historic traces of congealed blood in the bedroom. Lots of it. Yours and Anton's? We should have the analysis of those back shortly."

Melissa scowled. But Helen had seen her reaction to the mention of Castle Road and knew she had her on the run now.

"Anton didn't like to put down roots, did he? He was a man who liked to move around, cultivate an air of mystery. And there was a rumor that where he went, his cash went too. He didn't believe in banks, did he? And he always slept with a knife on his pillow. Now maybe you put two and two together or perhaps you heard the rumor. Either way, you needed the money, didn't you?"

"You're talking out of your fat arse."

"You had been evicted from your bedsit for nonpayment of rent and had large drug debts. You needed money. And Anton's stash fitted the bill perfectly. How much did he have?"

Melissa was about to respond, but swallowed it just in time. Clearly not enough, Helen thought, if the stash ever existed. Had she tortured and murdered her pimp for nothing?

There was a long, long pause, before Melissa finally replied: "No comment."

"I'm going to suggest we break now. During this interval you will have a chance to call a lawyer, which I strongly recommend you do. When we come back I'm going to caution you, then formally arrest you on suspicion of murder, GBH, wrongful imprisonment, theft and perverting the course of justice. Not to mention wasting police time. How does that sound?"

Finally, Helen's anger peeped through and Melissa was onto it in a shot. She was up on her feet, jabbing her finger at Helen across the table.

"Get Bridges."

"I'm sorry?"

"Get Tony Bridges. He'll sort this out."

"What do you—"

"Get him. NOW!"

As Helen walked back to the incident room, a dozen different scenarios spun round her mind, each one worse than the last. What did Melissa mean? What had Tony done? And why was she so confident he could straighten this out for her?

95

She pulled the freezer door open and let her forehead rest on the cool interior. Her head throbbed, the livid bruises on her face pulsed and she felt that she might be sick at any moment. The freezer compartment had frosted up through neglect and it felt like a cool, round hand cupping her face. For a moment, she felt at peace, almost calm. But then the cries started up again and reality bit.

Opening the fridge door, she pulled a Coke from the shelf. She drank it down in one go. Then, turning, she walked out, leaving the fridge door ajar, its weak light giving the dirty lino a sickly yellow hue.

Amelia was lying on the bed, screaming with hunger. She stared down at her baby for a minute, hating its dependence on her. Why her? Why couldn't this girl have been born to someone proper? Someone decent? She was the offspring of a whore and a killer. Damned before she'd even started.

Her head screamed worse than ever as the baby's cries rose in volume, so she quickly scooped her up and in one easy motion lifted up her top and guided Amelia's puckering mouth to her nipple. As her baby began to feed, she felt light-headed and dizzy. She hadn't slept at all last night, consumed with rage and despair, and now she felt weak and unsteady. Settling Amelia in the crook of her arm, she wriggled her way up the bed, so she could rest her head for a few moments. Amelia's tight grip on her nipple never weakened, the child blissfully unaware of her mother's anguish.

When she awoke moments later, Amelia was lying in her arms, sated and asleep, the milky residue of her feed coating her lips.

During the course of the night, she had thought of many ways to deal with her problem. At first she thought about leaving Amelia on the steps of South Hants Hospital or even giving her to someone in the street, but she knew she didn't want to hand her over to strangers now. She had lost faith in the milk of human kindness. Who knew what they might do to her? What torments she might endure? She couldn't go back to her family obviously, so that meant it was down to her.

After that, it was just a question of how she would do it. She couldn't strike her. Couldn't face the prospect of using a pillow either. Despite everything, she knew her nerve would fail her. Better to do it during a feed. Amelia liked the bottle well enough and if she crushed up the pills small . . . The chemist's would be open soon and she could get what she needed. Then it would all be over.

As simple as that. And yet she knew it would be the hardest thing she'd ever have to do. She knew she was bringing peace, so why did it twist her guts to think about it? She had killed without qualm, had enjoyed exterminating those filthy little weasels who called themselves fathers and husbands. *Pop, pop, pop.* But now she hesitated. It was not just that the baby was her flesh and blood—it was what she felt. She had fought it for months now, had tried to make herself *hate* the little thing, but she couldn't deny it any longer. She felt pity for it.

And that was an emotion she hadn't felt for a long, long time.

96

"I'm going to make this easy for you. Here."

Tony Bridges slipped an envelope across the pub table. Helen didn't break eye contact, trying to see inside the man she had always trusted.

"It's my resignation letter," Tony continued.

Helen hesitated, then finally dropped her gaze. Opening the envelope, she scanned the letter.

"Tony, this is premature. You've messed up big-time, but maybe there's a way we can deal with this, take you off operational duty, get you a desk job—"

"No. I need to go. It's best for me. And you. I . . . I need time to be with Nicola. I need to tell her what's happened. And see if I can earn her forgiveness. It's time for me to put her first for a change."

Helen could see he was resolute. She was gutted to lose one of her best officers—one of her best friends at the station—but he had made up his mind and there was no point fighting him.

"I thought you'd try to talk me round, so I also dropped a copy into Harwood's office on the way here."

Helen couldn't help but smile. This was typical Tony—diligent to the end.

"What happened, Tony?"

Tony looked her straight in the eye as he responded, refusing to duck his responsibility:

"I was weak. I wanted her and . . . It's not an excuse, but my life has been so . . . barren. So empty. And she offered me something I didn't have. Truth is, I'd probably still be with her if she hadn't . . . I needed to do it. Needed to remind myself what's important. What I love. I know now that I want Nicola. I want her to be happy, us to be happy. I've got some money put away, so . . . so I'm going to spend some time with my wife."

Helen was struck by his sense of purpose. For a man who'd been so lost, who'd fucked up so badly, Tony was suddenly completely clear in his mind what needed to be done. His strength of feeling was admirable, but it was still a terrible waste.

"I know I could try to wheedle my way out of it, but I've betrayed my wife and I've betrayed the force. When I first sat down with Melissa, I told her about Angel—what we knew, what we didn't know—and she created Lyra to fill in the gaps. Told me what I wanted to hear. She would never have been able to lead us down a blind alley if I hadn't revealed things, confidential things, about the investigation. I was suckered by the oldest trick in the book. To protect you, to protect the team, it's best I go."

Helen was about to interject, but Tony wasn't finished.

"If it's okay with you, I won't go back to the station again. I'd prefer that they remember me in a good light. As I was."

"Of course. I'll square it with HR and I guess your rep will be in touch. I'll try to get the best deal for you, Tony."

"You've done enough already. I'm just sorry that ultimately I did so little."

With that he stood up, emotion suddenly ambushing him. He clearly wanted to be gone and Helen didn't stop him.

"Take care of yourself, Tony."

He raised his hand as he left, but didn't turn round. He had been one of her most promising officers, her sounding board, and now he was gone. Angel was still out there and Helen was more alone than ever.

97

"What I'm about to tell you stays in this room. We can't afford any unnecessary distractions—this *cannot* leak out. So don't discuss it, don't tell your friends or partners. I want a total lockdown."

The team had assembled in the incident room at short notice, all except DC Fortune, who couldn't be found. Helen was loath to do this without everybody present, but she had no choice. She had to nip this in the bud.

"You've no doubt heard the rumors and I'm sorry to say that they are true. Tony Bridges had a sexual relationship with Melissa Owen and compromised the investigation."

The team clearly *had* heard the rumors, but it was still a hammer blow to have it confirmed.

"Lyra Campbell is a dead end, an attempt by Melissa to shift the blame for Anton Gardiner's murder onto someone else. She thought she could use Tony to get her off the hook. The only good thing to come out of this sorry mess is that she will do time for what she's done. Tony . . . Tony won't be coming back. He resigned this afternoon. Charlie will take over his duties."

Helen shot a look at Charlie, who for once wouldn't meet her eye. Helen hesitated, unnerved, then carried on.

"So we start over."

A couple of heads sank, so Helen carried on briskly.

"We have some new information that might be helpful. Forensics have done their analysis on the blood found at the cargo yard. There was plenty of blood on the crates and the ground that belongs to a female, blood type O, who is a heavy user of alcohol, sedatives and cocaine. More interestingly, there are raised levels of prolactin in her blood. Which strongly suggests that she's breast-feeding."

An audible gasp from the team. A surprising development and one that significantly raised the stakes.

"So maybe Angel has a baby, or recently gave one away, but either way, someone, somewhere will have come into contact with her. Could be a GP, a prenatal clinic, a drop-in center, Social Services, an A&E department or just the local branch of Boots. Thanks to Jason Robins, we now have a new e-fit of Angel that's strong on facial detail—DC McAndrew will distribute it—so I want everyone, and I mean everyone, out there asking the right questions in the right places."

The team was about to disperse, but was brought to a halt by DC Fortune's sudden appearance.

"The call was for the whole team, DC Fortune," Helen chided him.

"I know and I'm sorry, ma'am," replied the young officer, blushing. "But I was working on the techno angle with the boys . . . and I think I might have found something."

The team settled back down, expectant.

"We were trying to see if we could wriggle a way to the IP addresses of the other contributors on Bitchfest. See if we could locate any of the other men who'd had contact with Angel. We weren't having much joy but, looking over the posts, I noticed something. Certain recurring phrases and spellings."

He had Helen's interest now. She had an inkling where this was going, and if she was right, it changed everything.

"There were several men who used the forum a lot—anonymous contributors like 'PussyKing,' 'fillyerboots,' 'Blade,' 'BlackArrow,' who blogged their sexual encounters and encouraged other posters like Simon Booker, Alan Matthews and Christopher Reid to seek out Angel. They told them where they could find her and what she would do for them. I was rereading their posts while the techie boys were doing their thing and I noticed that on more than one occasion 'Pussy-King' had used the phrase 'splitting that bitch.' And I remembered that 'Blade' had used that phrase too. I noticed also that they both hyphen-ated 'blow-job,' as did 'fillyerboots.' Also, all three of them constantly misspelled the word 'Ecstasy' as 'Ecstacy.' So I pulled up all their posts and . . . the spellings, the punctuation, the typos are identical."

"So all this time we've been hunting down these three guys when actually—"

"They are all the same person," DC Fortune interjected.

"They are all Angel."

Even as she said it, Helen's head spun.

"She's been guiding her victims to her."

The team looked stunned. It was clear now why they had been unable to trace Angel's punters—because they didn't exist. How could they have got it so badly wrong?

"Right. We need to change tack immediately," Helen continued, rallying her shell-shocked troops. "We can assume the misspellings on the courier boxes were a deliberate attempt to make the killer appear ill-educated, even dyslexic. In fact she is educated and sophisticated. Her vocabulary is extensive, she is adept at using and manipulating IT and she has a phenomenally ordered brain, capable of planning and executing these murders with minimal risk to herself. She is not stupid. She is cunning, intelligent and bold."

The team was hanging on her every word as their first detailed image of their killer took shape before them.

"She is a heavy drinker and drug user and brought a baby to term recently. She probably has a history of prostitution, yet has never been arrested—her DNA is not in the national database. So she may be relatively new to the scene. She is presumably heavily bruised and perhaps injured following her latest attack. We have a lot to work with—we have the e-fit—but we have to be smart. Let's target the upper end of the market first—escorts, students—and think about the geography of these attacks. I'll bet she's hiding out somewhere in the central or northern parts of the city, so let's go find her."

The team hurried over to grab their e-fits, suddenly fired with a determination to bring this investigation to a close. The only one who didn't race over straightaway was Charlie. And Helen wanted to know why.

98

Charlie was heading away from the station fast—but not fast enough. Helen caught up with her before she made it across the road. She got straight to the point.

"What's going on, Charlie?"

"Sorry?"

"Normally you'd be right on this, but something's the matter."

Charlie looked at her boss. There was no point in lying to her; they were beyond that.

"It's Steve. He wants me to leave the force."

"I see," Helen replied. She wasn't surprised. "I'm sorry if I've made things worse for you. I could have handled Steve better."

"It's not your fault. It's been coming. Ever since . . ."

She didn't need to say it out loud.

"I understand. We need you. You know we need you, but ultimately you have to do what's right for you. I won't stand in your way and I'll back you whatever you decide, okay?"

Helen put a comforting hand on Charlie's arm.

"Thank you."

"And if you need to talk . . ."

"Sure."

Helen turned to go.

"And how are you?"

Helen paused, surprised by Charlie's question. Her eyes strayed to the newsagent's across the road and the *Evening News* board, which promised more revelations about Robert and Marianne. It wasn't hard to work out why Charlie was asking.

"I don't know how she does it."

"Who?"

"Garanita. She knows where I go, what I do. Who I see. She knows *everything*. It's like she's climbed inside of me and . . . I don't know how she does it."

"A leak in the team?"

"No . . . this isn't just about the investigation. It's about me. Personal stuff. She's just a ghost following me into every room of my life."

Helen hated looking lost in front of Charlie, but there was no point in concealing her profound hurt from someone who'd been through hell with her already.

"You've beaten worse than her. You mustn't let her win."

Helen nodded. She knew Charlie was right, but it was hard to be optimistic when she was so badly on the back foot.

"She's a worm," Charlie continued. "She's not worthy to stand on the same street as you. Whatever she's got, you're Helen Grace. You're a hero. No one will ever be able to destroy that. I believe in you and so should you."

Helen looked up, grateful for Charlie's support.

"As for Emilia Garanita," Charlie continued, "she'll get hers soon enough. Her sort always do."

Charlie smiled and Helen responded. Shortly after, the two women parted.

Walking back to the station, Helen was momentarily buoyed up—pleased to have received a pep talk from a woman she had tried so hard to push away. Reaching the atrium, she realized that her phone had been switched off since the news of Robert's identity had broken. When she turned it back on, a host of voice mail messages sprang up and with them the text from Robert.

It read simply: *Fuck you.*

99

It was late when Charlie got home. The clock read eleven fifteen p.m. and the house was quiet. There was no sign of—

"Hello."

Charlie jumped out of her skin as Steve's voice rang out. She turned to find him sitting in darkness in the living room. She crossed the room, flicking on the lights. He frowned, offended by the harsh glare of the halogen.

"I've been waiting for you for hours, but I guess you were working late."

His tone was neutral and there was none of the bitterness Charlie had been expecting. Still, his even tone unnerved her. He sounded businesslike.

"Where have you been?" she asked. She felt that something

momentous—something bad?—was about to be said, but she was still so relieved that he had come home.

"At Richard's."

His best friend. Charlie had called him when looking for Steve, and he had lied to her. She was not surprised.

"I've been doing a lot of thinking. And I've come to a decision," Steve continued.

Charlie tensed, saying nothing.

"I want to have a child, Charlie." Now it was his turn to sound upset. "I want a baby with you more than anything else in the world. But we can't do that when you're working like this, putting yourself in harm's way every day. I can't go there again. Do you understand?"

Charlie nodded.

"I'm asking you to leave. So we can have the life we always wanted. And if you can't do that, or won't . . . then I don't think I can stay."

There it was. The ultimatum that had been coming for eighteen months.

The legacy of the abduction that had nearly cost her her life.

100

It was past midnight and the incident room was deserted. Those officers who weren't chasing up leads were asleep in bed, aware that another punishing day awaited them tomorrow. Helen had gathered up the case files and was looking for something to put them in. It wasn't good practice to remove them from the station, but she wanted to take them home and pore over them once more with a fresh pair of eyes. Once again, she cursed herself for having been led so easily down a blind alley.

Clip-clop. Clip-clop.

Someone was coming down the deserted corridor.

Detective Superintendent Ceri Harwood. Immediately Helen's defenses were raised. She hadn't seen or heard Harwood for a while, and that suddenly made her very nervous.

"Working late?" Harwood asked.

"Just finishing. You?"

"Yes, but that's not really why I'm here so late. I wanted to talk to you alone and it seems the witching hour is the best time to find you."

A little insult casually thrown in. Helen had a nasty feeling she was being ambushed.

"I didn't want to do this when the team were here. These things are best done . . . gracefully."

"Meaning?" Helen replied.

"I'm taking you off the case."

There it was—out in the open.

"On what grounds?"

"On the grounds that you've ballsed up, Helen. We have no suspect, no one in custody and five bodies on the slab. And I have a chief investigating officer who's been so distracted protecting her bad-seed nephew that she failed to spot that her own deputy was fucking a key witness."

"I think you're being unfair. We've made mistakes, but we are closer than we've ever been to finding her. We're in the endgame now and with the greatest of respect, I would sug—"

"Don't pretend you've ever had any respect for me, Helen. I know what you think. And if you'd even vaguely tried to hide your . . . contempt, it might not have come to this. But the truth is that you're bad news, Helen. You spread contagion wherever you go and I have no confidence in your leadership of this investigation. Which is why I was forced to go to the police commissioner."

"Who's taking over?"

"I am."

Helen smiled bitterly.

"So just as we are finally getting close you climb on board? Is this how you work? Is this how you've climbed so high without ever actually *doing* anything?"

"Be careful, Helen."

"You're a glory hunter. A parasite."

"Call me what you will. But I am now in charge and you are out."

Harwood paused, enjoying her moment of victory.

"I'll handle the press—"

"I bet you will."

"And I'll tell the team tomorrow morning first thing. Why don't you tidy up here and take a week's leave? We'll find something else for you when you come back. Perhaps you can tidy up the Alexia Louszko murder?"

"You'll be lucky if you see me here again."

"That's entirely your decision, Helen."

Having said her piece, she left, flinging a cursory "Good night" over her shoulder. Helen watched her go, a riot of emotions firing through her as she realized the comprehensive nature of her defeat. She had been routed. The investigation and her career were now in ruins and there was nothing she could do about it.

101

She wouldn't look at him. However much he begged her to, she wouldn't look at him. Her eyes stared resolutely at the window, seeing nothing. Tony Bridges walked round to the other side of the bed, but as he neared Nicola's line of vision, she swiveled her glance the other way. As she did so, tears ran down her cheeks.

Tony was crying too. He had started to weep before he'd even finished his confession. An overwhelming sense of shame had crept up on him, making his mea culpa faltering and ragged. He had seen alarm in Nicola's eyes at first—concern perhaps that a family member had died or he'd lost his job—but slowly her eyes had hardened and narrowed as the nature of his crime became clear. So they remained apart in the small room, more apart than they had ever been in their whole married life.

What could he say to her? How could he make things right? He had sought in the arms of another woman something that his wife would never be able to give him.

"I know you probably hate me. And if you want me to leave, then I won't fight you. But I *want* to be here. I've resigned from the force, so I can start to repair the damage I've done, make some changes to my life, be the husband you deserve."

Nicola stared resolutely at the open doorway.

"I want to be how we were before. The early days when we never spent a night apart, lived in each other's pockets. I . . . I made a big mistake and though I can never make up for it . . . I'd like it to be a new beginning for me. For us."

Tony hung his head, once more ambushed by the possibility that Nicola would call time on their marriage and throw him out on the street. Why had he been so stupid? So selfish?

Still Nicola refused to react. In conversation, she would normally blink once for yes and twice for no, but so far her eyes had remained resolutely still. Her cheeks were wet, so Tony reached out to pat them dry with a tissue. Nicola closed her eyes and held them shut, refusing to look at him as he stroked her cheek.

"Maybe you'll never want me again, but I want to try. I really want to try. I'm not going to force it on you and if you want me to go and get your mother now, tell her what's happened, then I will. But if you want me, then let me try to make things better. No more nights apart, no more snatched conversations. No more caregivers, no more strangers. Just you, me . . . and Charles Dickens."

He walked round to the head of the bed and for the first time today she didn't look away.

"It's up to you, love. I'm in your hands. Will you let me try?"

The silence in the room was all-consuming—all Tony could hear was his heart thumping. He felt like he was about to burst, but then Nicola's eyelid finally moved.

It came down once and stayed shut.

102

The Student Counseling Centre was situated at the scruffy end of Highfield Road in Portswood. It was close to the University of Southampton campus, but also served students from Southampton Solent University and the National Oceanography Centre—if they could be bothered to trek that far north. DC Sanderson stood outside it now, rolling back and forth on the balls of her tired feet as she waited for Jackie Greene to turn up. Students are night owls and counselors are often kept up late as a result, but still it irritated Sanderson that Greene was late. She was a grown woman—the center's head of service and its most experienced counselor—surely she could be on time for a meeting with the police?

When the overweight Ms. Greene eventually turned up, the reason for her tardiness quickly became clear. She didn't really like the police. Was this because of her left-wing politics (there were National

Union of Students and Greenpeace stickers all over her desktop computer) or her solidarity with the students, who she believed had been roughed up by the police during recent demonstrations against cutbacks at the university? Either way, she was not keen to help. But Sanderson didn't mind. She was in a bad mood and up for a challenge.

"We are focusing on female students who are, or have been, sex workers. She probably uses drugs and alcohol, may be prone to violence, and we believe recently had a baby."

"That's a lot of 'may' and 'probably,'" Greene replied unhelpfully. "Have you spoken to the local maternity units?"

"Of course, but your organization caters to the whole student population, and as such you're best placed to help us," Sanderson replied, dismissing Greene's attempt to deflect her questions.

"What makes you think she's a student?"

"We don't know that she is. But she's young, articulate and very computer literate. This is not some brainless kid who dropped out of school. This is someone who had—has—a lot to offer but has gone very badly off the rails. If she does or did have a baby, it's essential we find her as soon as possible. We have an e-fit here that I'd like you to look at, to see if it jogs any memories."

Jackie Greene took the e-fit.

"She's probably heavily bruised or injured following a recent fight. If anyone like this has called or visited you—"

"I don't recognize her."

"Look again."

"Why? I've told you once I don't recognize her. So unless you're doubting my word—"

"I'm not sure you realize how serious this is. There are five people dead already and there will be more unless she is apprehended, so I want you to think. Has your organization been contacted by a student working in the sex industry who fits this description?"

"God, you really have no idea, do you?" Greene replied, shaking her head.

"I beg your pardon?"

"We have dozens . . . scores of girls matching that description phoning us every week. Do you know how expensive it is doing a degree these days? I'm guessing not."

Sanderson let the insult ride over.

"Go on."

"I'm not going to give you names. The sessions are completely confidential. You should know that."

"And you should know that in extraordinary circumstances—which these most definitely are—I can apply for an order of court forcing you to open up your files. Which means that we will pore over every detail of every student who's ever got in touch with you."

"You can threaten me all you like. I'm not giving you names."

"I'll ask you again. Has anyone matching the description been in touch?"

"Are you deaf, dear? There are *lots* of girls who match the description. They run out of money, turn to prostitution, can't handle it, but by that point it's too late. So they drink or take drugs to deal with it and many suffer violence, rape and pregnancy scares along the way. Some of these girls have courses that are six, seven years long, and Mum and Dad can't pay for them and the government's sure as hell not going to help them, so what can they do?"

Sanderson felt a little tingle down her spine, as a thought took hold.

"Back up a minute. Would you say that girls with longer courses are more likely to fall into prostitution?"

"Of course. Makes sense, doesn't it? It costs them tens of thousands of pounds to finish a course like that and prostitution pays better than bar work, so . . ."

"And what sort of courses last that long?"

"Vets, some engineering degrees, but mostly it's the doctors. Medicine."

"And have you recently had a medical student get in touch who might match our description?"

"More than one. But as I said, I'm not giving you any names."

Jackie Greene sat back in her seat, arms folded, daring Sanderson to go and get a warrant. She would if she had to, but she had another thought on how she could get what she needed. She left the counseling center and headed for the university's main administration building. An image was forming in her head and she wanted to run it to ground as quickly as possible. After all, who better to carry out a DIY thoracotomy than a former medical student?

103

She should have gone hours ago, but still Helen couldn't leave. It was nearly nine a.m.—the team would be assembling now—and Harwood would no doubt wait until they were all there before sweeping in and taking control. She was good at timing these things to maximum effect. She would get one of the startled team to bring her up to speed, before issuing tasks. All of which meant Helen had an hour, two tops, before she was out for good.

She had removed the case files from the incident room and holed up in a damp interview room that was generally avoided. All through the night she had been going over the vast cache of documents in the numerous files, trying to see through the mass of details to the important connections. Working backward from the most recent, messiest murder, she had been searching for correlations and parallels, hunting for pointers to why Angel had been driven to kill and what she would do next. Did these men have any connection to the student world? Had they used an escort service that recruited a "better" sort of woman? What had set her off? Who was she angry with? Questions, questions, questions.

As sunrise came and went without progress, Helen had gone back to first principles. Who was Angel and what had precipitated this killing spree? What was the spark that lit the fire?

Opening the Alan Matthews case file, she reread the details for the umpteenth time. She was so tired now that the words swam in front of her eyes. Throwing down another slug of cold coffee, she turned to the pictures from the crime scene instead. She had seen them numerous times, but they still made her feel nauseous—the bloated torso opened up for all to see.

For all to see. The phrase buzzed round her mind as she took in Alan Matthews's corpse. Suddenly her eyes zeroed in on the hood, which had been placed carefully over his head before death. Helen had always dismissed this as Angel's security—an attempt by a nascent killer to hide her identity in case it all went wrong and the victim escaped. But what if it signified something else? She had taken her time on the others—she had abused them, then split them open with a steady hand, enjoying herself. The DIY thoracotomy, as Jim Grieves had put it, carried out on Alan Matthews was more ragged, more brutal. Was this because she was an amateur or was something else at play? Was she nervous?

Helen shot a look at the clock. It was half past nine now. Surely her time was almost up. Yet she felt she was onto something, as if the jigsaw puzzle were trying to assemble itself in front of her. She had to keep going and hope against hope that she would not be found. Her phone started buzzing, but she ignored it. No time for distractions now.

The hood. Focus on the hood. The one distinguishing feature of the first murder. Angel might have wanted to conceal her identity in case the victim escaped *or* she might have done it because . . . she didn't want to look her victim in the eye when she carried out the mutilation. Was she scared of him? Scared her nerve would fail her? *Did she know him?*

The hood wasn't used to suffocate him and wasn't employed in the later murders, so what made her first victim unique? Did he have some kind of power over her? Why was Alan Matthews special? He was a hypocritical, corrupt sexual deviant with an interest in evangelical religion and a passion for beating his family . . .

An echo of a memory. Something calling to Helen. Suddenly she was tossing the files aside, looking for the surveillance file that DC Fortune and his team had assembled on the Matthews family. There was a mass of mundane details, time logs, all of which might help, but Helen discarded them for the photos from the funeral. Helen had been there, for God's sake—had the answer been under her nose all along?

Photos of the cortege leaving the house, of the mourners arriving, of the family departing the church. All of them inviting the same question. There was Eileen, being supported by her elder daughter, Carrie. And there were the twins, smart in their dark suits. But where was Ella? When he was alive, Alan Matthews had made great play of being a father of four, the fertile paterfamilias of a close-knit, disciplined and devout family, so where was his younger daughter? Why hadn't she turned up at the funeral? And, more important, why had the family never mentioned her—during police interviews, during the funeral orations. Why had Ella been airbrushed out of the family?

As that thought landed, another punched through. The heart. All the other hearts had been delivered to places of work, but not Alan Matthews's heart. That was delivered to the family home. Surely that had to be significant?

Helen's phone started buzzing again. She was about to reject it—expecting it to be an irate Harwood—but she recognized the number and answered it instead.

"DI Grace."

"Hi, boss, it's me," DC Sanderson replied. "I'm at the university's admissions office and I think I may have something for you. I was going through the list of students who dropped out of their studies this year, looking particularly at female medical students. One name came up."

"Ella Matthews?"

"Ella Matthews," Sanderson confirmed, surprised by her boss's prescience. "She was a good student for the first year, then went badly off the rails. Late work, turning up to classes drunk or stoned, aggressive behavior to other students. Her welfare officer suspected she may have resorted to prostitution because she had no money coming in from family. She was a mess. Six months ago she vanished."

"Good work—stay on it. Find her friends, tutors, anybody who can give us more information on where she liked to go, where she felt safe, where she bought her drugs, anything. She's our number one suspect—leave no stone unturned."

Sanderson rang off. Helen knew she had no right to issue orders, but now that they were finally onto something, she was damned if she was going to let Harwood mess it up. This case still felt like hers and she wasn't prepared to give it up yet. Bagging up the files, Helen hurried from the room.

Her time was limited, but she knew there was one person who could reveal the truth. And she was on her way to see her now.

104

It was past ten o'clock. They should both have left for work hours ago. But instead they lay there together, happy and warm in a postcoital glow, neither moving a muscle. After all the emotion and heartache of the past few hours, it felt so good just to be quiet and still.

After Steve had delivered his ultimatum, Charlie's initial instinct had been to kick back at him. She hated being boxed into a corner, forced to choose between being a mother or a copper. But even as she accused him of moving the goalposts, of breaking his word, she knew that the fight was going out of her. If it really was down to a choice of the job or him, then Steve would win every time. Charlie loved being a policewoman—it was all she'd ever wanted to be and she had paid a heavy price for that ambition. But she couldn't imagine life without Steve, and he was right. There *was* a hole in their life, the indelible shape of the baby Charlie had lost during her incarceration.

They had circled each other for hours, but eventually Charlie promised to leave her job. At that point Steve had cried. Charlie too. Before long they had ended up in bed, making love with a passion and urgency that surprised them both. They had eschewed contraception, a silent acknowledgment that things had changed and there was no way back.

It felt so nice, so decadent, to be lying here with him. She had turned her phone off and pushed away thoughts of Helen and the team, who were no doubt wondering where she was. She would call Helen later and explain.

If she felt a spasm of guilt at the thought—more than a spasm, actually—Charlie ignored it. She had made her decision.

105

Helen was sure Eileen Matthews would slam the door in her face, but for once luck was on her side. One of the twins answered the door and, on seeing Helen's warrant card, let her straight in. As he ran upstairs to fetch his mother, Helen took a detailed look at the living room. Everything she saw confirmed her suspicions.

Eileen Matthews marched into the room. She clearly had a speech prepared, but Helen wasn't in the mood to be lectured.

"Where's Ella?" Helen barked, nodding at the framed photos on the living room walls.

"I'm sorry?" Eileen retorted.

"I see photos of you and Alan. Lots of photos of the twins. And Carrie—at her confirmation, her wedding, holding your first grandchild. But I don't see *any* photos of Ella. You and your husband were very big on family. So I'll ask you again—where's Ella?"

It was as if she had just punched Eileen in the face. She was temporarily robbed of speech, her breathing short and unsteady. For a moment, Helen thought she might faint, but then finally she replied:

"She's dead."

"When?" barked Helen, incredulous.

Another long pause. Then:

"She's dead to us."

Helen shook her head, suddenly furious with this foolish, bigoted woman.

"Why?"

"I don't have to answer these quest—"

"You do, and if you don't start talking right now, I am going to drag you out of this house in cuffs. In front of your boys, in front of your neighbors—"

"Why are you doing this to us? Why are you making—"

"Because I think Ella killed your husband."

Eileen blinked back at Helen twice, then slowly collapsed onto the sofa. In that moment Helen knew that whatever else she'd concealed, Eileen had never even considered that her daughter might be involved in Alan's murder.

"I didn't . . . is she even in Southampton?" Eileen said eventually.

"We believe she's living in the Portswood area."

Eileen nodded, though how much she was taking in was hard to say. A long, heavy silence followed, which was suddenly and inopportunely broken by the sound of Helen's mobile ringing. Harwood. Helen rejected the call, then turned her phone off and seated herself on the sofa next to Eileen.

"Tell me what happened."

Eileen said nothing, still in shock.

"We can't bring Alan back. But we can stop others dying. You can do that, Eileen, if you talk to me now."

"She was always the bad seed."

Helen flinched at the phrase but said nothing.

"She was a sweet girl when she was young, but when she was a teenager, she changed. She wouldn't listen. Not to me. Not even to her father. She was rebellious, destructive, violent."

"Violent to whom?"

"To her sister, her brothers, kids who were smaller than her."

"So what did you do about it?"

Silence.

"What happened to her after these incidents?" Helen continued.

"She was disciplined."

"By whom?"

"By Alan, of course," she replied, as if confused by the question.

"Why not you?"

"Because he's my husband. The head of the family. I am his help-meet and I support him in any way I can, but it's his duty to correct us when we require it."

"'Us'? He disciplined you too?"

"Of course."

"Of course?"

"Yes, of course," Eileen replied defiantly. "I know the modern world frowns on physical punishment, but we and the other members of our church have always believed that beatings are necessary if people are to learn—"

"And is that what Ella received—beatings?"

"To begin with. But she *wouldn't* learn. When she was a teenager she would get into fights, go with boys, take drink—"

"And what happened to her then?"

"Then Alan disciplined her more firmly."

"Meaning?"

"Meaning he hit her. With my blessing. And if she still refused to be contrite, Alan took her down to the cellar."

"And then?"

"He'd make sure she learned her lesson."

Helen shook her head, stunned by what she was hearing.

"You may shake your head," Eileen suddenly erupted, "but I have three healthy, obedient children who know right from wrong, *because* of their upbringing. Because we brought them up to respect their father and through him—"

"Did Alan enjoy punishing his children?"

"He never shied away from his duty."

"Answer the fucking question."

Eileen paused, stunned by Helen's sudden outburst.

"Did your husband enjoy punishing his children?"

"He never complained about having to do it."

"And did he enjoy beating you?"

"I don't know. It wasn't about 'enjoyment'—"

"Did he ever go too far? With you?"

"I . . . don't—"

"Was there a time when you asked him to stop and he wouldn't?"

Eileen hung her head and said nothing.

"Show me the cellar."

Eileen resisted at first, but the fight was going out of her, and a couple of minutes later she and Helen were standing in the freezing-cold room. It was desolate and dark, four walls of rough brick, almost entirely empty except for a stacking chair in the middle and a locked plastic crate in the corner. Helen shivered, but it wasn't the cold making her shake.

"What's the chair for?"

Eileen hesitated and then said:

"Alan would secure Ella to the chair."

"How?"

"With handcuffs, round her ankles and her wrists. Then he'd use a whip or a chain from the box."

"Beat some sense into her?"

"Sometimes."

"Sometimes?"

"You have to understand what she was like. She wouldn't obey him. Wouldn't listen. So *sometimes* he had to use other methods as well."

"Such as?"

Eileen thought for a moment.

"It would depend on what she'd done. If she'd blasphemed, then he would make her eat excrement. If she had stolen, he would fill her mouth with coins and make her swallow them. If she'd been with boys, he . . . he would beat her between her legs to make sure she wouldn't do it again—"

"He tortured her?" Helen roared.

"He corrected her," Eileen retorted. "You don't understand. She was wild. Ungovernable."

"She was *traumatized*. Traumatized by your bully of a husband. Why didn't you intervene, for God's sake?"

Eileen could no longer look Helen in the eye. For all her conviction, without her husband present, nothing seemed certain anymore.

Helen continued in a more soothing tone:

"Why her and not the others?"

"Because they did as they were asked."

"Carrie—how old was she when she got married?"

"Sixteen. She finished her schooling, then married a good man."

"From the church?"

Eileen nodded again.

"How old was her husband? When they married?" Helen continued.

"Forty-two."

Eileen suddenly looked up, as if searching for Helen's disapproval.

"Young girls need discipline—"

"So you said," Helen interrupted firmly.

A heavy silence followed. This room had been so full of misery, so full of vitriol, hatred and abuse. How powerless must the young girl have felt down here alone with her bully of a father, while he abused her physically and verbally. It conjured up images of her own childhood long since buried, which Helen pushed away forcefully now.

The twins were getting restless, calling down to their mother. Eileen turned to go, but Helen caught her arm, stopping her in her tracks.

"Why did she leave?"

"Because she was lost."

"Because she wouldn't give up school and marry a guy old enough to be her father?"

Eileen shrugged, resentful now of Helen's presence and the judgment it brought.

"She wanted to study, didn't she? She wanted to be a doctor. In spite of everything that had happened to her, she wanted to help people?"

"It was the school's fault. They put ideas in girls' heads. We knew it would end in tears, and it did."

"What do you mean?" Helen responded.

"She walked out on us. Disobeyed her father, said she would find her own ways to fund her 'studies.' We all knew what that meant."

There was almost a bitter glee in Eileen's voice now.

"What happened to her?"

"She took to prostitution. Took money from strangers who . . ."

"How do you know this?"

"Because she told us. When she came home with a bastard child in her belly."

Helen breathed out, the full tragedy of Ella's life slowly taking shape in front of her.

"Whose was it?"

"She didn't know," Eileen replied, but now the glee had vanished from her voice.

"Why not?"

"She . . . she had got herself into trouble. A group of men who'd . . . who'd tricked her into going to their flat."

"And raped her?"

Suddenly Eileen was crying, her head hanging low, her shoulders shaking gently. For all the dogma, perhaps there was still a mother in there somewhere.

"Eileen?"

"Yes. They . . . they kept her there for two days."

Helen closed her eyes. She wanted to flee from the horror of Ella's ordeal, but the images forced themselves into her brain.

"Afterward they said they'd slit her throat if she told anyone," Eileen continued falteringly.

"And she came home when she discovered she was pregnant?"

Eileen nodded.

"And what happened?"

"Alan turned her away. What else could he do?"

She looked up imploringly, as if begging Helen to understand. Helen wanted to shout and scream at her, but swallowed down her rage.

"When was this?"

"Six months ago."

"And after that she was airbrushed out of the family?"

Eileen nodded.

"Before that, Alan had told people she was working overseas . . . for a medical charity. But afterward, he told everyone she was dead."

"And the photos?" Helen asked, hoping against hope for a recent picture of their killer.

Eileen paused, before once more looking up at Helen with tears in her eyes.

"He burned every single one."

106

Helen sprinted to her bike, switching her phone back on as she ran. Seven voice mail messages. They would all be from Harwood, but Helen didn't have time for that now. She dialed Sanderson instead.

It rang and rang. Then:

"Hello?"

"Sanderson, it's me. Can you talk?"

There was a momentary pause, then:

"Oh, hi, Mum, give me *one* second."

Clever girl. There was a longer pause, then the sound of the fire door swinging open and shut.

"I shouldn't even be talking to you," Sanderson resumed in a hushed voice. "Harwood is going nuts looking for you."

"I know and I feel bad asking for one more favor, but . . . I need you to find Carrie Matthews. Find out what she knows about her sister's movements and see if you can get a photo from her. If she hasn't got one, try the university. Alan Matthews destroyed all their photos of her after she turned up pregnant following a gang rape. Ella Matthews is our killer—I'm a hundred percent certain of that. The priority for you and the team now must be to bring her in before she kills again."

"On it. I'll call you when I have news."

Climbing the stairs to Jake's flat, Helen felt a mixture of panic and relief. Relief at seeing him, but also anxiety at the darkness rising within her. Strong as she was, there were always moments when it took her. The world was full of viciousness and sometimes she was thrust right back to a time when *she* was the world's punching bag, when she and her sister had taken the sins of the world upon their shoulders. She was jumpy now, unable to contain the panic spiking inside her, the feeling that any minute, she would be back there in that room.

Jake wanted to hold her, but she wouldn't let him. She chained herself up without being asked and told him to get on with it. She knew she was being rude and aggressive, but she needed this badly.

"Now."

Jake hesitated.

"Please."

Then he relented. Taking a medium-sized crop from his armory, he raised his arm and brought it down firmly on her naked back.

"Again."

He raised it again. This time he wasn't so reluctant—he could feel the charge flowing out of Helen's body, as her anxiety escaped. He brought the crop down again, then again, his excitement rising as the rhythm of the beating took hold. Helen was moaning now, demanding more pain. Jake gave it to her . . . faster and faster.

Eventually the beating slowed as Helen relaxed and before long everything was calm once more.

Helen relished this moment of stillness. Her life had been so fraught, so out of control, but whatever happened now, she could always come here. Jake was still the fix she needed when she was ambushed by the darkness. She didn't love him, but she needed him. Perhaps that was the first step on the road.

She was lucky. She had found someone. Ella hadn't. She had been the plaything of men who enjoyed controlling and abusing women. First her father with his taste for violence, sadism and cruelty. Then a group of men who took pleasure from imprisoning and torturing a vulnerable young woman. She had been left brutalized and pregnant. A single woman bringing up a child of rape.

Unbidden, Robert popped into her brain. And alongside him, as always, thoughts of Marianne.

107

It is amazing how calm you are when you know the end is near. Since she had made her decision, Ella had felt elated. She giggled, sang songs to Amelia, behaved like a dizzy child. The rage still lurked within her, seeking a chance to escape and reassert itself, but this morning she didn't need it.

She had lifted some smart baby clothes from Boots a few days earlier. She was pleased she had done so now. She wanted Amelia to be looking nice when they found her. Since she had delivered Amelia, alone and uncared for in this dirty flat, she had never known what to feel for her. She was the price of her sin, a present from her rapists, reminding her of the callousness of the world. Her first instinct had been to smother the screaming bundle. She had gone to do it, but . . . the girl looked just like her. Her attackers had been dark-skinned, with heavy stubble and black hair. Amelia was blond, with a cute button nose.

Her next thought had been to ignore the baby, to punish it for its existence by deliberately starving it of food. But then she'd felt the milk seeping from her breasts and knew that something bigger than herself was in play here. So she'd fed the baby. Occasionally she would brush her nipple against the baby's mouth, then withdraw it, goading the baby with its unfulfilled hunger. But after a while even that seemed cruel and stupid and she'd fed the baby willingly. She found she was happy when she breast-fed, nourishing the small child, and for those brief moments when they were joined together, she could forget the other stuff, the violence, the hypocrisy, the rage. One day she realized that she didn't *want* the baby to suffer, that she wanted to protect it. So when she went out at night, she slipped some Night Nurse into her formula. This kept her slumbering happily until her mother returned.

Sadness pulsed through her heart, but she shook it off. She was committed to this path, so no point having regrets. The pills were waiting for her in the kitchen. All she had to do was get some formula and then she would be ready.

There was no backing out now.

108

The two women stared at each other, refusing to back down. Harwood had been in full spate, castigating Charlie for her irresponsibility, when Charlie had thrown in her bombshell. She was resigning from the force with immediate effect.

Harwood, with that effortless ease that ambitious people possess, paused momentarily, then just steamrollered on. She refused to accept Charlie's resignation. She would give her time to reconsider, to pull back from the very serious mistake she was making, in order to fulfill her destiny within the force. Charlie wondered if Harwood had promised the police commissioner that she would step into Helen's shoes and that their very high-profile investigation wouldn't suffer as a result of Helen's abrupt departure.

"Charlie, we need you. The team needs you," Harwood continued, "so I'm going to ask you to swallow this for now."

"I can't. I've given my word."

"I understand that, but perhaps if I met with Steve? I know he
had a problem with Helen, but she's not a factor anymore."

"She is to me. Which is all the more reason why—"

"I appreciate loyalty, I really do, but you don't seem to be seeing
the bigger picture. We are about to bring this killer in and I need
every available body on the case. We *need* to bring this to a close.
For the good of everybody."

For the good of your career, Charlie thought, but she said nothing.

"At the very least I would expect you to work your notice period.
You know how funny HR can be about pensions and so on when
people break the terms of their contract. Do that for me at least and
help us see this thing to a close."

Charlie capitulated shortly afterward. The truth was she *did* feel
bad about deserting Sanderson, McAndrew and the rest at this crucial time. Nevertheless, it felt profoundly odd as she took her place
in the incident room. Without Helen, things were very different.

Sanderson had brought Harwood up to speed. The latter was now
briefing the team, but Charlie had zoned out, boringly aware of the
protocols Harwood would employ. They hadn't traced Ella yet, but it
was only a matter of time now—they had too much on her. Harwood
was getting to the point and Charlie snapped out of it as her new boss
finally bared her teeth.

"Priority is to bring Ella Matthews in as quickly and cleanly as
possible," Harwood announced. "She is a multiple murderer who will
kill again and again unless stopped. I have therefore asked for and
obtained an emergency court order allowing the use of deadly force in

her apprehension. Tactical Support are mobilized and will step up if required."

Charlie shot a look at the team, who looked surprised and uncomfortable, but Harwood carried on regardless:

"We have one simple task now. And that is to bring Ella Matthews in. Dead or alive."

109

She had approached the house with extreme caution and was surprised—and alarmed—to find that it wasn't necessary. The press pack had inexplicably deserted Robert's house. Calm had returned to this quiet cul-de-sac, but it was a mournful silence—the modest detached house looked lonely and desolate as the rain swept over it.

Helen stood still, getting more saturated with every passing second, as she debated what to do. Desperate to see for herself what Robert was going through, she had come to Cole Avenue in silent pilgrimage, but it was obvious now that something had happened. Something had driven the clamoring hacks away.

She was still standing there debating what to do next, when the front door opened. A middle-aged woman shot a look here and there, as if expecting to be jumped, then hurried to a small hatchback that sat in their drive. She deposited a suitcase in the back, then turned again toward the house. Then she paused and swiveled to take in the sight of a beautiful woman in biking leathers standing stock-still. Suspicion, then a moment of comprehension in Monica's face, before suddenly and unexpectedly she started marching toward Helen.

"Where is he?" Helen blurted out.

"What have you done?" Monica spat back, fury rendering her words shaky and unstable.

"Where is he? What's happened?"

"He's gone."

"Gone where?"

Monica shrugged and looked away. She obviously did not want to let Helen see her cry.

"Where?" Despite her shame, Helen's tone was angry and impatient.

Monica looked up sharply.

"He must have gone last night. We found a note this morning. He . . . he says he probably won't see us again. That it's for the be—"

She broke down. Helen went to comfort her, but was angrily shrugged off.

"God damn you for what you've done to him."

She marched away into the house, slamming the door viciously behind her. Helen stood in the rain, not moving. She was right, of course. Helen had wanted to save Marianne. She had wanted to save Robert. But she had damned them both.

110

Carrie Matthews's hand shook as she gave DC Sanderson the photo. It was of Ella. It was a selfie that Ella had taken and then e-mailed to her sister—a message of solidarity from her exile and something to remember her by. When Sanderson had turned up at Carrie's home in Shirley, her husband, Paul, had tried to take over proceedings, forcing his young wife into the background. He was a bull of a man—an elder of the church and the founding father of Christian Domestic Order. Sanderson had taken great pleasure in ordering him out of the room, threatening him with a very public arrest if he didn't comply. He seemed shocked—appalled might be more accurate—but eventually he'd done as he was told.

"Please find her. Please help her," Carrie begged as she withdrew the photo from its hiding place in the dresser and handed it over to Sanderson. "She's not what everyone thinks she is."

"I know," Sanderson replied. "We're doing everything we can."

But Sanderson knew even as she said it that the chances of this thing ending well were slim. Harwood was determined to stop Ella in her tracks by any means necessary and Ella was probably too far gone to fear death. Nevertheless, she reassured Carrie and went on her way, adding as she left that there were many organizations and shelters that could help her if she ever needed them.

As soon as she stepped outside, her radio squawked into life.

A woman matching Ella's description had just been seen shoplifting in a branch of Boots in Bevois. She had escaped the security guards and taken refuge somewhere in the Fairview estate.

Sanderson was in her car and on the road in seconds, her siren blaring as she bullied the midday traffic out of her way. This was it, then. The endgame had begun. And Sanderson was determined to be in at the death.

111

She slunk into the room like a thief. It felt shameful and wrong to be here, even though she had run things for so many years. Now she was an outsider, unnecessary and unwelcome.

Following her confrontation with Robert's mother, Helen had been adrift, reeling from the weight of the damage she had done. She had called Jake, but he was with a client. After that she had momentarily ground to a halt, unsure of what to do next. There *was* no one else to call.

Slowly her emotions had calmed and sense prevailed. There was one useful thing she could do. Though she had been taken off the case, she still had most of the case files with her, and besides, it was important that she set down her discoveries about Ella for Sanderson, Harwood and the others. If it ever came to court, every "i" would have to be dotted, every "t" crossed. She couldn't afford a mistake that would rob the victims' families of the justice they deserved. So, summoning up her last vestige of resolve, Helen had headed to Southampton Central to do her duty.

The desk sergeant had thought she was on leave and was surprised to see her.

"No rest for the wicked?" he offered jauntily.

"Paperwork" was Helen's deliberately jaded response.

He buzzed her through. She took the lift up to the seventh floor. A journey she'd done many times—but never as an outcast.

Once inside the room, she wrote up her report and left it and the case files on Harwood's desk. As she was about to leave, a noise startled her. She was momentarily confused—Harwood and the team were out chasing leads—then surprised. It was Tony Bridges, another victim of the wreckage. They stared at each other for a second. Then Helen said:

"You've heard?"

"Yes, and I'm sorry, Helen. If it had anything to do with me, I can ta—"

"It's nothing to do with you, Tony. It's personal. She wants me out."

"She's an idiot."

Helen smiled.

"Be that as it may, she's in charge, so . . ."

"Sure, I just wanted to give you . . . her . . . this. It's my report."

"Great minds," Helen said, smiling once more. "Leave it on her desk."

Tony raised a rueful eyebrow and headed for Harwood's office. As she watched him go, Helen could only think what a waste it all was. He was a talented and dedicated officer brought low by a moment of weakness. He had been stupid, but surely he deserved better than this. Melissa was a raw but artful character who'd seized an opportunity and mercilessly exploited Tony's feelings for her own ends. It was the commonly held view now that "Lyra" was a fiction. Helen was furious with herself at having been duped. How easily Melissa had pulled the wool over their eyes. On the say-so of one person, they had gone down a massive blind alley and compromised the invest—

Helen's internal tirade ground to a halt, frozen by the thought. Because of course Melissa hadn't been the only person who "knew" Lyra. There was another person who claimed to have met this fictitious phantom. A young woman. A young woman with a baby.

Helen's mind flew back to that interview—she pictured the young prostitute opposite her, awkwardly cradling her wriggling baby as she told them how she "knew" Lyra. The girl had been monosyllabic and seemed ill-educated, but now Helen saw something else in her. The shaved head and the multiple piercings had disguised her identity, but there was something in the shape of her face. Looking up at the most recent picture of Ella, which Sanderson had stuck to the board, Helen knew in an instant that the young girl—with her high cheekbones and wide, full mouth—was Ella.

She snapped out of it to find Tony staring at her. He looked concerned.

"You okay, boss?"

Helen gazed at him for a moment, hardly daring to believe it. Then she said:

"We've got her, Tony. We've got her."

112

Helen sped through the city center toward the north of the city. She was flagrantly breaking the speed limit, but she didn't care. She knew how to handle the bike, could outrun any cop car and was possessed by the idea of facing their killer.

Tony had tried to stop her, but she had stopped him in his tracks: "You never saw me, Tony."

What she was about to do was dangerous and broke every rule in the book. If Tony was associated with her actions in any way, he would lose his pension, service payments, everything. She couldn't do that to him. Besides, the more people who knew, the greater the chance that they would get to Ella before she did. And she was determined she wouldn't let that happen.

She had no idea what she was going to do. She was just gripped by a terrible urgency, a sense of things building to a horrible climax, and she knew she had to do everything in her power to prevent further bloodshed. A baby's life was at stake. Ella's too. In spite of everything she'd done, in spite of the appalling horror of her crimes, Helen felt sympathy for Ella and wanted to bring her in safely.

Soon she was in Spire Street. Pulling up outside the dilapidated tenement building, she killed the engine and hopped off her bike in one fluid movement. She looked around—there were no signs of life on this forgotten street. Sliding her baton into her belt, she stepped inside the building. The stairwell was cold and lonely, decorated with the detritus left by last night's crack smokers. The tired building was scheduled for redevelopment next year and in the interim had become home to a motley crew of squatters and junkies. They seemed to operate an open-door policy, people coming and going day and night, so it wasn't hard to gain access to the third-floor flat. Helen had last seen Ella here four days ago, snuggled up on the dirty sofa with other prostitutes and junkies. The shared company of the afflicted.

But Ella wasn't there now. Faced by a warrant card, the odorous man who "owned" the flat directed her upstairs. According to him, Ella lived at the top of the house in splendid isolation—just her and her baby tucked away from the prying eyes of Social Services. It was not the sort of house where people asked questions—the perfect hideaway for their invisible killer.

Helen paused outside flat 9, then gently turned the handle. It was locked. Helen placed her ear against the door, straining to hear if there was movement within. Nothing. Then a faint cry. She strained to hear more. But now it was quiet once more. Pulling a credit card from her pocket, she slipped it through the crack between the door and the architrave. The latch was old and weak and within twenty seconds it slid open. Helen was in.

She closed the door silently behind her and stood stock-still.

Nothing. She moved slowly forward. The old floorboards protested, so she changed her route, hugging the wall.

She paused at the doorway to the kitchen. She darted her head round quickly, but it was empty. Just a dirty sink and a large cannibalized fridge, humming happily to itself.

On Helen crept toward the living room—or what passed for it. Somehow she sensed Ella would be here, but as she stepped inside, she found it was also empty. Then she heard it—that cry again.

Now fear overrode her caution and Helen extended her baton and marched across the room, pushing the bedroom door roughly open. She expected an attack at any moment, but the room was bare— except for a crumpled old bed and a travel cot, in which a baby girl was stirring. Helen shot a look over her shoulder, expecting ambush, but all was still, so she hurried inside.

So this was her. The child that Ella had never asked for. But whom she had cared for nevertheless. Helen had been right to come. Placing her baton on the bed, Helen bent down and picked up the baby, who rubbed her sleepy eyes with her tiny bunched fist, as she awoke from her slumbers. The sight made Helen smile. Seeing this, the baby smiled back. Who knew what this baby had seen, what she had experienced, but she could still smile. Some innocence remained.

"What the fuck are you doing?"

Helen turned to find Ella standing not ten feet away from her in the living room. Ella's face was annoyed, rather than angry, but as soon as Helen turned, her expression changed. As she recognized Helen's face, she dropped her shopping bag and fled. Helen waited for the front door to slam, but instead she heard a drawer opening and shutting noisily. Seconds later, Ella returned, a large butcher's knife in her hand.

"Put her down and get out of here."

"I can't do that, Ella."

Ella flinched at her name.

"Put her down!" she screamed.

The baby started whimpering now, scared by this noisy face-off.

"It's over, Ella. I know what you've been through. I know how you've suffered. But it's finished. For your sake, for your baby's, it's time to hand yourself in."

"You give her to me right now or I will stab you through your fucking eyes."

Helen held the baby close to her, as Ella took a step forward.

"What's her name?" Helen asked, backing off, but maintaining eye contact.

"Don't fuck with me."

"Tell me her name, please."

"Give her to me."

Her voice was threatening, unstable, but she halted her advance. Her eyes flicked between her baby and Helen, weighing up her options.

"I am not going to do that, Ella. You'll have to kill me first. My only concern is for you and your baby's welfare. You're not well and you both deserve better than this place. Let me help you."

"You think I don't know what'll happen? As soon as we're out of here, I'll be in cuffs and I'll never see her again."

"That's not what'll—"

"You think I'll fall for that? Well, forget it. She's not leaving here and neither are you."

As Ella advanced, Helen turned to shield the baby from attack. Ella's eyes were black, she was panting with anger, and in that moment Helen knew she had made a fatal mistake.

113

Charlie hurried away from the Fairview estate, struggling to keep up with her superior. Harwood was spitting blood, furious that their "lead" had turned out to be a waste of time. They had sped to the estate, with Tactical Support and most of the station's CID team in tow—all of which was quite a surprise for the sixteen-year-old girl who was hiding out in her mate's flat, following her clumsy attempt to steal some makeup from Boots. She did look passingly like Angel, but she was far too young and, besides, her long black hair was genuine. Once she and her mate had recovered from the shock, they'd started to get lippy, asking if they always called out guys with guns to pick on young girls—none of which improved Harwood's mood. In another light, in another world, it would have been funny. But the stakes were too high for that, so Charlie followed behind, her heart in her boots.

"What the hell is *he* doing here?"

Charlie snapped out of it to see Harwood gesturing toward Tony, who was chatting to a uniformed officer he was friendly with. Harwood stared at Charlie, her eyes full of suspicion, but for once Charlie was innocent of all charges.

"No idea."

They hurried over.

"You can't be here," Harwood announced without introduction. "Whatever you think can be gained by coming down here—"

"Would you shut the fuck up?" Tony barked back at her, silencing her instantly. There was something in his eyes that brooked no argument.

"Helen knows where Ella is. She's gone to find her."

"What?"

"She wouldn't tell me where she was going. Or how she knew where she was. But I think she's in danger. We've got to help her."

The words poured from him, forced out at speed by his anxiety.

"How the hell did she know?"

"She wouldn't say. I came to the seventh floor to hand in my report and then . . . She told me not to say anything . . . but I can't do that to her."

"Get uniform onto it. I want to hear from anyone who's seen her or her fucking bike. Check the traffic cameras—see if we can trace her route," Harwood said, turning to Charlie. "Get McAndrew back to the nick. Get her to go through Helen's write-up. See if there's anything in there."

"What about her phone? If we can triangulate that—"

"Do it."

Charlie hared off, Harwood following close behind.

"What about me? What can I do to help?" Tony asked.

Harwood paused, then turned:

"You can go to hell."

114

She was trapped. Helen had backed into the tiny bedroom to escape Ella's advance, but was now boxed into a corner. For days she had been praying for this moment—when she would finally come face-to-face with their killer—but now it was here and death would be the only outcome. Helen hugged the baby closer to her chest as Ella took another step toward them.

Had she deluded herself that she might be able to save Ella? That there would still be some residual humanity within her? She had to engage her if she could. Look past the madness and find a way in.

"So you kill me—then what? The whole of the force is out looking for you. They know your name, what you look like. They know you have a baby. Swampy downstairs knows I'm here, knows who *you* are, so you can't stay. What are you going to do—go on the run with a baby?"

"She's not coming with me."

"What do you mean?"

"I don't know what'll happen to me, but it ends here for her. She's been through enough."

"You don't mean that."

"Why do you think I got the fucking formula?" Ella shouted back. "I've got the pills. I was going to give them to her today. It could all have been so . . . right."

"She's just a tiny baby. For God's sake, Ella, you're better than that."

"Stop saying my name. Ella is *dead*. The kid is going to join her and if I have to kill you to get to her, I bloody will."

She took a step closer. She was only a foot away from Helen now. Helen tensed, expecting her to strike at any moment. Then:

"Do it then. I'll make it easy for you."

Helen bent down, placing Amelia on the bed.

"If you really want to kill her, I'll make it easy for you. There she is. Do it."

Surprised, Ella looked from Helen to her baby and then back again. The baby kicked out on the bed and—freed from Helen's warm embrace—started to cry.

"GO ON!" Helen shouted suddenly.

Still Ella hesitated. Helen had been coiled tight, ready to spring if Ella made the slightest move toward the baby, but she didn't. And in that moment, Helen knew she had an opportunity.

"Ella, listen to me. I know, okay? I know that you are in hell, that you feel the world is against you, that it's full of vicious, violent men who want to hurt you. And you're right. It is."

Ella eyed her suspiciously, unsure if this was a trick. Helen took a deep breath and continued:

"I was raped when I was a kid. More than once. I was sixteen, trying to find my way out of care, but I made bad choices. And I paid. I'm still paying. So I know where you are right now. I know you believe there is no way back, but there *is*."

Ella paused, staring intently at Helen.

"You're making shit up."

"Would you look at me?" Helen replied, suddenly angry. "My bloody hands are shaking . . . I've never told a soul about this, not a single soul. So *don't* accuse me of lying."

Ella didn't break her stare. Her hand gripped the knife tightly.

"I can't pretend to know you," Helen continued. "I don't know what your dad did to you, what those men did to you, but I *know* this doesn't have to be the end. You can get through this. Whatever you've done, you did for a reason and when Amelia is older she will want you. She will *need* you. Please don't abandon her, Ella, I beg you."

For the first time, Ella dropped her gaze to her baby.

"I know you have goodness inside you. I know you can do the right thing by your little girl. So please, let me help you. For her sake."

Helen reached out her hand. She knew in that moment that it all came down to this. Her last shot at redemption. Her final chance to save Ella.

115

They were floundering in the dark—hapless figures scrabbling for a foothold as the ground kept giving way beneath them. Racing back to the station, Charlie had taken the lead. Harwood might be the boss, but she had the operational experience and she refused to trust anyone else with this—there was too much at stake. But they were getting nowhere.

McAndrew had read Helen's files twice already but had unearthed no clues as to Ella's whereabouts. They had tried triangulating Helen's mobile phone signal, only to find that her phone was turned off. It had last been used six hours ago, when she was at the nick, so would be no use to them now. Traffic cameras had picked Helen's bike up speeding north, but then lost her as she left the city center. Where the hell was she? What had she seen that no one else had?

Charlie marched along the corridor, then down the stairs and out of the station. The team would continue to do their work as directed, but Charlie felt she needed to be out doing something. And as she neared her car, she slowed. A thought was forming, a past conversation coming back to her. Slowly an idea took hold and, electrified, she jumped in the car and roared off. Suddenly she knew exactly where to go.

Heads turned as Charlie marched between the line of desks, making a beeline for the office at the back. The security guards and receptionists, whose protests she'd ignored, hurried after her, but she had too big a lead on them and she was in Emilia's office before they could get to her. Slamming the door shut, she rammed a chair under the handle and turned to face the startled reporter.

"Where is she?" Charlie demanded.

"Where's who?"

"Helen Grace."

"I have no idea and frankly I'm not sure what you think you're—"

"How do you do it?"

"Do what? Make sense, please, Char—"

"You know where she is, you know who she is with."

"For God's sake, why would I—"

Charlie was across the room before Emilia could finish her denial. Grabbing the reporter by the throat, she thrust her hard against the brick wall.

"Listen very carefully to me, Emilia. Helen's life is at stake here and I promise you that if you do not tell me what I need to know *right now*, I will nail your head to this wall."

Emilia was choking now, Charlie's hands growing ever tighter round her throat.

"I have been through too much to let her down, so tell me how you do it. Are you bugging her phone? Intercepting her messages?"

Emilia shook her head. Charlie cracked it hard against the wall.
"Tell me!"

Emilia made a gurgling noise as if she was trying to speak, so Charlie loosened her grip. Emilia mumbled something.

"What?"

"Her bike," Emilia croaked.

"What about it?" Charlie demanded.

"There's a tracking device on her bike."

So there it was.

"How do you follow her?"

"It's linked to my phone. As long as she's within a five-mile radius of me, I can find her."

"Good," Charlie said, releasing her victim. "Take me to her."

116

The baby shrieked wildly on the bed, working herself up into a frenzy. Neither woman made a move to comfort her. They were frozen in time, on the cusp of salvation or destruction. Helen's eyes remained glued to Ella. She had refused to take Helen's hand or drop her knife. She was just staring at her screaming baby as if trying to penetrate some insoluble mystery. Helen thought that if she moved suddenly she could disarm Ella, now that she was distracted, but she daren't risk it. Not now that she seemed so close to bringing her round.

"I didn't mean for this to happen."

Helen was startled when Ella spoke.

"I didn't want this to happen."

"I know."

"It's his fault."

"I know your dad was a cruel man—"

"I've done those other kids a favor."

"The twins?"

"And Carrie. I've freed them."

"You're right, Ella. He was a bully and a sadist."

"And a fucking hypocrite. Do you know what he said to me? He said I was evil. Dirty. He said I had a black heart."

"He was wrong."

"After those guys . . . did what they did, I was on booze, drugs, pills, whatever I could get . . . I was killing myself, I . . . I'd vowed I would never ask for their help again. I hated him. And her."

She shot a glance at Amelia.

"But I was seven months gone. And I . . . I begged for their help. *Begged* them to find a home for her. Somewhere away from *me*. And they shut the door in my face. Told me that being raped was too good for me."

The words shot out, fractured and bitter.

"He looked me in the face . . . and said the most diabolical things and then . . . and then . . ."

"You saw him again, didn't you? Later on? You saw him picking up a prostitute."

Ella turned and now her eyes were full of rage.

"It was only a few weeks later . . . And they *knew* each other. He was a bloody *regular*. And then I got it—every Tuesday night for God knows how long he'd been . . . After everything he'd said, after everything he'd *done* . . ."

"He lied to you, he lied to your mum."

"When I did him, he never even knew me. A bloody black wig and a few nose rings . . . but I could have been wearing my school bloody uniform with a big smile on my face. All he could think about was what he was going to get, what 'Angel' would let him do to her. He was a pig and he got what he deserved."

Helen said nothing. Amelia was growing puce now with crying, a barking cough racking her body.

"We need to pick her up, Ella. You need to pick her up."

Ella snapped out of it, casting a suspicious look at Helen.

"We can't leave her crying like this. She's going to choke."

The volume of Amelia's cries rose still further, then the barking cough started up again. Ella hesitated.

"Please, Ella—put the knife on the bed, pick up your baby and let's all walk out together."

Ella looked at Amelia, then at the knife in her hand. This was it, then—do or die.

"Let's end this," Helen said.

117

Up, up, up. The Tactical Support team mounted the stairs at double speed, climbing to their vantage point on the top floor of the crumbling building. The stairs were broken and unstable and Harwood had to pick her path carefully, as she followed in their wake. Behind her she heard McAndrew put her foot through a board, cursing loudly as she did so.

"Be quiet, for God's sake," Harwood hissed at her.

Before long they were in place. Looking down, Harwood could see Helen's bike parked outside the squat opposite. Charlie had already entered it—the people living there had confirmed that Ella Matthews lived at the very top of the building. Across the way, Tactical Support was now in place and searching for their quarry.

"What've you got?" Harwood demanded, her nerves jangling.

"Two females."

"Grace?"

"And another."

"What's happening?"

A long pause.

"I can't see. They are kind of locked together. It's hard to get a good angle from here."

"There's nowhere else to go, so work with it. Can you see a weapon?"

"Negative."

"Can you get a clear shot?"

"Negative."

"Well, what the fuck can you give me?"

"You want to be hauled up in front of the IPCC, be my guest," the irritated sniper replied. "But I can't get a clear shot and I'm not doing anything until I can. You know better, then take over, please."

He spat the words out without once looking up, his vision locked on the drama playing out across the road. Harwood scowled inwardly. She knew he was right, but it didn't make it any better. She had staked a lot on this investigation and it had to turn out right.

What the fuck was going on in there?

118

Helen refused to drop her gaze. Ella was virtually eyeball to eyeball with her. Helen could smell her rank breath, could feel the cold steel of the knife pressing against her leg. Still Ella refused to relinquish it.

"Why do you want to save me, Helen?" Ella asked suddenly.

"Because I think you've been wronged. Because I think the world owes you."

"You think I'm good?" A snarl came and went in her voice.

"I *know* you're good."

Ella smiled bitterly.

"Well, then, you listen to me. I want you to know something."

She was about to speak, then paused, distracted by a sudden squeak from the living room. A board creaking. Helen knew immediately that they had company. Charlie? Tony? Tactical Support? Helen wanted to scream at them to stay the fuck away, but she stayed stock-still, not breaking eye contact, not breathing. Ella hesitated for a second, then leaned in closer.

"I don't regret it, Helen. Whatever I say afterward, I want *you* to know. I don't regret a single thing."

Helen said nothing. Ella's pupils were dilated, her breathing unsteady.

"Those men . . . those hypocrites . . . they *deserved* to be exposed," she continued. "They were happy enough to flaunt their wedding rings, play the husband and father. They weren't so happy to be seen with girls like *me*. Well, I changed all that. I showed them up for what they really are. Sometimes the world needs a wake-up call, right?"

She looked at Helen fiercely for a moment; then the fire seemed to die in her eyes.

"But I want to do right by Amelia. So I'm going to trust you. Can I trust you, Helen?"

"You have my word. I won't let you down."

"Then thank you."

Slowly she turned the knife in her hand. Gripping the blade, she held the handle up for Helen to take.

Immediately there was a sharp crack and Ella lurched sideways, crashing into the wardrobe next to her.

Helen froze for a moment, stunned. Then, snapping out of it, she rushed to Ella. Even as she knelt down to help her, she could see that it was hopeless. The bullet had entered through Ella's temple and she was already dead.

Charlie burst in, but it was too late. Helen was cradling the killer's corpse and on the bed, spattered with blood, her baby continued to cry.

119

Helen walked from the building, clutching Amelia to her chest. Colleagues rushed to help, photographers buzzed around her, but she didn't see any of them. She pushed them roughly aside and carried on, keen to put as much distance as possible between herself and the carnage.

People were calling to her, but their voices were just noises. Her body was shaking with the trauma of what she'd just experienced, her brain playing and replaying the sharp snap of the sniper's bullet on an endless repetitive loop. She had tried so hard to save Ella, to rescue her from the wreckage of her life. But she had failed, and once more she had blood on her hands.

Passing an attending squad car, Helen caught sight of her reflection in the windscreen. She looked like a monster—crazed, disheveled, her hair matted, her clothes stained. She now became aware of Charlie guiding her toward the paramedics, gently imploring her to seek medical assistance for herself and the baby.

She allowed herself to be helped into the ambulance, but once there she refused to cooperate. Despite the best endeavors of the paramedics, Helen would not relinquish her grip on Amelia, who had calmed now and clung to Helen with her tiny, delicate hands. Licking her thumb, Helen began to wipe the blood from the child's face. The baby smiled at the contact, as if enjoying being tickled. Helen could hear the others talking around her. They assumed she was in shock, that she wasn't thinking straight, but they were wrong—she knew exactly what she was doing. While Amelia was in Helen's arms, nothing could happen to her. For a brief moment at least, she would be safe from a dark and unforgiving world.

120

EPILOGUE

Helen paused outside the Guildhall, pulling her compact from her bag to check her appearance. Two weeks had passed since Ella had died, and though Helen's face still looked tired and drawn, she had lost the look of blank horror that had characterized her expression for days afterward. She had hardly been outside her flat since it happened, and suddenly she felt sick with nerves. The Guildhall usually hosted bands and comedians but today it was packed with Hampshire Police's finest, all gathered together to honor outstanding officers— Helen among them. She could think of easier ways to ease herself back into normal life and her strong instinct was to turn tail and run.

As soon as she stepped inside the building, however, she was assailed by an enormous wave of goodwill. Smiles, pats on the back, rounds of applause. The team from the seventh floor swarmed round her, hailing the return of their leader, welcoming her back into the family. They had obviously been worried about her, fearing perhaps that she would never return, and Helen was moved by their affection and concern. As she received their congratulations she realized that though she might constantly castigate herself for her failings, to Charlie, Sanderson and the rest, she was a hero.

Her nerves grew steadily as each award was given out; then finally it was her turn. An official police commendation handed over in person by the deputy chief constable himself. Standing next to him, waiting patiently to shake Helen's hand, was Detective Superintendent Harwood.

"Well done, Helen."

Helen nodded her thanks, before leaving the stage. As she walked back to her seat in the front row, a feeling of quiet satisfaction crept over her. The coverage of the case had been extensive during the last fortnight—pictures of Helen carrying Amelia from the building had been splashed across the front pages of all the newspapers, both local and national. Helen's team had pinned the cuttings up on the wall with pride, saving center spot for the profile pieces in the *Southampton Evening News,* which went out of its way to praise Helen's character and actions. Harwood's name had been all but absent from the reports, a forgotten presence. Maybe there was some justice after all.

The team virtually carried Helen from the Guildhall on their shoulders. Awarding themselves an extended lunch break, they frog-marched her to the Crown and Two Chairmen to celebrate the conclusion of this high-profile investigation. Coppers are strange beasts—even though they knew Helen didn't drink, there was no question of going anywhere other than this much-visited pub. Helen didn't mind; it was comforting in its familiarity and she was pleased to see the team looking so happy and carefree again.

Finishing her drink, Helen slipped off to the loo, keen to have a moment by herself away from the adulation and praise. But her ordeal wasn't over yet.

"Friends?"

Emilia Garanita. She had been there at the commendation ceremony and here she was again. Helen's shadow.

"What is it with you and toilets, Emilia?" Helen replied.

"You're a hard woman to get on your own."

Helen said nothing. She had called a truce with her nemesis in the immediate aftermath of the case, agreeing not to charge the reporter with attempting to blackmail a serving police officer and worse, in return for a promise not to pursue or expose baby Amelia as she grew into her new life. Helen knew there would be numerous dissections of the Matthews family—as Alan's brutality and perversions were explored in endless column inches—but she wanted to protect the innocent. Emilia had honored the deal, keeping the spotlight firmly on Alan Matthews, while simultaneously lavishing praise on DI Grace and her team in double-page spreads, but it cut little ice with Helen. She had made the deal with Emilia for pragmatic reasons. As for the rest of it—particularly the callous dismantling of Robert's life—she would not forgive, nor would she forget.

"I'm pleased we've come to an arrangement," Emilia continued, breaking the silence, "as I would like us to go on working together in the future."

"Not jetting off to London?"

"I'm working on it."

Clearly Emilia's scoop hadn't quite earned her the dream move she was after, but Helen resisted the temptation to put the boot in.

"Well, good luck with that."

Helen made to leave, but Emilia stopped her.

"I'd like this to be a fresh start for us and . . . well, I wanted to say sorry."

"For tracking me? Threatening me? Or for ruining a young man's life?" Helen countered.

"For being unprofessional."

Typical Emilia, Helen thought. Defiant even in apology.

"I'm sorry, and it won't happen again."

It wasn't much, but Helen knew it still cost Emilia to say it. She accepted her apology and left. Emilia was keen to buy her a drink to cement their détente, but Helen demurred. Pubs weren't her natural habitat and she didn't feel much like celebrating.

Besides, there was somewhere she needed to be.

121

Clutching a small posy of flowers, Helen hurried along the pathway. Fallen leaves lay all around, a rich red-and-gold carpet that was oddly beautiful. Even the sun had obliged this morning, poking its head through the clouds to add a warm, hazy glow to the scene.

The cemetery was all but deserted. It was a nondenominational, Her Majesty's Prison graveyard on the edge of town. Few people knew about it—it was the final resting ground for the undesirable and the unclaimed. Ella Matthews fitted both of these categories.

Her mother and most of her family had abandoned her in death, as they had in life. They had put their house on the market, shunned the press and tried to act as if they were in no way responsible for what had happened. Helen knew otherwise and despised them for their cowardice.

But there was one who hadn't forgotten. Someone who'd refused to discard a beloved sister so easily. Carrie Matthews looked around as Helen approached and smiled sheepishly. The pair of them stood together silently for a moment, looking down at the anonymous wooden cross, each reflecting on the prize and price of sisterly love. They at least would never forget.

A few yards away, a bright red baby stroller stood out amid the rows of gray headstones. In it, Amelia slumbered peacefully, blissfully unaware of her surroundings. After Ella's death, the tiny baby had been placed with emergency foster caregivers while a more permanent solution was sought. As usual, her relatives were contacted, but nobody seemed to want the blameless baby, until at the last moment Carrie Matthews had come forward. Unable to have children herself, Carrie was determined that her niece would not be brought up in care. Helen had been moved to tears when she'd heard the news—more relieved than she could say that Amelia would escape the fate that had befallen Marianne and herself all those years before. Many trials lay ahead, no doubt, but for now Amelia was safe and well in the bosom of her family.

Carrie exchanged a few words with Helen, then laid her flowers on the grave and kissed the cross. She had defied her husband to be there, rejecting dogma and bullying in order to grieve for her sister properly. Though fully aware of the possible consequences, she still had come. Watching her, Helen could see that there was already something different about Carrie Matthews—a new strength and determination born of a desire to do right by Amelia. Maybe this would be Ella's legacy, then, the flowers that would bloom on her grave. *Perhaps after all,* Helen thought to herself, *there is still hope.*

Don't miss Detective Helen Grace's next chilling case.

THE DOLL'S HOUSE

Available from New American Library
in February 2016

1

Ruby tossed fitfully in her bed after a disturbed night's sleep. She seemed to have been in and out of consciousness for hours—not fully awake, but not truly asleep either. Wild anxiety dreams collided uneasily with the odd sensation of her mother carrying her to bed. That had felt nice but was impossible, of course. Ruby lived alone and it had been fifteen years or more since her parents had had to do that.

Ruby regretted her session at Revolution last night. Angry with life, she had been in a self-destructive mood, unable or unwilling to turn down the free drinks offered by hopeful lads. There had been pills and cocaine too—the whole thing was a blur. But had she really drunk so much, taken so much, that she should feel *this* bad?

She turned over again, burying her throbbing head in the sheets. She had important stuff to do today—her mum was coming round soon—but suddenly Ruby couldn't face any of it. She just wanted to hide away from the world, cocooned in her hangover, safe from the intrusion of family, responsibility, betrayal, and tears. She wanted her life to go away—for a couple of hours at least.

Putting her head under the pillow, she groaned quietly. It was surprisingly cool underneath—cooler than usual—and for a moment she felt refreshed and soothed. This would be a good hidey-hole for a litt—

Something wasn't right. The smell. What was it about the smell of the sheets? They smelled . . . wrong.

Alarm started to burrow through her hangover. Her sheets always smelled citrusy. She used the same fabric softener her mum did. So why did they now smell of lavender?

Ruby kept her eyes closed, the pillow clamped over her head. Her brain ached fiercely as it spooled back over last night's events. She had snogged a guy, flirted with a few more . . . but she hadn't gone home with anyone, had she? No, she had made it back to her flat alone. She remembered dropping her keys on the table, drinking water straight from the kitchen tap, taking some Nurofen before flopping into bed. That *was* last night, wasn't it?

She could feel her breathing becoming shallow now, her chest tightening. She needed her asthma inhaler. Stretching out her arm, she groped for the bedside table—drunk or not, she always left her inhaler within easy reach. But it wasn't there. She reached out farther. Nothing. The *table* wasn't bloody there. Her hand collided with the wall. Rough brick. Her wall wasn't like th—

Ruby pulled her head off the pillow and sat up. Her mouth fell open, but only a weak gasp came out, her body frozen in breathless panic. She had gone to sleep in her nice, cozy bed. But she'd woken up in a cold, dark cellar.

2

The sun was high in the sky and Carsholt Beach looked magnificent, a long swath of golden sand merging effortlessly with the gentle waters of the Solent. Andy Baker patted himself on the back—Carsholt was literally at the end of the road, so even though the beach was beautiful, there was hardly ever anybody down here. Cathy, he, and the kids had the place to themselves and were set fair for a perfect Saturday by the sea. Picnic, bit of Frisbee, a few beers—already the stresses of the working week were melting away.

Leaving the boys to dig their trench—a prelude to pitched battles between his boisterous twins—Andy set off by himself toward the water's edge. What was it that was so calming about this place? The isolation? The view? The sound of the sea lapping the shore? Andy let the water run over his toes. He had been coming here since he was a kid. He'd brought his wife—his first wife—and the boys here. That hadn't ended well, of course, but looking over toward Cathy, digging and joking with Tom and Jimbo, Andy now felt blessed.

This place was his sanctuary and he looked forward to it all week. Running a security business sounded good on paper, but it was nonstop aggro. You used to be able to get decent people on your books, but not now. Maybe it was the influx of foreigners or just modern times, but every third employee seemed to have a drug problem or an eye for the girls. Last month, he'd been sued by a nightclub owner who'd caught one of his guys dealing ketamine in the club toilets. He was getting too old for stuff like that—perhaps it was time to think about retiring.

A noise made Andy look up sharply. It came from behind him. From the direction of the boys. They were shouting. No, they were screaming.

Already Andy was sprinting across the sand, his heart beating sixteen to the dozen. Was someone hurting them? He could see Cathy, but where were the boys?

"Cathy?"

She didn't even look at him.

"Cathy?"

Finally, she looked up. Her face was ashen. She tried to speak, but before she could say anything the boys crashed into her, holding on to her for dear life.

Andy stared at them, confused and fearful. As Cathy clasped the boys to her chest, her gaze remained resolutely fixed on the trench. Was it something there that had spooked them? A dead animal or . . .

Andy approached the lip of the trench. He had a sense of what he would find. Could see it in his mind's eye. But even so, his heart skipped a beat when he peered into the hole. The sides were steep, the trench was deep—three feet or so—and there at the bottom, perfectly framed by wet sand, was the pale face of a young woman.

3

Snow blindness studded her vision and her chest tightened still further. Ruby was in the midst of a full-blown asthma attack now, her panic making her breathing short and erratic. She could feel her heart thundering out a remorseless rhythm, as if it were going to explode. What the hell was happening? Was this *real*?

She sank her teeth into her arm. The pain coursed through her fleetingly, before she released her grip to try to suck in more air. It *was* real. She should have known by how bloody freezing she was. Shivering, she lay down on the bed and tried to calm herself. The thought of not having her inhaler was freaking her out, but she had to try to control her panic or she would black out. And she couldn't do that. Not here.

Calm. Try to be calm. Think nice thoughts. Think of Mum. And Dad. And Cassie. And Conor. Think of fields. And rivers. And sunlight. Think of being a kid. And playgrounds. And summers in the garden. Running through the sprinkler. Think happy, happy thoughts.

Ruby's chest was rising and falling less violently now, her breathing a little less desperate. *Keep your cool. It will be fine. There will be a simple explanation for all this.* Propping herself up on her pillows, she took a deep breath and suddenly called:

"Hello?"

Her voice sounded strange, her words flopping dully off the exposed brick walls. The room was in darkness, save for the light that stole under the bottom of the door, providing just enough illumination to reveal her situation. The room measured about fifteen by fifteen and would have looked like any other bedsit—a bed, a table and chairs, an oven and kettle, some bookshelves—except for the fact that there were no windows. The boards that formed the low ceiling betrayed no cracks or chinks of light.

"Hello?" Her voice quavered, as she fought to suppress the panic that gripped her. Still no answer, no sign of life.

Suddenly she was on her feet—anything to keep from sitting still and thinking horrible thoughts. She crossed the room to the heavy metal door and worked the handle, but it was locked. Frantically she did a circuit of the small room, looking for some means of escape, but found nothing.

She shivered. She was scared half to death and cold to the bone. Her gaze fell on the cooker. It was an old gas one, with two ovens and four hobs. She was suddenly seized with the thought of turning it on. The four hobs would warm the place up and brighten it a little too. She turned the dial of one of the hobs and pressed the ignition. Nothing. She tried the next, then the next. Still nothing.

She walked round the cooker to check out the back. She didn't know the first thing about cookers, but perhaps there was something obvious.

It wasn't connected. There were no pipes at the back connecting it to a gas supply. It was just for show. Ruby slumped to the ground. Tears came fast now, as her confusion collided with fear.

What was this place? Why was she here? Questions spun round in Ruby's head, as she tried to process this strange reality. She was slipping fast into despair, tears rolling off her chin onto the floor.

Then suddenly a noise nearby made her look up.

What was it? Was it upstairs or down here?

There it was again. Footsteps. Definitely footsteps. They were coming closer. Stopping outside the door. Ruby jumped to her feet, alive to the danger.

Silence. Then suddenly a wicket hatch in the door slid open and a pair of eyes filled the slit. Ruby stumbled backward, pressing herself into the corner of the room—she wanted to be as far away from the door as possible.

The sound of bolts being unlocked.

"HELP!" Ruby screamed.

But she didn't get any further. The door swung open, flooding the room with light. Ruby clamped her eyes shut, blinded by the sudden burst of illumination. Then slowly, cautiously, she opened them again.

A tall figure stood in the doorway, silhouetted by the light behind him. She couldn't make out his features. He was just a shadow—hovering, watching.

Then, as suddenly as it had opened, the heavy door slammed shut again. They were together in darkness now.

Ruby covered her face with her hands and prayed to a God she didn't believe in, pleading with him to have mercy on her. But for all her praying, she couldn't block out the sound of the footsteps approaching her.

4

The wind buffeted DI Helen Grace as she sped along the coastal road. She hadn't been down this isolated spit of land before and she liked what she saw. The wildness, the isolation—it was her kind of place. With the road open before her, she ratcheted up her speed, pushing hard against the strong headwind.

Soon the crime scene came into view and she eased off on the throttle, bringing her Kawasaki's progress down to a respectable thirty miles per hour. DS Lloyd Fortune was waiting for her by the fluttering police tape. Young, smart, the poster boy for ethnic-minority policing in Southampton, Lloyd was destined for great things. Helen had always liked and respected him, yet still it felt odd having him as her number two. Charlie had been temporarily promoted to DS during their pursuit of Ella Matthews, but her elevation had never been made permanent. And as soon as she had announced her pregnancy, it became academic—she would remain at her former rank of DC for the foreseeable future. It wasn't fair, but that was the way it worked, the odds forever stacked against working mums.

The old team was breaking up. Tony Bridges had left the force for good, DC Grounds was due to retire shortly and Charlie was on maternity leave, a few weeks shy of giving birth. Lloyd was the new DS and they had two new DCs—the Major Incident Team had a very different feel now. If she was honest, it made Helen uncomfortable. She hadn't got a handle on the new personalities, was yet to establish an easy rhythm with the freshly assembled team. But the only way to do that was to go through fire together.

"What have you got for me, Lloyd?"

They were already making their way under the police cordon and across the sand toward the trench.

"Young female. Buried about three feet down. Found by a couple of kids an hour or so ago. They're over there with their parents."

Lloyd indicated the family of four, huddled in police blankets, giving their statements to a uniformed officer.

"Any connection to the victim?"

"No. They come here most weekends. Usually have the place to themselves."

"Anybody live near here?"

"No. The nearest houses are three miles away."

"Does it pick up any illumination from the lighthouse at night?"

"It's too far round."

"Making this a pretty good burial site."

They walked in silence to the lip of the trench. Meredith Walker, Southampton Central's chief forensics officer, was at the bottom, carefully excavating the body. Helen took in the scene, the white-suited forensics officer crouching sinisterly over a woman who looked completely at peace, despite the wet sand that stuck to her hair, eyes and lips.

The woman's face, shoulders, upper torso and arms had been revealed. Her limbs were painfully thin and the skin very pale, which made her single tattoo stand out even more. Despite the partial decomposition, she was a strangely beautiful sight, her black hair still framing those vivid blue eyes. It reminded Helen of the Grimms' fairy tales, of Gothic damsels awaiting love's true kiss.

"How long has she been down there?" Helen asked.

"Hard to say," replied Meredith. "The sand at this depth is cold and wet—ideal conditions to preserve the body. There are no animals or insects to get to her here either. But it's not recent. Given the levels of decomposition, I would say two, three years—Jim Grieves will be able tell you more once he gets her back to the mortuary."

"I'll need the crime scene photos tonight if possible," Helen replied.

"Will do. Though I'm not sure how much help they'll be. Whoever did this was careful. Her earrings and nose studs were removed. The fingernails were cut. And you can guess what time and tide have done to any residual forensic evidence."

Helen thanked Meredith and walked down to the water's edge to get a better view of the scene. Already her nerves were jangling. This was a careful, premeditated disposal by someone who knew exactly what they were doing. This wasn't the work of an amateur. Which strongly suggested to Helen that their killer had done this before.

5

"Stay away. Don't come near me."

Ruby was backed into a corner of the room. She held out her arms to ward off attack, but knew immediately that it was an empty gesture.

Click. A powerful torch beam fired straight at her. Her heart raced as she watched the torch beam roam over her, creeping down from her face, over her chest to her thighs and then her feet. Despite her determination to appear strong, her composure abandoned her now and she started to sob.

"Don't be frightened."

His voice was measured and steady. She didn't recognize it, though the Southampton accent came through clearly.

"Please let me go," she gushed through tears. "I won't tell anyone. I—"

"Are you cold?"

"Please. I just want to go home."

"If you're cold, I can get you an extra blanket. I want you to be comfortable."

His calm pragmatism was crushing. He was speaking as if nothing unusual had happened. As if this were *normal*.

"Are you hungry?"

"I want to go home, you motherfucker. Stop . . . stop talking to me. Just . . . take me home. The police will be looking for me—"

"Nobody's looking for you, Ruby."

"My parents are expecting me. My mum's coming round today—"

"Your parents don't love you."

"What?"

"They never have."

"Why are you say—"

"I've seen the way they treat you. What they say about you when you're not around. They want rid of you."

"That's not true."

"Really? You walked out on *them*, remember. So why should they come looking for you?"

The horrible logic of it rendered Ruby speechless.

"No . . . no. You're wrong. You're lying. If you want money, they've got—"

"I'm just telling you the truth. They don't want you. But I do."

Ruby sobbed louder. This couldn't be happening.

"I want to go home," she whimpered.

The torch beam moved still closer. He was beside her now. Ruby hung her head, clamping her eyes shut. She could feel his breath on her. She flinched when she felt him stroke her hair.

"That's good to hear, my love."

His voice was a warm whisper.

"Because this is your home now."

ABOUT THE AUTHOR

M. J. Arlidge has worked in television for the past fifteen years, and he lives in England. His debut novel, *Eeny Meeny*, has been sold in twenty-six countries.

CONNECT ONLINE
twitter.com/mjarlidge

7/21-22 R's Dream: Rich verging shot?
Some 1 needs shot of   Some 1 to 7K
"son-of-diabetes"   shot?

Strapping Tape